Caroline Fry Wilson

The Listener

Caroline Fry Wilson

The Listener

ISBN/EAN: 9783741186141

Manufactured in Europe, USA, Canada, Australia, Japa

Cover: Foto ©Andreas Hilbeck / pixelio.de

Manufactured and distributed by brebook publishing software
(www.brebook.com)

Caroline Fry Wilson

The Listener

BY

CAROLINE FRY,

AUTHOR OF

"THE ASSISTANT OF EDUCATION, ETC

IN TWO VOLUMES.

VOL. I.

TENTH EDITION.

LONDON:

JAMES NISBET AND CO., BERNERS STREET.

M DCCC XLVII.

PREFACE.

THE office of Listener is not one of very honourable note, especially when determined to tell what he hears: but, to deprecate the wrath of my readers against so treacherous an intermeddler with their studies and their sports, I entreat them to consider that good may be wrought of that with which we usually work evil. If I have the misfortune to have no business of my own, and a peculiar talent for observing other people's—if my sight is so keen, and my hearing so acute, as to perceive what is passing where I am not present, to see through the roof, and to hear through the walls—what can I do but endeavour to make the best use of so dangerous an endowment, and employ it for the benefit of others? I whisper no idle tale in gossip's ear; I write no satires upon innocent mistakes—no dry lectures

upon well-known evils; but I bear about with me,
as it were, a reflecting glass, which I present to the
actors in the scenes before me, that, seeing in it what
is, they may haply discover what better might be.
I may sometimes listen, and sometimes dream, and
sometimes be forced to perform the task without the
benefit of either; but, however it be, I hope my
young friends will accept my monthly communication, without being too curious as to how I came by
my information, granting me always the privilege of
hearing and overhearing whatever I think proper.

CONTENTS OF VOLUME I.

No.		Page

THE LISTENER.

No. I.

MUSIC.

> ....Music oft has such a charm,
> To make bad good, and good provoke to harm.

IT was one of those still Autumn nights, when the silence of nature bears rather the character of death than of repose—when, the ear listening in vain for so much as the falling of a withered leaf, a momentary sensation steals upon the mind that we only are remaining in existence, while all is extinct besides. There was not so much as a ripple to break the moonbeam that was sleeping on the water, a still, pale streak of unvarying brightness. A few dark sails hung motionless upon the surface, soliciting the breeze in vain; but most, in despair of further progress, had dropped the anchor and betaken themselves to the hold, whence a gleam of light now and then glanced upon the water to give the only token of existence. The moon hung in solitary splendour midway in the heavens, and the outline of every object was as distinctly traced as in the full light of day; seeming to gain magnitude and sublimity by the loss of colouring. The cliff appeared to have grown to immeasurable height, the woods to impenetrable thickness. There was not in all the heavens a cloud, nor on all the earth a vapour. Thoughts of lightness and folly can find no welcome in the mind at such an hour as this. That Being with whom we seem to be left alone in the universe, becomes more sensibly the guardian of our path. When removed from all other observation, we grow more conscious of His presence; and the sensation is powerful, though mistaken, that persuades us He can more distinctly mark our feelings in the solitude of night than amid the noise and bustle of the day.

It was so I felt and so I thought, as I walked between the huge dark cliff, and the far-receded waters, listening in vain for any sound that might break on the imperturbable stillness of the evening. I was now drawing near to the habitations of men, that, stretching from the town, spread themselves at unequal distances along the cliff; rare, at first, but increasing in thickness as they drew nearer to the centre from which they emanated. Here too all was silent. Small store of fire and candles had bidden the peasant early to his rest—the cottage door was closed—the honest were wrapt in wholesome slumber, and the nightly depredator had not yet come forth on his errand of mischief. I paused a moment to consider the mercy of Him who watches over the unguarded pillow of the one, and forbears the punishment due to the deeds of the other, when a sound, as of distant music, came upon my ear. Walking a little forward, I perceived that it proceeded from a house, yet at some distance, that stood between me and the town. The notes, as far as I could distinguish them, were soft and plaintive; and in the silence of such a night, there seemed to me something in them almost celestial. My feelings at that moment told me music was the gift of Heaven, and therefore must have been given for our good; and rapidly my mind ran over the various uses that have been made of it.

In every age and every country, music has been made the emblem of whatever is most lovely and enchanting; and whether the tales that are told us of its influence be truth or fiction, they equally prove the general perception of its power over the feelings and affections of humanity. From the coarse whistle of the ploughboy riding homeward on the fore-horse of his team, to the loud peal of the organ amid the chorus of some hundred voices, music seems to be the most natural language of the happy, the spontaneous solace of the sad. With every idea of things beautiful, pure, and delightful, music has been associated; but we never mix it with the images of things base, vicious, and disgraceful. No heathen savage ever pictured to himself a future heaven, but he placed music among the first of his delights; and in those bright prospects of eternal bliss, so often opened to us in the Holy Scriptures, music is always made a part, real or emblematical, of our promised enjoyment.

A power so universal in its influence on our feelings, so naturally combined with whatever is good and fair, and honoured with so much notice in the commands and promises of God, must surely be a gift from heaven, for the use of which we are responsible. Given, as we must suppose it, to our first parents in Paradise, it was there the language of gratitude and joy. The first use of music upon earth, perhaps, was to sound forth the praises of the Creator; and certainly it is the only one of our talents, of the continuance and purpose of which hereafter any mention has been made. Surely, then, it is a gift too sacred to be used as an instrument of folly and impiety. It is not my purpose here to disclose the worst uses to which it has been perverted—may my readers long and ever continue strangers to them!

My loitering steps now brought me near to the window whence the delightful sounds had issued. I heard them still, and could distinguish voices mingled in natural and simple harmony. Imagination supplying what I did not hear, I fancied it the language of piety going forth from glad and grateful hearts, and stealing through the silence of the night to find gracious acceptance at the throne of mercy; and now my propensity to know more than was intended for my observation became strong within me—ascending a mound directly opposite to the inviting window, I set myself to see what might be passing within.

The room was dressed with flowers, and gaily lighted, shining with many a fair and happy countenance. There was not a brow amongst them that seemed to bear the weight of twenty years, and some not half that number. The little group were variously occupied. Some were examining the wild-flowers, or turning over the shells and pebbles that had been gathered in their morning walk—others were spreading forth prints and drawings for the amusement of their friends. Of the younger, some were deeply intent on the intricate puzzle; of the elder, one was placed at the piano, while another tuned the harp, and the leaves of the music-book were rapidly turned over in search of the selected song.

My active fancy now found ample business. There was so much innocence in the employments, and so much pleasure in the countenances, of the young assembly, that all seemed in unison with my previous feelings. I imagined it some happy birthday night, which the inmates of the mansion had assembled their friends to celebrate. I looked on each countenance separately, and saw not on one a frown of ill-humour or a shade of sorrow. Here then at least, I whispered to myself, is the use of music not perverted. Some child beloved has completed another of her early years, and the hearts of those who love her are glad and grateful. Strains of moral feeling, perhaps of cheerful piety, are going forth from hearts as yet untainted with the follies and the fashions of the world; from lips that no unholy jest, no thoughtless impiety, as yet has stained. The music began; the air was plaintive. If it had not the sublimity of our best sacred music, it was feeling, chaste, and beautiful. I descended quickly from the mound, and placed myself near enough to the window indistinctly to catch the words. But my dreams of grateful devotion and moral purity, how were they dissipated, when the first words I distinguished were an impassioned address to a heathen god, beginning " Dieu d'Amour," and going on with a great deal about " les Astres," " les Parques," and other objects of a pagan's worship : My pleasure was past ; but curiosity retained me on the spot, and I waited patiently another and another song. The second was Italian, the sweetest language of music, and the most perverted. The best I could hope here, was, that performers and audience were alike ignorant of the nonsense, not to say indelicacy, of the words they were singing. At last I distinguished the accents of our native tongue, and something of a better hope revived—for now the young performers at least must know the meaning of their words. I heard the name of God—the Christian's God : and listened with redoubled earnestness : though, in truth,

there seemed something of profanation in the mix-
ture; but, alas! it was more in accordance than I
thought. That sacred name was used but as an
expression of earnestness on subjects with which the
thought of Him could not possibly combine. How
I wished I were at that moment on the mound, to
see if a blush did not suffuse the cheeks of the singer,
as she uttered a name she could not be accustomed
to profane: Or can it be, that the lips of innocence
may sing without thought, or feeling, words they
dare not speak—sentiments they would blush to feel
—breathe out a mockery of prayer under cover of a
foreign language, and make sport of names, at the
mention of which, angels in heaven bow their heads
with reverence? The best that can be said is, that
they think no wrong; and, in the enjoyment of the
music, give no heed to the meaning of the words;
but that is not the less a danger to which we are
insensible; and custom has gone far indeed to do its
work of mischief, if words of folly and impiety *can*
pass our lips without exciting our attention. Again
my mind recurred to what music might be—to what
it ought to be. Its powerful influence on our hearts
—its fitness to excite and to express the best and finest
feelings of our nature—above all, its peculiar suitability to speak the feelings of a grateful heart, at
peace with God and with itself. I listened no more
that night.

No. II.

TIME.

I saw the leaves gliding down a brook—
Swift the brook ran, and bright the sun burn'd—
The sere and the verdant, the same course they took;
And sped gaily and fast, but they never return'd.
And I thought how the years of a man pass away,
Threescore and ten—and then where are they?

H. NEELE.

" THREESCORE years and ten," thought I to my-self, as I walked, one rainy morning, as a sailor walks the quarterdeck, up and down a short alcove, extending before the windows of a modern house. It was one of those days in June in which our summer hopes take umbrage at what we call unseasonable weather, though no season was ever known to pass without them. Unlike the rapid and delightful showers of warmer days, suddenly succeeding to the sunshine, when the parched vegetables and arid earth seize with avidity and imbibe the moisture ere it becomes unpleasant to our feelings, there had fallen a drizzling rain throughout the night; the saturated soil returned to the atmosphere the humidity it could

no longer absorb, and there it hung in chilling
thickness between rain and fog. The birds did not
sing, for their little wings were heavy, and their
plumage roughed. The flowers did not open, for the
cold drop was on their cheek, and no sunbeam was
there to welcome them. Nature itself wore the garb
of sadness; and man's too dependent spirits were
ready to assume it: those at least that were not so
happy as to find means of forgetting it. Such was
the case with my unfortunate self. I had descended
to the breakfast-room at the usual hour, but no one
appeared—I looked for a book, but found none except Moore's Almanack and Paterson's Road-book.
The books were kept in the library, beyond all
dispute their proper place, had I not been in a
humour to think otherwise. The house was too hot,
and the external air was too cold; and I was fain to
betake myself to that last resource of the absolutely
idle, a mechanical movement of the body up and
down a given space. And from the alcove where I
walked I heard the ticking of the timepiece—and as
I passed the window I saw the hands advance—every
time I had returned they had gone a little further.
" Threescore years and ten," said I to myself, " and
a third or a fourth of it is nature's claim for indispensable repose—and many a day consumed on the
bed of sickness—and many a year by the infirmities
of age—and some part of all necessarily sacrificed
to the recruiting of the health by exercise. And
what do we with the rest?" Nothing answered me

but the ticking of the clock, of which the hands were traversing between nine and ten. They had nearly met at the latter hour, when the party began to assemble within : and each one commenced, for aught I could discover, the functions of the day—for neither their appearance nor their remarks gave any intimation that they had been previously employed. One, indeed, declared the weather made her so idle she had scarcely found strength to dress herself—another confessed he had passed an additional hour in bed, because the day promised him so little to do up. One by one, as they dropped in, the seats at the breakfast-table filled; and as a single newspaper was all the apparent means of mental occupation, I anticipated some interesting conversation. I waited and I watched. One ran the point of his fork into the table-cloth—another balanced her spoon on the tea-cup—a third told backwards and forwards the rings on her fingers, as duly as a friar tells his beads. As such actions are the symptoms sometimes of mental occupation, I began to anticipate the brilliant results of so much thinking. I cried Hem! in hopes to rouse them to expression, and not quite unsuccessfully : for one remarked it was a wretched day, another wished it was fine, and a third hoped it shortly would be so. Mean time the index of the clock went round—it was gaining close upon eleven before all had withdrawn from the table. My eye followed one to the window-place, where, with her back to the wall, and her eyes fixed without, she passed a full half-hour in gazing at the prospect, or wishing, perhaps, the mist did not prevent her seeing it. A very young lady was so busy in pulling the dead leaves from a geranium, and crumbling them in her fingers, I could not doubt but some important purpose was in the task. A third resumed the newspaper he had read for a whole hour before, and betook himself at last to the advertisements. A fourth repaired to the alcove—gathered some flowers, picked them to pieces, threw them away again, and returned. " Cease thy prating, thou never-resting timepiece," said I to myself, " for no one heeds thy tale. What is it to us that each one of thy tickings cuts a link from our brief chain of life ?—Time is the gift of Heaven, but man has no use for it."

I had scarcely thought out the melancholy thought, when a young lady entered with an elegant work-box, red without and blue within, and filled with manifold conveniences for the pursuance of her art. Glad was I most truly at the sight. By the use of the needle the naked may be clothed—ingenuity may economise her means, and have more to spare for those that need it—invention may multiply the ways of honest subsistence, and direct the ignorant to the use of them ; most glad was I, therefore, that the signal of industry drew more than one wanderer to the same pursuit—though not till much time had been consumed in going in and out, and up and down, in search of the materials. All was found at last—the party worked ; and I, as usual, listened. " I think this trimming," said one, "will repay me for my trouble, though it has cost me three months' work already, and it will be three months more before it is finished."—"Indeed," rejoined her friend, "I wish I were half as industrious: but I have been working six weeks at this handkerchief, and have not found time to finish it: now the fashion is past, and I shall not go on."—"How beautifully you are weaving that necklace!—is it not very tedious?"—"Yes, almost endless; but I delight in the work, otherwise I should not do it—for the beads cost almost as much as I could buy it for."—"I should like to begin one this morning," interposed a fourth, "but the milliner has sent home my bonnet so ill trimmed, it will take me all the day to alter it. The bow is on the wrong side, and the trimming at the edge is too broad. It is very tiresome to spend all one's life in altering things we pay so much for."—"I wish," said a little girl at the end of the table. "that I might work some trimmings for my frock, but I am obliged to do this plain work first. The poor lame girl in the village. who is almost starving, would do it for me for a shilling. but I must save my allowance this week to buy a French trinket I have taken a fancy to."

"Poor thing! she is much to be pitied." said the lady of the trimming; "if I had time, I would make her some clothes."

And so they worked, and so they talked, till I and the timepiece had counted many an hour which they took no account of—when one of them yawned and said, " How tedious are these wet days !—it is really impossible to spin out one's time without a walk."

" I am surprised you find it so," rejoined the lady of the beads ; " I can rarely make time for walking —though keeping the house makes me miserably languid." And so the morning passed. It was four o'clock, and the company dispersed to their apartments. I pretend not to know what they did there ; but each one returned between five and six in an altered dress. And then half an hour elapsed, in which, as I understood from their impatience, they were waiting for dinner, each in turn complaining of the waste of time occasioned by its delay ; and the little use it would be to go about any thing when it was so near. And as soon as dinner was over, they began to wait for tea, with exactly the same complainings. And the tea came—and, cheered by the vivifying draught, one did repair to the instrument, and began a tune,—one did take up a pencil, and prepare to draw,—and one almost opened a book. But, alas ! the shades of night were growing fast— ten minutes had scarcely elapsed before each one resigned her occupation with a murmur at the darkness of the weather ; and though some person suggested that there were such things as lamps and candles, it was agreed to be a pity to have lights so early in the midst of summer, and so another half hour elapsed.

The lights, when they came, would have failed to

relumine an expectation in my bosom, had not their beams disclosed the forms of various books which one and another had brought in for the evening's amusement. Again I watched, and again I listened. "I wish I had something to do, mamma," said the little girl. "Why do you not take a book and read?" rejoined her mother. "My books are all up-stairs," she replied; "and so near bed-time, it is not worth while to fetch them."—"This is the best novel I ever read," said a lady, something older, turning the leaves mean time so very fast, that those who are not used to this method of reading, might suppose she found nothing in it worthy of attention. "I dare say it is," said another, whose eyes had been fixed for half an hour on the same page of Words-worth's poems—"but I have no time to read novels."—"I wish I had time to read any thing," said a third, whom I had observed already to have been perusing attentively the title-page of every book on the table, publisher's name, date, and all; whilst a fourth was too intensely engaged in studying the blue cover of a magazine to make any remark whatever.

And now I was much amused to perceive with what frequency eyes were turned upon the dial-plate, through all the day so little regarded. Watches were drawn out, compared, and pronounced too slow. With some difficulty one was found that had outrun his fellows, and, determined to be right, gave per-mission to the company to disperse, little more than twelve hours from the time of their assembling, to recover, as I supposed, during the other twelve, dressing and undressing included, the effect of their mental and bodily exertions. "So," I exclaimed, as soon as I found myself alone, "twelve times round yonder dial-plate those little hands have stolen, and twelve times more they may now go round unheeded. They who are gone to rest have a day the less to live, and record has been made in Heaven of that day's use. Will He who gave, ask no reckoning for His gifts? The time, the thoughts, the talents — the improvement we might have made, and made not— the good we might have done, and did not — the health, and strength, and intellect, that may not be ours to-morrow, and have not been used to-day—will not conscience whisper of it ere they sleep to-night? The days of man were shortened upon earth by reason of the wickedness the Creator saw. Threescore years and ten are now his portion, and often not half the number. They pause not; they loiter not—the hours strike on—and they may even go—for it seems they are all too much. The young, with minds as yet unstored, full of error, full of ignorance in all that it behoves them most to know, unfit alike as yet for earth or heaven—the old, whose sum of life is almost told, and but a brief space remaining to repair their mistakes, and redeem the time they have lost— the simple and ungifted, who, having from nature but little, need the more assiduity to fulfil their measures of usefulness, and make that little do the most it may—the clever and highly talented, who have an almost appalling account to render for the much received—they all have time to waste. But let them remember, time is not their own—not a moment of it but is the grant of Heaven — and Heaven gives nothing without a purpose and an end. Every hour that is wasted, fails of that purpose; and in so far as it is wasted or ill spent, the gift of Heaven is misused, and the misuse is to be answered for. Methinks I would be allowed to whisper nightly in the ears of my young friends, as they lie down to rest, "How many minutes have you lost to-day, that might have been employed in your own improvement, in your Maker's service, or for your fellow-creatures' good?"

No. III.

CONVERSATION.

Conversation is the daughter of reasoning, the mother of knowledge, the breath of the soul, the commerce of hearts, the bond of friendship, the nourishment of contentment, and the occupation of men of wit.

" HOLD your tongue, Miss Julia; little girls should be seen and not heard," said Mrs B.'s nursery governess to a little sprite of seven years old, who was essaying to take a turn in the chatter of the breakfast-table. For I would not have my readers suppose that a nursery breakfast passes without chatter. I who traverse houses from corner to corner, and listen from behind the doors, know better. From the nursery to the kitchen, from the school-room to the parlour, all is chatter, and one might conclude the power of talking increases in inverse ratio with the information possessed. But be it not thence concluded that I am no friend to talking. We listeners are considerably interested in the furtherance of the custom : and it may even appear, ere the end of my tale, that I have a very different object in view than that of putting my young friends to silence.

It is objected by some, that young people talk too much, and by others, that they talk too little; and each remark is just—for they do both. But here, be it observed, I speak only of persons under twenty; far be it from me to suppose that any lady above that age can be charged with the habit I presume to censure.

When young people are alone, freed from the constraints of society and the presence of those who are older and wiser than themselves, their ceaseless volubility, the idleness, uselessness, and folly of their conversation is all too much; not a pause to reflect upon their words—not a moment to weigh the sentiments they hear—not a care for the time they waste, or for the habits of trifling and exaggeration they acquire. But in society they talk too little. An unreasonable fear of exposing their sentiments loses to them the best means of ascertaining if they are right. A want of that simplicity of mind, which, conscious of no design, does not look to be charged with a wrong one, makes them fear to be thought ostentatious—while the real difficulty of expressing themselves, from want of being accustomed to it—a difficulty their indolence would rather keep than make an effort to subdue—prevents their joining in conversation on subjects on which they are fully able to speak, and would gain information by doing so: Modesty forbids them to suppose they can contribute to the pleasure of the conversation, and pride is not well pleased to take the benefit and contribute nothing.

I have wondered often how all this befalls—but now methinks I have stolen a key that may unlock the mystery. Little Julia was to be seen and not heard—that is to say, she was to ask no questions when her infant mind was struggling to enlarge itself by increase of knowledge—she was to express no feeling that moved her little bosom, or thought that awakened in her dormant intellect. But Julia was to listen, I suppose; and much may be learned by silent attention. She listened—and so did I—and we learned a great deal—for we heard all that the footman had told the cook, and the cook had told the nursery-maid—and we gained an insight into our neighbours' affairs, and heard many wonders, the incredibility of which never failed to secure belief; whereas what was simply true and certain was warmly contested. Added to all this, were the schemes of deception and petty artifices that I do not judge it honourable to disclose.

This, then, I thought within myself, is little Julia's first lesson in the art of talking; a lesson she will probably repeat after her own manner, the first time she escapes with her younger sisters to a private corner; and not being allowed to inquire, her mind must work, for work it will, upon the hopeful materials it has gathered; and I heard her in truth, not long after, exaggerating, and mimicking, and wondering, and disputing, as fast as her happy little tongue could move, to evince its delight at the resumption of its powers.

The powers of speech are among the most important committed to our charge; and as capable as any other of a right or a wrong cultivation; there is this only difference: that while other powers lie dormant from neglect, these will be in action whether cultivated or not, and if we do not direct them to the right, will most certainly expend themselves on the wrong. If a young person is not allowed, or not encouraged to speak with her parents and equals, she will requite herself by talking to her waiting-maid: and if she be not accustomed in society to converse rationally and sensibly, she will most surely spend the powers given her for better purposes, in idle gossip or mischievous slander.

From the lessons in the nursery, Julia passes to the school-room. She there learns much, and perhaps thinks much, but has little opportunity to communicate. If the discipline be strict, she is desired to hold her tongue, and mind her lessons: if it be indulgent, she may talk, indeed, as fast as it pleases her—she may repeat, with the more exaggeration the better, all the tittle-tattle she has heard elsewhere—what this person says, and that person does, and the other person wears—but no one takes any care to lead her to subjects useful and improving, to correct her misconceptions, and false ideas, and rash assertions. And here I entreat my readers to attend—for if the fault has been hitherto charged to the nurse and to the governess, it now becomes their own.

And so it was, that some years after my first acquaintance with Julia in the nursery—It was a cheerless night—the heavens were hung with the thick pillowy clouds that betoken coming snow— scarcely might here and there a pallid star peep forth, perceived but a moment ere it was gone, and returned no more. I watched them long, and they became fewer and fewer—and one by one I saw the clouds close over them, as time closes over the joys that are past. And now the vapours united into one unshadowed and unbroken mass of blackness. The winds just whispered through the leafless trees, a low and melancholy sound, and I began to feel the cold droppings of the fleecy shower. More silent than the thief upon his midnight errand, unheard and unsuspected from within, the snow stole down upon the iron earth, to prepare for the returning sun far other landscape than that he shone upon before he set. I was some distance yet from home, and liking to observe nature in all her varied aspects, I sought shelter in the porch of a handsome dwelling- house that fronted the path I was treading. There, through an opening in the crimson curtains of an adjoining window, I looked upon a scene strikingly contrasted with that which was without. A blazing fire, recently fed with the dry log, crackled and sparkled on the hearth. The reeking urn, with the tall candles by its side, was hissing on the table. The downy rug and many-coloured carpet, with the deep crimson of the curtain, gave a glow, a tone of warmth to the picture, strikingly opposed to the growing whiteness of the scene without. A number of young persons were in the room; the plainness of their dress, their easy familiarity and small numbers, did not indicate a party, and yet there were more than might belong to a single family. This was not hard to understand. And how powerfully came to my mind, at the moment, the boundless munificence of that Being, who has provided enjoyments for every season, comforts for nature's most sad and cheerless hours: What was to them the chilling shower that fell without, or the frost that bound the palsied earth in iron hardness? In the enjoyment of present pleasures, other, but not less, they sighed not at recollection of the tints of autumn or the summer's sun. And then came into my gladdened mind all the delights of social intercourse—of sentiments sweetly responding to each other—of feelings tenderly participated—of argument without dispute—reproof without unkindness. And I thought, if I might not share it, I might now at least contemplate it: and so I tried to list what passed within. To ordinary persons this might have been difficult. But what can professed listeners not hear?

The youthful party, for such it was, had recently met, as it seemed to me, to pass a social evening, all on familiar terms and intimately acquainted; therefore there was neither reserve nor form to check their communications. The tea was making, and as they sipped the fragrant draught, the talk went

blithely round. It began as usual with the weather.
I do not exactly object to this; because something
must be said first; and as the beginning address is
a great difficulty to the reserved and modest, it is
very well to have an established form of commencement, fitted for all circumstances. But I did think
half an hour something too long for this prelude.
And I did think besides, that when one called it
miserable weather, and another said it was a wretched
day, and a third declared it put her quite out of
temper, and a fourth wished she could sleep till it
was finer, the speakers either did not well regard
the meaning of their words, or had formed an extraordinary estimate of misery and wretchedness, as
well as of the value of time, and the preservatives of
good-humour. And I began to be something impatient, when one remarked at some length on the
wonderful shortening of the days, which, as it usually
occurs in November, I thought scarcely might need
a remark, much less an expression of surprise or
complaint. The subject next in succession was that
of dress. Here, too, the gentle critic must concede
something to what makes a necessary part of a
woman's business; and so I was very patient for a
while. But, indeed, this subject so far outlived its
predecessor, the remarks were so useless, the eagerness so disproportioned to the occasion; the importance attached to it so much too great, and the expenditure of thought on it so very obvious, I began
to be well-nigh weary of my listening, when it

diverged a little from dress in the abstract, to dress in the application, and all the dresses of all the ladies in the parish, red, blue, and black, Sunday and working-day, were numbered, described, and discussed.

But wo to him whose discontent would have a change at any rate, before he knows for what! From the dress we passed to the persons, and from the persons to the affairs, of others. What was before but useless, now became mischievous. Words were repeated, tales were told, surmises were whispered, peculiarities were mimicked, falsehoods were circulated, and truths were ridiculed. The only hope that promised some limit to the evil circulated was, that as all talked at once, no one could receive much impression from what another said. But I, the silent Listener, did—for I observed that one in particular was so addicted to exaggeration, that if she told a truth, it became a falsehood on her lips—another was so possessed with the image of self, that even in talking of others, she never failed to push in the *I* and the *me* at every sentence, either by the way of comparison, or simile, or illustration—and another was so, if not envious, at least censorious, that she replied with a *but* to every the least suggestion of merit, or palliation of demerit, in another —in a fourth, I remarked that her opinion changed so rapidly, in one thing only was she decided, that of differing from whoever happened to be heard last —another was so absolutely certain of every thing, one was almost constrained to believe her an eye-witness of all that had passed in the three kingdoms since she was born, and for twenty years before. But no one more displeased me than a little lady, who could assume every body's countenance, mimic every body's tone of voice, and caricature every body's manners.

Full two good hours more had elapsed before the conversation had progressed through all these shades of subject, and there came a transition for which I could not well account; it having arisen in a corner whence I could not distinctly hear amid the tumult. But suddenly it seemed to me, from certain words I caught, that my young party were speaking of religion. I was not long in doubt how the conversation might have passed from things so frivolous to a theme so important; for I soon was doomed to know that the frivolity of talk does not depend upon its subject. These young critics were talking, indeed, of preachers, and of sermons, and of last Sunday's congregation, and who was there, and who ought to have been there and was not. And one minister was compared with another, and one extolled, and the other depreciated. And the last sermon at their parish church, which seemed to be tolerably well remembered, was closely criticised—one liked this part, and one did not like that part, and some ridiculed and even mimicked the peculiarities in the expression and manner of the preacher. And then the mistakes and inconsistencies of all the religious

people in their circle of acquaintance were hinted
and wondered at, and very conscientiously bewailed.
It was a point as difficult, indeed, as it seemed to be
important, to determine, amid conflicting opinions,
who amongst them were to be considered religious,
and who were not. And so they went on—But I
forbore to listen. The night's increasing chillness
warned me thence—and as I betook myself to my
solitary home, I tried in vain to recall, of what I
had heard, one single expression of feeling, one
thought that bespoke reflection, one breathing of
piety, cultivation, or good sense. Yet had I reason
to believe the young persons possessed all these—
they had been carefully, politely, and religiously
educated—they knew much, and probably felt much
—Why then was it so? From habit simply—habit,
unresisted by others when they were younger, and
now unresisted by themselves, growing every year
more inveterate, shortly to become too difficult to
conquer. Dispersed in society where good sense,
piety, and intellect, give the tone to the discourse,
these young people would be found silent, reserved,
and embarrassed, wishing in vain they had words in
which to clothe their thoughts, or courage to express
their feelings, and ask elucidation of their doubts.
And their minds must have more than the ordinary
power of resistance, if they come not eventually to
prefer the company of the trifling, the frivolous, and
the senseless.

Mean time the Oracle of Wisdom has declared,

" The thought of foolishness is sin." What sin, then, in its habitual and confirmed expression, become by habit the language of our lives! What sin in the perversion of that power whose use is unlimited in good—in telling forth the praises of God—in speaking comfort to the suffering—in giving information to those that know not—in adding the highest zest to intellectual pleasures—the most exquisite enjoyment to social intercourse! Rational conversation is the means above all others calculated to correct our mental errors, to shame our selfish passions, to correct the false estimate we form of ourselves, and induce a liberal and benevolent consideration of the feelings of others. It is the genial fire applied from time to time, to save the heart from the icy coldness that steals upon it 'mid the selfish occupations of the world. It is the overflow of feelings too big for the bosom to hold and be at peace. It is the gentle consolation that neither age, nor sorrow, nor infirmity, forbids to us—the draught oblivious, in which suffering, the most poignant, can for a while forget itself—the offspring of confidence and love, better thriving on the hearth of domestic privacy, than in the sullen splendours of dissipation.

And is it even so, that of a gift like this, we make an instrument of folly—to dissipate every serious thought—to put to the blush every right feeling—to disseminate falsehood and mischief—wound others, and corrupt ourselves ?

No. IV.

POLL PEG.

She for her humble sphere by nature fit,
Has little understanding and no wit,
Receives no praise; but though her lot be such,
Toilsome and indigent, she renders much—
Just knows, and knows no more, her Bible true.

COWPER.

ALL who enter on the world are in pursuit of happiness; each one questions of another where it is, or fancies he perceives it from afar; but very few confess that they have found it. The young, starting into life with sanguine hopes and spirits gay, expect it every where: the more experienced, having sought it long and found it not, decide that it is nowhere. The moralist tells us there is no such thing. The historian almost proves it by the miseries he details. Poverty says, It is not with me—and Wealth says, Not with me. Splendour dashes by the cottage door, heaves the rich jewel on her bosom with a sigh, and says the dwellers there are happier than she is. Penury looks out upon her as she passes, loathes her own portion, and silently envies what she must not share. Ignorance, with dazzled and misjudging eye, admires the learned, and esteems them happy. Learning decides that "ignorance is bliss," and bewails the enlargement of capacity it cannot find enough to fill. Wherever we ask, the answer is still, "Seek further." Is it so, then, that there is no happiness on earth? Or if it does exist, is it a thing of circumstance, confined to certain states, dependent on rank and station—here to-day and gone to-morrow, in miserable dependence on the casualties of life? We are often asked the question by those by whom the world is yet untried, who, even in the spring-time of their mirth, are used to hear the complaints of all around them, and well may wonder what they mean. We affect not to answer questions which never were answered yet—but we can tell a story of something that our ear has heard and our eye has seen, and that many besides can testify to be the truth. And well may we, who so often listen to what we like not, be allowed for once to tell a pleasant tale.

Distant something more than a mile from the village of Desford, in Leicestershire, at the lower extremity of a steep and rugged lane, was seen an obscure and melancholy hovel. The door stood not wide to invite observation; the cheerful fire gleamed not through the casement to excite attention from the passenger. The low roof and outer wall were but just perceived among the branches of the hedgerow—uncultured and untrimmed—that ran between it and the road. As if there were nothing there that any one might seek, no way of access presented itself, and the step of curiosity that would persist in finding entrance, must pass over mud and brier to obtain it. Having reached the door with difficulty, a sight presented itself such as the eye of delicacy is not used to look upon. It was not the gay contentedness of peasant life that poets tell of, and prosperity sometimes stoops to envy. It was not the labourer resting from his toil, the ruddy child exulting in its hard, scant meal, the housewife singing blithely at her wheel, the repose of health and fearlessness—pictures that so often persuade us happiness has her dwelling in the cabins of the poor. The room was dark and dirty—there was nothing on the walls but the bare beams, too ill joined to exclude the weather, with crevices in vain attempted to be stopped by rent and moulded paper. A few broken utensils hung about the room—a table and some broken chairs were all the furniture, except what seemed intended for a bed, yet promised little repose. The close and smoky atmosphere of the apartment gave to it the last colouring of discomfort and disease. Within there sat a figure such as the pencil well might choose for the portrait of wretchedness. Quite grey, and very old, and scarcely clothed, a woman was seen sitting by the fire-place, seemingly unconscious of all that passed around her. Her features were remarkably large, and in expression harsh—her white hair, turned back from the forehead, hung uncombed upon her shoulders—her withered arm, stretched without motion on her knee, in form and colouring seemed nothing that had lived—her eye was fixed on the wall before her—an expression of suffering, and a faint movement of the lip, alone giving token of existence.

Placed with her back towards the door, she perceived not the intrusion, and while I paused to listen and to gaze, I might have determined that here at least was a spot where happiness could not dwell—one being, at least, to whom enjoyment upon earth must be forbidden by external circumstance—with whom to live was of necessity to be wretched. Well might the Listener in such a scene as this be startled by expressions of delight, strangely contrasted with the murmurs we are used to hear amid the world's abundance. But it was even so. From the pale shrivelled lips of this poor woman we heard a whispering expression of enjoyment, scarcely articulate, yet not so low but that we could distinguish the words, " Delightful," " Happy."

As we advanced with the hesitation of disgust into the unsightly hovel, the old woman looked at us with kindness, but without emotion, bade us be seated, and, till questioned, showed very little inclination to speak. Being asked how she did, she at first replied, " Very ill," then hastily added, " My carcass is ill—but I am well, very well." And then she laid her head upon a cold, black stone, project-

ing from the wall beside the fire-place, as if unable
to support it longer. We remarked that it was bad
weather. "Yes," she answered—then hastily correcting herself—"No, not bad—it is God Almighty's
weather, and cannot be bad."—"Are you in pain?"
we asked—a question scarcely necessary, so plainly
did her movements betray it. "Yes, always in pain
—but not such pain as my Saviour suffered for
me—his pain was worse than mine—mine does not
signify." Some remark being made on the wretchedness of her dwelling, her stern features almost relaxed
into a smile, and she said she did not think it so;
and wished us all as happy as herself. As she
showed little disposition to talk, and never made
any remark till asked for it, and then in words as
few and simple as might express her meaning, it was
slowly and by reiterated questions that we could
draw from her a simple tale. Being asked if that
was all the bed she had on which to sleep, she said
she seldom slept, and it was long that she had not
been able to undress herself—but it was on that
straw she passed the night. We asked her if the
night seemed not very long. "No—not long," she
answered—"never long—I think of God all night,
and when the cock crows, am surprised it comes so
soon."—"And the days—you sit here all day, in pain
and unable to move—are the days not long?"—
"How can they be long? Is not He with me?
Is it not all up—up?" an expression she frequently
made use of to describe the joyful elevation of her

mind. On saying she passed much time in prayer, she was asked for what she prayed. To this she always answered, " Oh! to go, you know—to go— when He pleases—not till He pleases." To express the facility she found in prayer, she once said, it seemed as if her prayers were all laid out ready for her in her bed. But time would fail us to repeat the words, brief as they were, in which this aged saint expressed her gratitude to the Saviour who died for her—her enjoyment of the God who abode with her—her expectations of the heaven to which she was hasting—and perfect contentedness with her earthly portion. It proved on inquiry to be worse than it appeared. The outline of her history, as gathered at different times from her own lips, was this :—

Her husband's name was Peg; her own being Mary, she was usually known by the appellation of Poll Peg, and had been long remembered in the village, as living in extreme poverty, and going about to beg bacon at Christmas time. Her youth had been passed in service of various kinds ; and though she did not know her age, it appeared from public events which she remembered to have passed when she was a girl, that she could not be less than eighty. Later in life she had kept sheep upon the forest hills, and, in the simplicity of her heart, would speak of her days of prosperity when she had two sheep of her own. She could not read—but from attending divine service had become familiar with the language of Scripture, and knew, though hitherto she did not regard, the promises and threatenings it contains. We know nothing of her previous character; that of her husband and family was very bad— but we are not informed that hers was so. The first earnest religious feeling she related of herself, was felt some short time previous; when walking alone in the fields, she bethought herself of her hard fate —a youth of toil, an old age of want and misery— and if she must go to hell at last, how dreadful was her portion! Struck with the appalling thought, she knelt down beneath the hedge to pray—the first time, perhaps, that heartfelt and earnest prayer had gone up to Heaven from her lips.

Not very long after this, as we understand, the old woman was taken ill, and unable to move from the straw, at that time her only bed, in a loft over the apartment we have described—where, little sheltered by the broken roof and less by the rags that scarcely covered her, she lay exposed to the inclemencies of the weather, without money to support or friend to comfort her. It was in this situation that her mind, dwelling probably on the things that in health passed by her unregarded, received the strong and lasting impression of a vision she thought she beheld, probably in a dream, though she herself believed that she was waking. In idea she saw the broad road and the narrow, as described in Scripture. In the broad road, to use her own expressions, there were many walking; it was smooth and pleasant, and they got on fast—but the end of it was dark. On the narrow road she herself was treading, and some few others—but the way was rugged—some turned back, and others sat down unable to proceed. She herself advanced till she reached a place more beautiful, she said, than any thing to which she could compare it. When asked what it was like, she could not say, but that it was very bright, and that there were many sitting there. Being questioned who these were—she said they were like men, but larger and more beautiful, and all dressed in glitterings—such was her expression—and one was more beautiful than the rest, whom she knew to be the Saviour, because of his readiness and kindness in receiving her. But the most pleasing impression seemed to be left by the Hallelujahs this company were singing. She was told by Him she knew to be the Saviour, that she must go back for a little time, and then should come again to dwell with them for ever.

Thus ended her vision—but not so the impression it made. The recollection of the scene she had witnessed, and of the bliss that had been promised her, was the source of all her happiness. Turning her eye from earth to heaven, and fixing all her thoughts on that eternity to which she was hastening, it left her, not what she before had been, wretched on earth and unmindful of any thing beyond—but with a heart deeply impressed with the love and mercy of God, fully and undoubtedly relying on her Saviour's promise, and proving the reality of those feelings by earnest devotion, and most cheerful acquiescence in her Maker's will. It was not the fervour of a first impression—the enthusiasm of an excited imagination. She survived six or seven years, but time made no change on her feelings. She passed those years in the extreme of poverty, dependent on the alms of some few persons who knew and visited her: she passed them in pain and helplessness; mocked and ill-treated by her husband and her sons, and insulted often by her unfeeling neighbours, who came to laugh at her devotion, and ridicule her hopes. For these, as well as for some who visited her for kinder purposes, she had but one answer—she wished them all like her; prayed that they might only be as happy as herself. When told what she had seen was a mere dream and a delusion, she said it did not signify to tell her that—she had seen it, and it was the recollection of it that made her nights so short and her days so happy. "And what does it signify," she added, "that they swear at me, and tell me I am a foolish old woman—don't I know how happy I am?" During the many years that she survived, the minister of the parish saw her constantly, and found little variation in her feelings, none in her firm adherence to the tale she at first had told, and the persuasion that what she had seen was a blessed reality, sufficient to make her happy in every extreme of earthly wretchedness. And he saw her die, as she had lived, in holy, calm, and confident reliance on her Saviour's promise.

To what I have written, I could find much to add, having notes of all that passed during the protracted years of this devoted woman's life. But my purpose was not to make a story. I have witnessed only to what I saw, and repeated only what my ear has listened to. And I have repeated it but to prove that the happiness which all men seek, and most complain they find not, has sometimes an abode where we should least expect to find it. This is an extreme case—extreme in mental enjoyment as in external misery. But it is true. And if it be so, that a being debarred the commonest comforts of life, almost of the light and air of heaven, suffering, and incapable even to clothe herself, or cleanse her unsightly dwelling, could yet pass years of so much happiness, that her warmest expression of gratitude to her benefactors was to wish them a portion as happy as her own—what are we to say to those, who, amid the overflow of sublunary good, make the wide world resound with their complainings? How are we to understand it, that, while blessings are showered around us as the summer rain, there is so little real happiness on earth?—Because we seek it not aright—we seek it where it is not—in outward circumstance and external good, and neglect to seek it, where alone it dwells, in the close chambers of the bosom. We would have a happiness in time independent of eternity—we would have it inde-

pendent of the Being whose it is to give; and so we
go forth, each one as best we may, to seek out the
rich possession for ourselves. Those who think they
are succeeding, will not list our tale. But if there
be any, who, having made a trial of the world, are
disposed to disbelieve the existence of what they
seek—if there be any among the young, who start
at the report, and shrink from the aspect of their
already clouded prospects, we would have them hear
a brighter tale. There is happiness upon earth.
There is happiness for the poor and for the rich;
for the most prosperous and the most desolate.
There is happiness, but we will not have it.

No. V.

TRUTH.

So much of the happiness of social life is derived from the use of language, and so profitless would the mere power of language be but for the truth that dictates it, that the absence of the confidence which is placed in our declarations may not merely be in the highest degree injurious to the individual, but would tend, if general, to throw back the whole race of mankind into that barbarism from which they have emerged.

DR BROWN.

WALKING one morning in the garden at an hour when there is little to listen to, except the small twittering of the wakeful lark, the distant footsteps of the cattle, and the coarse voices of their drivers preparing to go forth to their labour, I desired at least to hear, what all who will listen may, a word of truth from the still voice of nature. There is so striking an affinity between the moral and the natural world, resembling consequences so surely resulting from resembling causes, one might imagine the world of things inanimate had been formed and framed but as a picture to show forth what is passing within us, and warn us of the things that affect our moral welfare: a fable, as it were, of which we are

to find the moral, and apply it to ourselves. There
is scarce a moment of our lives in which, if we be
pleased to pause and look around, we may not learn
a useful lesson from something that is passing among
the natural objects that encompass us.

The garden that morning was very gaily dressed
—the Moss-rose drooped its head, overladen with
the weight of dew that was upon it, more beautiful
in its tears than when opening in full splendour
to the mid-day sun. The pale Lily, scentless and
colourless, seemed in its spotless purity to shun the
charms that embellished other flowers. And the
Pink, and the gay Pansy, and numberless others,
were there, all ranged in correct and beautiful order,
unmixed with any noxious or unsightly weed: except that on one single spot I marked the first germ
of something that did not seem to be a flower, and
yet, having no distinct form, could not well be determined to be a weed. I paused a moment in thought
to pull it up—But what harm was there in it? It
bore but two small leaves, and why not let it grow?
And so it grew—and in a few weeks it spread far
and wide its rank, luxuriant branches—the flowers
that crept upon the soil were smothered beneath it,
while its taller neighbours were encompassed by its
leaves. And each morning as I renewed my walk,
I marked the growth of the unsightly weed, spreading farther and farther to mar the neatness and
beauty of the border. Its roots had mingled with
the roots of the tender flowers, its branches had

interwoven with their branches, and it would now be a task of difficulty to part them without injury.

And on the last morning that I walked there, I bethought myself of what this weed might resemble. that from so small and innocent a beginning, had grown into such speedy and abundant mischief. Alas! there were many things that it resembled but too closely. Many were the vices that came into my mind as the results of early indulgence—But in as much as this garden had been richly cultivated and fairly kept, and but for the rapid growth of this neglected weed, had seemed almost without a blemish, there was one thing in particular it seemed to me to resemble; for I had known that vice to subsist in minds of considerable cultivation, and hide itself under very highly-polished manners; the single blemish of an else fair character.

As the ground, accursed for our sake, when left unwatched, brings forth the poisonous weed, so the human heart, if unchecked in its propensities, will bring forth evil—but none, perhaps, so spontaneously as falsehood. There seems to be from earliest infancy a disposition to it, and it is generally the first great fault a child becomes guilty of.

Falsehood, in its grosser form, is so palpable a sin, and so revolting, that we need say nothing here to prove it so. The full-grown weed not any one would spare, could they find means to root it out. But the weed was a weed, before it seemed so, and the poison was already in its root. And so are there forms of falsehood that excite no disgust, and create but small alarm, if any, when first detected in the character—nay, are too often fostered and encouraged.

Had Anna told a direct falsehood in her infancy, she would have been corrected with seriousness—the guilt of it would have been made plain to her, and every proper means employed to prevent a recurrence of the fault. But no one gave heed to the slight inaccuracies into which she was betrayed by a lively imagination and a hurried mode of expression—her mistakes excited mirth, and were not seldom repeated in her presence, as proofs of wit or subjects of amusement. So welcome a lesson was promptly learned, and what was at first carelessness soon became design. The plain and simple truth gained no attention ; a very little exaggeration would make mirth for herself and her companions. In all this Anna meant no sin—and during her childhood, perhaps, it scarcely might amount to sin, because it deceived no one and injured no one. But the rank weed grew apace. From exaggerating by design, she grew so accustomed to it, that it became almost impossible to her to speak literally. One hour was, by her reckoning, always three—five hundred stood for twenty—every rood was a mile, and every common accident a marvel, if not an impossibility. These may seem trifles, and so perhaps they were—but they did not long continue so—The prattle of the child grew into the converse of the

woman—and where was then the truth too sacred
to be sacrificed to Anna's wit? The words of others
distorted, their actions misconstrued, and their affairs
misstated, to make them ridiculous and herself amusing. From exaggeration to invention is but a pass
imperceptible—no matter who was wronged or who
deceived—habit had absorbed the sense of wrong,
and a laugh had become the price current for a lie.
These lies, perhaps, were not meant to injure—
but every falsehood may injure, whatever be intended. Anna, at first, gave pain without knowing
it. But she could not stop here. There are occasions in every one's life where a falsehood may serve
our present interests—where a falsehood may gratify
our resentment, may shield us from disgrace, or
secure us a triumph over those who contend with us.
Would Anna pause when these occasions came?
Would she, who told falsehoods daily without a
motive, hesitate when it could serve some important
purpose? When passion was excited and interest
at stake, would she, for the first time in her life,
stop to consider the criminality of saying what was
not true? No—Anna will surely tell at last, if it
serves her purpose, the most injurious and deliberate
falsehood.

Now, however the world may join in with the
laugh, however willingly the idle may listen and the
thoughtless applaud, such a character is not esteemed.
The gay and the giddy may seek them when they
would be amused, but friendship takes them not to

her bosom—feeling holds no communion with them —sorrow asks of them no comfort—wisdom takes with them no counsel—candour, simplicity, and good sense, shrink instinctively from their touch. However brilliant, and however entertaining, however innocent, even in intention, the person whose words are habitually not true, is lowered in the scale of moral creatures—their opinions have very little weight, their testimony is but little regarded, and their sincerity but rarely trusted: even though they were never yet guilty of a mischievous deception. But we must look higher than this. There is One above us who himself is Truth, and to whom all that is not, must be hateful. He has promised to bring into judgment every idle word, and has already passed sentence upon the guilt of " whosoever loveth and maketh a lie." Surely they are dangerous weapons these to make us sport with. With the utmost caution we may use, we shall not escape the condemnation, should He be extreme to mark our words. There is so much deception in our hearts, that we rarely even know the truth exactly; and there is so much temptation to disguise or discolour it, that perhaps scarce a day goes by us in which we are not betrayed into some evasion. The weed is too surely indigenous to the soil, and every hour that we spare to check its growth, we spare an enemy that will spoil the lustre of our garden. The best, and the sweetest, and the purest in moral loveliness, will be attainted by its unhallowed touch.

Early let us go to our garden, and look if the small germ be there—and every morning return to see if it be coming. And mark well the manner of its growth. It does not come at once, a bold and mischievous falsehood. Being in society, we hear something that hurts or offends us—desiring that another should share our indignation or redress our wrong, we add to it, perhaps, no more but an aggravative tone. It is but wounded feeling, or just abhorrence of sin: True—but it is falsehood. Walking by the way-side, we meet an object of distress—anxious to interest others for their sake, we exaggerate the picture of suffering, or conceal its alleviation. Our motive is but benevolence: True—but it is falsehood. We have been witness to some incident, or listened to some recital—a very little embellishment will make it highly marvellous, and excite interest or afford amusement—no one can be harmed by it: True—but it is still falsehood. Well, the weed is fair and green—shall we let it grow on another day? We have committed some fault—if we confess it, we shame ourselves for ever, and sink in the esteem of those we love. A falsehood for this time will conceal it, and we will do the wrong no more. True—but another sin, and probably a greater, is added to the first, and He who knows all is left out of the account. Being innocent, we have been wronged, or we have been the unwilling occasion of wrong; by a falsehood, mischief may be prevented—With no other defence in our power, we may surely prevent crime, and secure ourselves from injury. But this is no more than to choose to ourselves the culprit's part, and, being innocent, voluntarily to claim guilt on our behalf—It is better to suffer innocent, than guilty to escape. We are brought unawares into a situation in which, if the truth be not denied, we shall seem unkind, ungrateful, insincere. We know that we are not so, though appearances are against us; falsehood becomes here but the servant of truth—we use it only to prevent mistake. Methinks our fatal weed is growing now apace. That which at first seemed the handmaid of generous feeling, hath passed over to the service of self—not yet, it is true, to serve any evil propensity or indulge any culpable desire. It seems but a fair background to set off our flowers. Let it grow on. Hard service truly has that propensity which once is enlisted to wait on the selfish interests of man. Envy, jealousy, and emulation, anger, resentment, and revenge, ambition, vanity, and pride—all these make a part of human selfishness, and claim to be served in their turn. The weapon is in a hand well practised to its use. When better feeling predominates, the use of it seems to be for good. But when passion surprises us, can the well-practised hand forbear the ready weapon? Envy can, by a word of falsehood, bear down its proud superior— emulation can, by a falsehood, pass over the head of its rival—revenge can sate itself, anger can safely spend itself in falsehood—pride, and vanity, and ambition may be served by it. And thus we have the weed full grown! We may use it oftener or seldomer, as the temptation arises, or as passion impels —but that we shall use it when occasion urges, is not doubtful. And who now can tell the deformity of the weed we have spared? It may misrepresent the most pure intention, it may blight the fairest character, it may attaint the holiest mind, bring ridicule on the most sacred truths, betray the most generous trust, destroy all confidence and honest intercourse in society, and provoke and insult that high, holy, and omniscient Being, whom nothing can deceive, and who will bear with no deception.

Faintly we have sketched the mischiefs, and faintly described the manner of the growth—We have given some examples, but they are a few among a thousand. We warn you of the danger of the first departure from truth—of the playful brandishing of so dangerous a weapon. Thus much, at least, must be acknowledged—falsehood is sin—sin can never be a trifle or a jest.

No. VI.

CHRISTMAS TIME.

O nuit bienheureuse, en laquelle est né le Christ, le Seigneur, je te trouve beaucoup plus claire et plus resplendissante que tous les beaux jours de l'année; car tu as été éclairée de ce bel soleil d'en haut, au regard duquel le soleil même n'est que ténébres! Bien-heureuse nuit, en laquelle on chante le triomphe dans le ciel, et on publie la paix en terre aux hommes, auxquels Dieu prend son bon plaisir!

DRELINCOURT.

In every period of nature's story, attached to every creed, and making a part of every mode of worship, religious festivals of some kind have been observed; and they have for the most part worn a character not ill-becoming the Deity in whose honour they were held. The Greek kept his festival with arms in hand, and in doing honour to his warrior gods, could find no fitter celebration than games of agility and feats of strength. The more savage Roman, in whose hard bosom inhumanity was the proudest vir-tue, feasted his deities with gladiatorial sights. The dark Indian, not very much mistaking the spirit he serves, holds festivals in honour of the Devil, in which his scalped and tortured enemies make at once the offering and the sport. While to his obscene, unholy gods, the unchaste Hindoo holds feasts of infamy, pollution, and dishonour.

Far other festival was theirs, who, mid the darkness of an idolatrous world, were taught to serve the God of truth and love. They kept their Passover with fasting and prayer. In their year of Jubilee, the oppressed had restitution, and the prisoner went free. Where superstition overclouds our holy faith, the religious festivals have assumed a like character. Saints and martyrs who have come in to share their Maker's glory and divide his worship, have all their festivals; and if we note the idle pomp, and useless offerings, and heartless ceremonies, with which they are celebrated, we must confess them not ill-suited to deities of earth, introduced with worse than Pagan polytheism, into the worship of the Christian Church.

Restored, in profession at least, to the simplicity of the gospel faith, disencumbered of all that man had intermixed with the spiritual worship demanded of us from God—forming their church, whether Episcopal or otherwise, on that which they believe to be the scripture model, Protestants have left their religious anniversaries but few and simple. Christmas and Easter are the two great festivals of their year —the latter only partially observed—the former, we believe, universally. How do we keep it? As suitably to our profession as the Hindoo to his? As much in accordance with the character of Him we serve,

as the Olympic games with the battle-loving gods of
Greece?

It was thus I questioned myself, as one evening
I sat pensive and alone, close on the hearth of my
solitary chamber. No one was nigh to answer to
my doubts. I trimmed my candle, and stirred my
fire, and listened as if something should bring me a
reply. Silence, indeed, there was not—for there was
a sound within of eager footsteps passing to and fro.
But what had I to do with that? And there was a
noise of carriage-wheels without—but what had that
to do with the subject of my thoughts? The books
that lay crowded on my table were my sole companions. Could I not question them? I opened one,
and it said, When the wise men beheld the star that
announced the Saviour's birth, they rejoiced with
exceeding great joy; and when they found him, they
fell down and worshipped him. And it said again,
that when that birth in Bethlehem was announced,
there appeared a multitude of the heavenly host,
praising God, and saying, Glory to God in the highest, and on earth peace, good-will toward men!

On earth and in heaven, then, this season was a
season of rejoicing; and we keep it in memory of
an event the most important that ever happened in
this nether world—so important, that exulting angels
shared the triumph of the news they brought. We
keep it in honour of Him, who on earth despised
the pomps and vanities of life, disowned the turbu-
lence of earthly passion, turned aside from the paths

of idleness and folly, and spoke with his sacred lips full many an awful "Woe" on all who loved them. His holy soul was bent on other purposes—his eyes wept tears of pity for the world's insensibility—his heart was rent and broken for its sins—and his hallowed spirit at last surrendered, to purchase manumission for the bond-slaves of the earth, and make them heirs of bliss eternal. And now in heaven he sits in unspotted purity enthroned, watching with eye compassionate the people he has loved on earth to save them from the dangers and temptations that encompass them; to win their hearts to penitence, and faith, and love.

And what to us was that event we celebrate? What share have we in the joy that was proclaimed in heaven at his coming? Ruined, lost, degraded, and condemned, his coming was to us, if it was any thing, pardon, and peace, and restoration to the favour and the likeness of God. The deepest humiliation that such an interference was needed, the most exalted joy that our need was thus provided —joy, greater than when the captive is set free —joy, greater than when the sentenced criminal is pardoned, becomes us at this season. But what joy? When we celebrate the memory of one we love, we tell fondly of his deeds—we bring to mind things that had nearly stolen from our thoughts—we repeat his sayings—bring forth each valued memento of his love—seek the scenes, and renew the employments, that best remind us of him; if he has been renowned for any thing, our music, our decorations, and our sports, bear all some reference to his character or his doings. Christmas is the celebration of our Saviour's birth. When angels told it, they gave glory to God on high. When wise men heard it, they fell down and worshipped. When Christians celebrate it, they —— I had not time to finish all I might have said of chastened gaiety, of warm and humble gratitude, of pious recollections, joyful praises, and confiding prayers, when a great increase of noises called off my attention to what was passing beyond the precincts of my solitude.

Our Christmas festival is not confined to the single day set apart by our Church for religious service. The season of rejoicing we usually call Christmas, extends to the length of weeks, distinguished from all others in the year by frequent festivities peculiar to itself; especially among the younger part of the community, to whom it is usually a time of holiday and domestic indulgence. And I soon perceived this was one of those nights which peculiarly develop what we mean by Christmas-time; and I recollected besides, that it was the New-year's Eve, a night of no common distinction among the distinguished. What a happy opportunity to solve my previous doubts, and set my mind at rest! I went out of my chamber in haste, to listen what might be passing. As I drew nigh to the spot, to which a glare of lights and a sound of music attracted me, I saw many an airy figure passing and repassing in the distance. I drew near—but why need I pause to describe it? Who does not know what is meant by a Children's Ball at Christmas? Many a beautiful little creature, whose cheek in the morning had been flushed with health, was already paling in the midnight glare—their glistening eyes and panting bosoms betrayed an unnatural excitement, while their unclothed and fragile limbs already moved with listlessness and languor. I thought the glittering trinkets on their bosoms did but attaint their purity, and their splendid and fantastic dresses transform the most exquisite of nature's works into the likeness of the mimic puppet-show. But they, it seems, thought otherwise—and so did the parents and elder spectators who lined the circumference of the ball-room. The beauty of one, and the elegance of another, and the dress of a third, engrossed all eyes, and set all tongues in motion. On one pale cheek, I saw the blush of mingled modesty and pride grow deeper and deeper as repeated words of admiration met her ear. I saw a second, whom Christmas balls had already cured of that first weakness, send her bright eyes round in search of the admiration at which she blushed no longer. I traced in some the restlessness of envy, the skulk of inferiority, and the languor of perceived neglect. In none — no, not in one of all that fairy crowd, saw I the calm of innocence or the simplicity of childhood. Unnatural exultation, or premature depression, was the expression of every countenance there. Mean time, the fête went on.

They looked at their watches—I looked at mine, and perceived they were preparing for the midnight hour. 'Tis well, I said, to note it; for, at its sounding, another year is stricken off from their short tale of life. Of the threescore years—perhaps of the twenty—or the ten—it may be not half of that, granted them by the Creator to give him glory and make ready for eternity, here is one more numbered off, and gone to make report in heaven of its use. How much of gratitude they owe for all the happiness in that year enjoyed—how much regret for all the errors and neglects with which they stained it—what remembrance, what love of Him, without whose birth on earth, at this season celebrated, each closing of the year would be but the signal of approaching and eternal misery! How much humility and holy awe at thought that even now it may possibly be so! It is a moment of no common interest. The year is closed—its pleasures can no more be enjoyed, its wasted moments can no more be used, the deeds that were done in it cannot be recalled, its dangers are escaped and its sufferings are over—very brief has it been, and the one that succeeds it will be no longer. Our last it may be—one less to us it must be.

Midnight struck. The music became louder and gayer than before—the dance went on with redoubled energy—every cheek glowed, and every eye kindled —old and young, all were now engaged—my eye searched every feature, to find if one of all these thoughts were written there—forgetfulness, absolute inebriation as to every rational recollection, was all the expression I could trace—a senseless joy because a year they had misused was gone, and another they meant to misuse was come, and the eternity they had forgotten was brought nearer, and the life they delighted in was receding. How long the intoxication lasted, I cannot say, for I withdrew to my chamber to reflect on what had passed.

This, then, is the festival Christians hold in honour of their God—in remembrance of that meek and suffering Lord!—Remembrance, alas! who remembered him in that gay room? Was not their object rather to forget him? How dissonant to their ears would have come the mention of his name— how little appropriate any emblem of his love—how almost profane to have made mention of his deeds or reference to his character!—Remembrance! Oh! if there had come, indeed, to any bosom there, a recollection of the meaning of Christmas, of the stable where the holy babe slept for our sakes on the cold manger—of the meanness and contempt with which the Son of the Most High in mercy clothed himself —the life of sorrow to which he was at this season born—how meek, how holy, and yet how wronged —by ourselves how much neglected and forgotten— surely the thought had marred their gaiety, and put to shame their strange festivity!

Was this forgetfulness the glory angels sung! Was this indifference the worship wise men offered! Yet thus we teach our children to celebrate the birth-time of their Saviour. Instead of the innocent, domestic treat, the game of healthful play, the holiday sweetened by previous industry, the useful or amusing present, things that formerly would constitute their Christmas gambols, it is the seed-time now for implanting every sinful feeling and unholy passion. Pride, and vanity, and rivalship, and envy, are to be awakened, time wasted, health impaired, and spirits exhausted. Many a long day expended, in thought at least, about the dress they are to wear; many another in weariness and languor, and disgust of less-exciting occupations; attention untimely called to the advantage of personal attractions; a false estimate induced of the comparative value of internal and external excellence. These are the evils now, without which so many of our young people cannot pass a happy Christmas—cannot celebrate—how strange the distortion!—the love and mercy of that holy Being to whom the very touch of evil is most hateful; who turns aside his head from the first movement of that sin which bound his sacred brow with thorns. He to whose glory and service our time, and thoughts, and health, and spirits are due, is to be honoured at this season by the more than usual want and perversion of them all. He to whose memory the fêtes are held, is to be more totally forgotten, if possible, at this season than in all the year besides. The expression of our joy may be the ball, the theatre, the rout—any thing, in short, so it have no reference to that which is our professed cause of rejoicing. We must be happy, because it is Christmas, the time of our Saviour's birth into the world—but do not remind us of the circumstance, lest it make us sad.

Would we have no rejoicing then? While heathens rejoice in their Apollo or their Vishnu, are Christians to go all the year in weeds of penitence, with mournful and downcast looks? No season of peculiar joy and exultation? Nay, surely not. Let Christmas be the happiest season of the year—there is much reason that it should—let the poor have their sober feasts and our children their glad holidays. But let us not be more inconsistent than heathens are, excluding from our feasts the thought of him we affect to celebrate, and offering him only what we know he loathes.

Would we know what are consistent and what are inconsistent modes of rejoicing at such a season, methinks mere common sense might tell us. We need be at no loss to discover what amusement consists with the glad remembrance of our Saviour's coming, the circumstances, cause, and consequence of that event—with all the love and obedience we owe to him because of it. We can surely discern what employment reminds us of him, and what disposes us to forget him : what, if he were yet on earth, he would consecrate with a blessing, and what he would turn from with a keen reproof or a compassionating tear. Yes, we do know—our ignorance is a feint— we know very well when we are about a thing,

whether we would rather that the eye of our God and
Saviour were averted, and his ear deafened, or at
least that nothing should remind us of his presence;
or whether it is pleasing to us to think that he is
near, checking our propensities to wrong, guarding
us from ill, prospering our pursuits, and sanctifying
our enjoyments. Whatever consists with the grateful
remembrance and desired presence of our Saviour, is
a fit amusement for the season—whatever excludes
them cannot be so.

If we say that on these terms we can have no
mirth, no amusement, and our children and our servants no enjoyment of their Christmas — then, in
truth, I know not what to say, but that our children,
and our servants, and ourselves, are in a strange
case:—we cannot rejoice in our Saviour's coming,
unless we may forget him—we cannot keep his birth-
time, unless we may offend him. If this be so, we
had better at least change the name of our festival,
and the pretext for our festivities—for though we
may be very glad it is the 25th of December, or
the 6th of January, we are clearly not glad it is the
day in which man's redemption was proclaimed from
Heaven, or in which wise men fell down and acknowledged their infant King. There was a period
in our country's history in which the same season
of the year was kept in honour of Woden, or some
Saxon god. In the North of England the common
people still make a sort of little images at Christmas,
which they call Yule Doos—this in modern language

would be Christmas Gods—a custom no doubt derived from their pagan ancestors: in them it is no idolatry, as they attach no meaning to it whatever, and only do it because it always has been done. But let us look to ourselves, lest, under a Christian name, we but keep the heathen's feast; serving therein some God of our own devising; doing honour to time and sense, and the world, and ourselves—to every thing but Him by whose holy name we call our unholy sports.

No. VII.

FEARS.

The butler desired me, with a very grave face, not to venture my-self in it after sunset, for that one of the footmen had been almost frightened out of his wits by a spirit that appeared to him in the shape of a black horse without a head—to which he added, that about a month ago, one of the maids coming home late that way, with a pail of milk upon her head, heard such a rustling in the bushes that she let it fall.

ADDISON.

I DO not desire to make great things of small, or to magnify into vices the little discrepancies of character that so incessantly blemish the moral prospect around us. Vice is one thing, folly is another. In their importance, no comparison can be made. Against vice, in its fairest and most delusive form, we hope we shall be found ever to protest, whatever sanction custom, fashion, or opinion, may have given it. But there are some things which are not vices, which cannot be called morally wrong, and which yet need to be reported of as follies, where the whisper of admonition may be timely heard. Next to being good, it is desirable to be agreeable—next to being virtuous, it is essential to be wise. When we have weeded our garden, we trim and prune our flowers to make them bloom the fairer. So if, in my silent wanderings through a noisy world, I make report of some things I have heard, that to my readers seem not to bear the character of wrongs, I beg it may not be believed I thought them so, or listened to them with feelings no less painful than to some other things by which man is injured and the Deity offended. But we are not content to mix up the bitter wormwood in our dishes, because it is not the poisonous nightshade. Must we encourage a folly because it is not a vice, and torment each other and ourselves because it does injury to no one? Of the extent of the folly I leave the wise to judge; of the grievousness of the torment, I presume to judge myself, having amply proved it, as I trust to make it appear.

It was my misfortune once to visit a family of people, very excellent, and very amiable, and for any thing that I desire to say to the contrary, very wise in things of moment. Besides the mother, there were several young people of different ages, reaching from infancy almost to womanhood, all happy, all compliant, and all obliging—except when they happened to be assailed with what they were pleased to call fear — but as fear has always respect to danger, fancied, real, or possible, I should prefer to find some other name for it, because I can prove that it existed where danger was not possible, nor even by themselves apprehended. What influence these attacks had upon their own happiness it is hard to judge, because some people find their enjoyment in the miseries they create for themselves—but they made woful inroads on the enjoyments of others; and for compliance, good-humour, and good-breeding, poor chance, indeed, had they to stand against the influence of these vehement emotions.

Though the hour was late, I had scarcely laid myself down to rest on the night of my arrival, ere I was aroused by the buzzing of voices, and the sound of soft, stolen footsteps in the adjoining gallery. The young ladies had been disturbed by extraordinary sounds, or such at least as would have been extraordinary, had not the hearing of them recurred every other night. One was afraid to go to bed, and another was afraid to get up—one could not come into her room, and another could not come out of it. Some thought they heard, and others were sure they heard, but nobody knew what. Nor was it easy to perceive the purport and end of the commotion— for no one made any attempt to ascertain the real ground of alarm; probably because they knew not where to look for it—or, more likely, because they were too much used to their own fears to expect to find any ground for them at all. And so, after much listening, and starting, and whispering, they were pleased at last to go to rest, and generously allowed me to do the same.

I ventured in the morning to suggest, that the indulgence of unreasonable fears was not the con-

comitant of a strong mind, and did in itself much
tend to weaken it: that in the presence of real
danger it unfits us for exertion, and in the absence
of it, costs us as much suffering as the evil itself
might do. I was answered by stories manifold and
various, of things that had been, and things that
might be; and the absolute certainty they still retained of having heard noises, though not one in
their morning senses really supposed there had been
any thing to make the noise.

Willing to close a conversation I thought so little
improving, I proposed to two of the younger girls
to walk with me in the grounds. It was agreed to
with pleasure; they were polite, cheerful, and obliging, till we had walked—must I own, not more than
some few hundred yards?—when a small frog jumped
out from the grass before us, and passed to the side
of the path. A scream that might have startled
even the insensible frog, broke from one of the young
ladies, and they both protested they would go no
farther on that path. It was in vain I represented
to them that a frog is the most harmless of living
things, having neither bite nor sting with which
to wound; and that, moreover, whether it were
harmless or harmful, it had taken itself willingly
away from us. They replied only that it was a
hideous, shocking creature, and frightened them to
death. Equally in vain I urged my wish to reach
the place to which that path would lead us — my
wishes had no weight against their fears—they would

not go, and excused themselves by saying they were
dreadfully afraid of live things. We turned aside
and took another path.—But alas! not far had we
pursued it, when I saw upon the green turf, where
it had untimely fallen, a sweet little bird already
dead and cold, its pretty eye unclosed, and not a
feather ruffled. I picked it up to admire it, when
suddenly both my companions let go my arm, and
stepped some paces back, protesting loudly that they
were dreadfully afraid of dead things, and should
never like to walk that path again. Methought
their path of life would scarce be easy, to whom the
living and the dead were thus alike terrific.

We now pursued our walk, but soon in utter
hopelessness, on my part, of any thing like comfort
or enjoyment. If we were to cross a meadow there
was a cow, or at least a horse in it—whichever way
we turned my companions saw a man, or a dog—
and when there was neither man nor dog, nor any
thing else, alive or dead, the way was so lonely they
were afraid to go forward. They could not sit in
the shade, lest the inhabitants of the bushes should
descend on their head—they could not sit in the sun,
lest the winged insects should settle on their clothes.
If I presented them with a flower, they let it fall,
because they mistook the green leaf for a caterpillar.
I wished them most heartily at home, and made
what haste I could to rid myself of such troublesome
companions.

But scarcely had we reached the house, when,

for the promoting of the day's amusement, a drive was proposed to view some neighbouring ruins. It will be believed I was comforted to find my walking companions were to be changed for some a little older, to whom I hoped the live things and dead things might be less alarming. But alas! we had now no need of either. When the carriage went up-hill, they were afraid it would run back; when it went down-hill, they were afraid it would run forward. If the horses ran slowly, they were sure they would never go on; if they went fast, they were sure they would never stop. The drive was romantic and beautiful in the extreme, but the ladies saw nothing except the ruts in the road. I attempted conversation, but was interrupted by a scream every time the carriage lost its exact perpendicular. And at last, when the ebullition of their fears could be forborne no longer, they insisted on stopping the carriage to enquire if the road was not very bad, and if it was safe to go forward. The former was too obvious to need the asking, the latter they were determined not to believe. When the carriage could not stop, they insisted upon getting out to walk, and then, having made the driver go slower and slower, till the fleet hours of days were nearly spent, they discovered that they should surely be benighted before their return, and of course be murdered, over and above having their necks broken by the badness of the road. These were certainly no pleasing anticipations; and, if I did not partake the imaginary ills, I was sufficiently tired of the real ones, to oppose returning without the accomplishment of our purpose ; and listened all dinner-time to assertions, proved and explained, of the absolute impossibility of reaching the place to which we had set out.

'All dinner-time, did I say? It might have been so, had not an unhappy wasp presented itself with the sweets of the second course. There was other company besides myself at table, but that could not signify when a wasp was in the case. The servants were all put in requisition with tongs, poker, and shovel ; the children started and jumped, and overset every thing in their way ; and the dinner remained to cool till the murder of the foe almost restored peace to the society—but not quite—for one was still sure it would crawl. Having a little girl next me, of whose good sense I had on some occasions formed a favourable opinion, I ventured to ask her why she was so much afraid of a wasp. She replied, as I expected, because it might sting her. I asked her if she had ever been stung by one. She assured me she had, in endeavouring to drive it from the table, whence, had she left it alone, it would probably have gone of itself quite harmlessly. I asked her of the pain, and how long it lasted, and whether it was difficult to bear. Her answer implied, that though the pain was acute it was short, and that the remainder of my question seemed to her ridiculous. I then submitted it to her candour, whether, in the worst issue of the case, which, considering the number of wasps that fly, and the number of people who will not let them fly in peace, occurs but seldom, the quantity of pain was really equal to the quantity of fear she had betrayed; and whether, in the certain anticipation of just so much pain by any other cause, she should have felt any fear at all? She confessed that she should not; because, as she sensibly remarked, a slight and temporary inconvenience from bodily pain was not worth a complaint, much less an anticipatory fear. But all this did not seem to her, reason why she should not scream at the sight of a wasp. Nor indeed was it, as she gave me occasion to learn before the lapse of many hours—for the entrance of a moth, that never yet in the memory of man was known to sting, created to the full as much commotion later in the evening: so much, indeed, that most of the party retreated out of the room in the midst of our musical festivities, and left me to play to myself.

Well I know, that ladies who have grown up in the indulgence of such fears, and have come at last to persuade themselves there is a degree of delicacy and refinement in them, must go on unto the end under the penalty due to their folly; that of tormenting themselves and annoying others. But as my whispers are for the ears of those with whom nothing is yet too late, I would represent to them the absolute inconsistency of such fears with good sense and a rational mind. All extravagance is folly —because sound sense mainly consists in giving to things their due degree of importance, and proportioning the sentiment to the occasion that calls it forth. Fear, therefore, beyond the occasion, must be folly, even when some degree of danger exists: and though, as a passion inherent to our nature, we cannot but be subject to it, we believe it will generally be found greater or less in proportion as the mind is strong or weak. The unreasonable indulgence of fear—we speak now of that fear which has a real object and occasion — is surely not inconsistent with the calm and humble trust we profess to repose in a superintending Providence, without whose knowledge harm cannot by any means befall us. If it be urged that we ought to foresee and provide against danger, that is true—but fear, so far from accelerating this provident care, usually unfits us for using the means we have of avoiding or resisting evil; the courageous will escape, where the timid must inevitably suffer. But that sort of fear, if, for want of another term, we so must call it, which is our present subject of reprehension, has nothing whatever to do with danger — call it timidity, sensibility, or whatever we may, it is nothing but weakness and folly; and we may depend upon it, that being purely selfish, it is always unpleasing. It is constitutional in some minds, no doubt, more than in others; but if we have a constitutional weakness of frame, we use all means to overcome it, and often with success. Then why not so with this, our mental weakness? But, in fact, much more depends on habit and education than on nature. Some children are absolutely taught it, and others are foolishly humoured in it, till it is no longer in their own power, or in the power of any one, to subdue it. I am certainly inclined to make an exception in those very extraordinary and wonderful cases of natural antipathy, of which the existence is too certain to be disputed, and too inscrutable to be understood; where an instinctive horror of some one particular thing gives such a keen perception of its presence as nothing can baffle or deceive. This, perhaps, it may be impossible to conquer. But this bears no analogy whatever to the multifarious fears, and horrors, and dislikes, of which we have been speaking, by which reason and good sense are offended, selfishness fostered and indulged, and the feelings and convenience of others generally sacrificed to our own.

Addressing myself exclusively to my younger friends, I would induce them to consider that most of those living things for which they have conceived a horror, are in themselves beautiful, and should be objects of our admiration. I believe there is not in the whole creation a thing that can properly be termed disgusting. It may be troublesome and annoying, if it obtrudes itself where comfort and cleanliness forbid its entrance, and may justly be removed, or, if necessary, destroyed. But in themselves, both reptiles and insects are most curiously and exquisitely wrought, and instead of shrinking from them with senseless horror, we may accustom ourselves to look at them with sensations of extreme pleasure, as the works of Him whose wisdom and power they manifest, and of whose bounty they partake, in the enjoyment of the existence he has bestowed on them. It is to some persons, and might be to all, if they would cultivate the feeling, a source of infinite delight to watch the swarms of insects that people the whole creation in the mid-day of a summer sun. There are those who receive as much pleasure from the insect that settles on their finger, as from the wild-flower that blossoms under their feet. This complacent feeling in the contemplation of nature's living works, and that of persons who shrink from them with disgust, are merely habits of mind: the one may just as well be cultivated as the other.

In respect to the fear of accidents and injuries from our fellow-creatures, I believe the best cure for it is an abiding sense of the ever-present Providence of God; and if we are constitutionally timid, we cannot better subdue it than by cultivating this consciousness of the Divine protection, in such a manner that it may recur to our minds on the first movement of alarm; in short, so as to become influential on our habits and sensations, and make a part of all our thoughts and feelings.

No. VIII.

THE SABBATH.

Is there a time when moments flow
More lovelily than all beside ?—
It is, of all the times below,
A Sabbath even in summer tide.

EDMESTON.

IT was a Sabbath evening in the height of summer.
The sun had been some half-hour gone, but his beams
still lingered in the clear horizon, and still the fleecy
cloud was tinged with a fading touch of red.   The
blue vault had not yet deepened into grey, nor the
landscape become obscure in the growing twilight.
And yet there was a mellowing tint upon the scene,
that gave of softness what it stole of splendour—
like the brilliant and gifted spirit that religion has
chastened into stillness.   The flower that had drooped, and the leaf that had withered in the noonday
heat, were already recovered by the evening's fresh-
ness; while the Thrush prolonged her song, and the
Red-breast lingered on the bough, as if unwilling
to part from such a day. Peace and repose were
the character of the scene, and fancy well might

picture that the task of life was done, and all things ready for eternal rest.

In all there seemed a fitness for the day, and for the feelings with which I was returning from the evening service. The words of love and peace had dropped like holy balm upon the bosom, and put to rest its agitating cares. Shame and contrition had sunk the soul too low for opposition, and mercy had won it into grateful acquiescence. At peace with God, because it had drunk deeply of his grace and truth, at peace with the world, because it seemed no longer worth contention, at peace with itself, because self was degraded and dethroned, the spirit partook of the evening's Sabbath hue, and only wished it could be always so. "And will it not be always so," I thought, as I walked slowly homeward, "when our life's working-days are over, and the eternal Sabbath dawns upon our souls? A little while, and what is now but a brief foretaste, a passing semblance of celestial peace, will be an eternal and unchanging reality. A little while, and the smile of our Father will no more be averted, the world renounced will no more resume its power, and self-submitted will no more rebel. And if there be such pleasure in an early Sabbath, interrupted as it is with our coldness, and carelessness, and earthliness, what will be the bliss of that eternal Sabbath for which we are preparing?" And then I considered the goodness of God in this institution, by which one day in seven is separated from the rest, to be employed in making happy what the occupations of the other six too often tend to make wretched, and to sanctify what they are too well fitted to corrupt. Prone as we are to sin, and subject as we are to sorrow, our most lawful occupations are fraught with anxiety and danger—What comfort, then, that there is one day in which it is our duty to neglect them, to forget them, and give up ourselves entirely to thoughts and pursuits of which the fruits are love, and holiness, and joy : to have nothing to do but to acquaint ourselves with God and be at peace ! I passed the day-labourer in his clean white frock, his Bible and prayer-book tucked under his arm, and thought how he must enjoy the repose of such a day, his only means of instruction, perhaps his only pause from effort and endurance. I overtook the pale mechanic, and fancied, from the expression of content upon his features, that he was telling over the stores of consolation he had gathered, to feed on in his close workshop all the week. The children of charity were tripping by my side, in their plain round bonnets and dark frocks, the bag of books on their arm, or the basket in their hand—I looked at them, and hoped something had that day been taught them that would sweeten the rude lot for which they were preparing. A little longer musing, and I should have persuaded myself the Sabbath was a day that all men love, and the calm of nature what all were sharing, and the song of gratitude what all were singing. But truth was at hand, and fancy must give place.

When I turned from the meadows into the public road, the passengers began to thicken on my path. The town had poured out her population in every direction for their evening walk, and the hills and the pathways were scattered thick with figures of various appearance, all well-dressed and neat, and seemingly free from care. There was nothing at first strongly to invade my previous feelings. I could still fancy that the poor labourer, or richer tradesman, was enjoying with his wife and children the beauties of creation and the grateful recollection of a day well spent : and in many a lowly hovel, as I passed it, I saw, in interesting group, the father attentively perusing his Bible, while the mother was setting out the plain spare supper, where every thing looked clean once in the week at least. Truth might indeed have told, that some who enjoyed the leisure of the day had thought nothing of Him whose day it was, and some who were tasting of nature's charms felt nothing of gratitude to Him who gave them ; but so much was not written on their brow ; and they wore at least an air of enjoyment that became the hour.

Not so, when, proceeding a little further, I met the gay equipage returning from an evening drive— Not so when I saw the light skiff, with sails unfurled, gliding merrily towards the shore. Whoever was within them, here was the day of God profaned by the direct breaking of his holy law. He had said, Remember that thou do it not—they did it, and boldly denied the harm. Whatever innocence might be assumed in those who took the pleasure, they were guilty of the sin of those they taught and paid to pursue on the Sunday the occupation of the week, and unhallow in thought and deed the day that God made sacred. They would say, perhaps, they spent an hour in a recreation very harmless, and no way inconsistent with their thoughts of holiness—but for their one hour of harmless recreation, others must toil many—the cattle that were used must be cleaned, the hand that plied the oar for them would ply for others, encouraged by their example—the words of God are plain and positive, and impossible to mis- construe; therefore the breach of them is a bold refusal to comply with his command, made openly in the face of earth and heaven. They would urge, no doubt, that they had enough kept holy the day, in going twice to the service appointed. Alas! if they had been there, it should almost seem to make their guilt the greater—for there they had heard the command enforced, and there they had prayed to be inclined to keep it, and thence they had re- turned resolved to break it, and deny the wrong.

The evening was closing fast — already the dark outline of form was all that remained distinct; and as I entered the town, the doors were closing and lights were beginning to gleam from every window. My pleasing reverie had been painfully dissipated— my mind was occupied in considering of the way in which Sunday evening is usually passed—and, presuming that when windows stand open, no secrets are passing within, I set myself to observe how people were employed in the various houses as I passed them; not without hope that I might gather something useful, in the way of warning or example for my readers.

I passed a window where noisy mirth bespoke the late dinner party; where it was evident the company would not, and the domestics could not, remember it was the Sabbath—except in so far as they sighed in secret that decency allowed them not to dance or play at cards—but there I paused not. There was nothing doubtful among these. They, too, had been to church—themselves—but not their servants, who had this dinner to make ready. As soon as they came forth from the sacred walls, they had passed with all speed from house to house to make their morning calls—I say not, to wipe off the serious impression of the service, for it had made none, but to get rid of the time till the bells should chime again. Unless they preferred a drive, they had gone a second time to church—they had plenty of time to dress for dinner, and then, thanks to this party, there was no more trouble about disposing of the hours till bed-time.

Neither did I stop long, where, in a more decent way, but with much the same purpose, a few friends had called in upon some other few, for the charitable purpose of passing away an evening on which they thought it right to be quiet and abstain from their weekly occupations, and yet found it very tedious. But I made a longer pause when I arrived under a window where there were clearly none present but the family that abode there, and it was pretty evident that no one had lost the recollection that it was the Sabbath. Knew I this from the smile of gratitude and heavenly peace that shone on their features? My readers shall judge. "I wish it was bed-time," said a little girl, not usually in haste to go to bed; "I am so tired of having nothing to do!" Though in truth she had risen two hours later than usual that morning.

"I think our clock must be too slow," replied her brother. "You know we were hardly dressed for breakfast when the bells began to ring this morning. It must be more than half-past nine:" and with a weary yawn he threw himself on the rug to play with the spaniel.

All were not alike unfortunate—for I observed a young lady at her writing-desk, folding and sealing as many letters as one can reasonably suppose she might have occasion to write in a week. How happy for her correspondents, that one day in seven was a leisure day—a day on which the hours, being less valuable, could be better spared than on any other! As I could not see within the letters, I am bound in charity to suppose the subject of them was in unison with the feelings and previous occupations of the day. How should they be otherwise? A heart that, from the rising till the going down of the Sabbath sun, had been in earnest devotion before God, had mourned in many a prayer the consciousness of sin, and grown light under the sweet assurance of its pardon—and had trembled at the awful denunciations pronounced on the dissembler, and been moved, amazed, overwhelmed, with the contemplation of the Redeemer's love and the Father's fond forbearance—It was impossible that such a heart could turn immediately to common themes, the amusements of yesterday and the business of to-morrow, and the thousand trifles that bespeak a mind unoccupied by deeper interests. If I could not penetrate the letters to find where the heart had been, and where the thoughts, I was at least certain that they had been together, and that the language of the letters had gone after them; and I felt much grief at a practice that could leave it doubtful whether they might not altogether have gone wrong. No common observer could know that a young lady who kept all her letters to write on a Sunday, did so that they might wear a deeper tone of piety, be the more faithful mirror of her better feelings, conveying greater good to others and more glory to God. Common observers might even go so far as to suppose it was a profane compounding between her conscience and her choice—permitting her to send her spirit to scenes where in person she dared not go, and to occupy her thoughts with things she dared not do. I could not but bewail the bad example of a practice so equivocal, where the deed was plain to all, the inducement to it a secret between herself and God.

Reclining on a sofa opposite, I observed another lady intent upon the perusal of a newspaper. Therein, at least, was nothing equivocal; for the contents of a newspaper are known to all: and doubtless, the mind that had been fed all day upon the high and holy things of heaven and eternity, must have found it a seasonable draught of temporalities to rid itself of the effects or impressions that might remain. I had some reason to doubt, from all I heard, whether this young lady would not have thought it wasting time to read the newspaper on a Monday, because she had so many other things to do. But on Sunday, alas!—on Sunday, on that day which is God's and not our own, it was a relief to find any thing that might be done. And all together could not stay the weariness with which they turned their eyes towards the lagging time-piece, that seemed but to go the slower for their impatience to be rid of a day, which, though shortened at either hand, was still too long.

And yet these people, and thousands who do like them, are going, so they tell us, and take it but ill that we should doubt it, to that blessed dwelling-place where there is no employ but one, the very one of which they grow so weary here: where the utmost reach of happiness is no more but the completion and duration endless, of that which they are so little willing to begin—a rest from the agitating cares of time and sense, and a devoting of time, and thoughts, and powers to the worship of the Deity, the contemplation of his works, and the performance of his will. This is a happiness that is not for us here, we cannot reach it if we would. But that we may taste of it, that we may cultivate a desire and a liking to it, an imperfect Sabbath has been at certain intervals appointed us, in which we are permitted, nay, commanded, under all the penalties of disobedience, to take of the food on which our perfected spirits will eternally be fed, if the feast of heaven be preparing for us. The day comes round, and finds so little welcome, it is but an impórtunate intruder on our enjoyments, an interruption to our business. The food we are required to take is so unpalatable, we are obliged to mix with it as much as possible of our weekly fare to enable us to take it. So averse are we to this faint semblance of the eternal state, that not even the terrors of God's broken law can force us to partake of it. The aversion must be strong indeed that will make us risk so much by disobedience, rather than make the sacrifice of a few brief hours. And to what is it we are so averse? Let us consider.

No. IX.

FRIENDSHIP.

For Friendship is no plant of hasty growth;
Though rooted in esteem's deep soil, the slow
And gradual culture of kind intercourse
Must bring to it perfection.

JOANNA BAILLIE.

THERE are a great number of things that every
body says for no reason that can be perceived, but
because every body always has said them; and,
whatever be the recommendation to these current
opinions, or rather assertions, for opinion has little
to do with them, it is certainly not their truth. There
is not one in ten of the persons who talk on these
universal topics, that has ever considered whether
what it is customary to say, be true or not; and
though they are matters of everyday experience,
they seldom pause to compare their habits of talking with their actual observation on the subject.
But observation, unfortunately, we most of us make
none, till past the age at which it would most avail
us. We take up our sentiments, and not seldom our
very feelings, upon trust, and it is not till after many

a hard rub and bitter pang, we come to perceive
that, had we felt more justly, we need not have suffered.   Perhaps this is an evil in some degree
irremediable ; there are many who cannot, and more
who will not, think and judge on their own behalf—
what they were taught in their youth they will believe in their age, and what they said at fifteen they
will go on saying at fifty; though the whole course
and current of their observations, had they made
any, would go to disprove it.   But if this is the
case, and if it must be so, it is but of the more importance what habits of thinking and feeling young
people receive, on entering a world that will not
change its course to meet their expectations, or show
overmuch indulgence to their mistakes.   If the mischief ended where we began to trace it, with the
mistaken sentiments given forth in the talk of society, it would be small, and we would let it pass as
a harmless fiction—but not seldom it goes to the
dearest and tenderest interests of our bosoms, to the
very vitals of our earthly happiness.   It may indeed
do worse—for it may assail our virtues and attaint
our souls with sin, by giving a check to the benevolent affections, and inducing a morose and cynical
habit of feeling towards our fellow-creatures, the
very reverse of what Christianity enjoins.

These reflections, something long, as those may
have thought who are in a hurry to know what they
mean, were excited in my mind by a conversation I
recently heard in a party of young ladies, and which

I take as a pattern and semblance of twenty other conversations I have heard in twenty similar parties. Friendship was, as it very often is, the subject of the discussion, and though the words have escaped my memory, I can well recall the substance of the remarks. One lady boldly asserted that there was no such thing as friendship in the world, where all was insincerity and selfishness. I looked, but saw not in her mirthful eye and unfurrowed cheeks any traces of the sorrow and ill-usage, that, I thought, should alone have wrung from gentle lips so harsh a sentence, and I wondered where, in twenty brief years, she could have learned so hard a lesson. Have known it, she could not ; therefore I concluded she had taken it upon trust from the poets, who are fain to tell all the ill they can of human nature, because it makes better poetry than the good. The remark was taken up, as might be expected, by a young champion, who thought, or said without thinking, that friendship was—I really cannot undertake to say what—but all the things that young ladies usually put into their themes at school—something very interminable, illimitable, and immutable. From this the discussion grew, and how it was, and what it was, went on to be discussed—I cannot pursue the thread of the discourse, but the amount of it was this. One thought friendship was the summer portion only of the blest ; a flower for the brow of the prosperous, that the child of misfortune must never gather. Another thought, that all interest being

destructive of its very essence, it could not be trusted
unless there was an utter destitution of every thing
that might recommend us to favour or requite affection.   This lady must have been brought to the depth
of wretchedness ere she ever could be sure she had
a friend.   Some, I found, thought it was made up of
a great deal of sensibility, vulgarly called jealousy,
that was to take umbrage at every seeming slight,
to the indescribable torment of either party.   Some
betrayed, if they did not exactly say it, that they
thought friendship such an absolute unity, that it
would be a less crime to worship two gods than to
love two friends ; and therefore, to bring it to its
perfection, it was necessary that all beside should be
despised and disregarded.   Others, very young, and
of course soon to grow wiser, thought it consisted
in the exact disclosure of your own concerns, and
those of every body else, with which you might
chance to become acquainted ; others, that it required such exact conformity in opinion, thought, and
feeling, as should make it impossible to differ ; and
others, that it implied such generous interference
even with the feelings as well as affairs of its object,
that it should spend itself in disinterested reproaches
and unasked advice.   But however differing else,
all were sure that friendship but usurped the name,
unless it were purely disinterested, endlessly durable,
and beyond the reach of time and circumstance to
change it ; and all were going forth in the full certainty of finding friends, each one after the pattern

of her own imagination; the first speaker only excepted, who was fully determined never to find any, or never to trust them if she did.

I marked with pained attention the warm glow of expectation so soon to be blighted, and reflected deeply on the many heartaches with which they must unlearn their errors. I saw that each one was likely to pass over and reject the richest blessing of earth, even in the very pursuing of it, from having sketched in imagination an unresembling portrait of the object of pursuit. "When friendship meets them," I said, "they will not know her. Can no one draw for them a better likeness?"

It is the language of books and the language of society, that friends are inconstant, and friendship but little to be depended on; and the belief where it is really received, goes far to make a truth of that which else were false, by creating what it suspects. Few of us but have lived already long enough to know the bitterness of being disappointed in our affections, and deceived in our calculations, by those with whom, in the various relationships of life, we are brought in contact. Perhaps the aggregate of pain from this cause is greater than from any other cause whatever. And yet it is much to be doubted, whether nearly the whole of this suffering does not arise from our own unreasonable and mistaken expectations. There are none so unfortunate, but they meet with some kindness in the world—and none, I believe, so fortunate, but that they meet with much less than they might do, were it not their own fault.

In the first place, we are mistaken in our expectation that friendship should be disinterested. It neither is, nor can be—it may be so in action, but never in the sentiment—there is always an equivalent to be returned. If not, it may be generosity, it may be benevolence, but friendship is not the name for it. As soon as we intermingle with our fellow-creatures, we begin to form preferences to one above another. The circumstances that decide this preference are infinitely various; but be they what they may, the movement in the first instance is purely selfish. In the advances we make, the attentions we pay, and the attempts to recommend ourselves to their affections, it is our happiness, not theirs, of which the increase is in our view. In some way or other, they pleased us before we began to love them; our friendship therefore is a purchase, not a gift; a part of the price is paid, and the rest is in expectation. If we examine the movements of our own hearts, we must be sure that this is the case; and yet we are so unreasonable as to expect our friends should be purely disinterested, and, after having secured their affections, we neglect to pay the price, and expect they should be continued to us for nothing. We grow careless of pleasing them, inconsiderate of their feelings, and heedless of the government of our own tempers towards them—and then we complain of inconsistency if they like us not so well as when dressed out in our best for the reception of their favour. Yet it is in fact we that are changed, not they.

Another fruitful source of disappointment in our attachments is, that while we are much more quick in detecting the faults of others than our own, we absurdly require that every one should be faultless but ourselves. We do not say that we expect this in our friends; but we do expect it, and our conduct proves that we expect it. We begin also with believing it. The obscurity of distance, the veil that the proprieties of society cast over nature's deformity, the dazzling glitter of exterior qualities, baffle for a time our most penetrating glances, and the imperfect vision seems all that we would have it. Our inexperienced hearts, and some, indeed, that should be better taught, fondly believe it to be all it seems, and begin their attachment in full hope to find it so. What wonder, then, that the bitterest disappointment should ensue, when, on more close acquaintance, we find them full of imperfections, perhaps of most glaring faults, and we begin to express disgust, sometimes even resentment, that they are not what we took them for. But was this their fault or ours? Did they not present themselves to us in a garb of mortal flesh; and do we not know that mortals are imperfect, soiled with sin—nay, sunk so very, very low in it, that however the outside be fair, the interior is corrupt and altogether vile? He who knows all, alone knows how corrupt :—the heart itself, en-

lightened by his grace, is more deeply in the secret
than any without can be—but if the thing we love
be mortal, something of it we must perceive—and
more and more of it we must perceive as we look
closer—and if this is to disappoint and revolt us,
and draw harsh reproaches and bitter recriminations
from our lips, there is but One on whom we can fix
our hearts with safety—and He is one, alas! we
show so little disposition to love, as proves that, with
all our complainings and bewailings of each other's
faultiness, our friends are as good as will at present
suit us.

Another cause of mortification is, that we expect
too much from those who do truly and really love
us.   We expect that they should prefer our interests,
feelings, and purposes to their own.   This is not, and
cannot be.   Truth has recorded many instances, and
fiction has invented an abundance more, in which,
on some great emergency, this has been the case;
and in the common relationships of life, we may
every day see the most lovely and endearing instances
of self-negation in favour of those on whom our
hearts are fixed.   But these are sacrifices, they are
efforts against the current; they ought never to be
presumed upon, and never exacted, if it be possible
to avoid it.   But instead of this forbearance, the
most willing hand becomes the most hardly taxed—
the more kindness we receive the more we demand
—the friend who professes to love us must yield
every thing for us; bear every thing from us, and

do every thing for us; and if it come out at length that he have interests, and purposes, and feelings of his own, we are wounded and surprised, and exclaim against the fallibility of human affections. Yes, they are fallible, and they are limited, as all things finite are; and if we did not persist in disbelieving this truth, we need not suffer those bitter disappointments. There never was but One whose love confessed no limit; and he was more than man. The more he was provoked the more he loved; his kindness grew upon the injuries that repulsed it, and the greater the burdens heaped upon him, the lower bowed his sacred head to bear them. His favour neither grew on our deservings, nor is chilled by our demerits; he gives all and takes nothing in return; and the more we demand, the more we confide, so much the more is he willing to bestow on us. But this is the portrait of no earthly friend, and unless it bear some resemblance to ourselves, we have no right to expect it should be.

And then the mutability of all sublunary things—Is it in the power of human constancy to fix them? However determined to keep them, can the pleasures of to-day be the pleasures of to-morrow, drunk on with unsated appetite? Does the waste of years, and the growth of knowledge, and the change of habits, make no change in our feelings and tastes? We part from our friend in the full glow of reciprocal affection, and think to meet again exactly as we parted. Our attachment may indeed outlive the

separation, and from youth to age be substantially
the same. But mean time the character of each is
slowly changing, new habits are acquiring, and new
judgments forming. We meet again and are surprised to find no more the unity of spirit that once
united us, the assimilation of feeling that once made
our society so delightful to each other. And again
in bitter disappointment we inveigh against the false-
ness and versatility of those who once took so much
delight in us. But are they to blame? Is it not
the common course of all things earthly, on which
changed and changeable is irrevocably written?

And lastly, but not least productive of these painful issues, there is the false system under which we
form our friendships, as we do all things else that
concern us upon earth—a system of error as it regards ourselves, our situation, and our destiny. We
forget that we are strangers and pilgrims upon earth,
hurried forward to a distant and far other state. Our
friends may be our fond companions by the way,
they may assuage our sorrows and heighten our delights, and with a transient tenderness may hold our
hands and assist us in our task; but their bosoms
must no more be our resting-place than any other
thing on earth—they are treasures that must be
parted from, they are possessions that time must
steal, they are goods that must corrupt and pass
away. Heaven has pronounced it so, and so it must
be. And if in this, as in all other things, we persist in acting, feeling, and expecting, as if the world

were our home, and the things of it our lasting heritage, instead of being, as they might, our sweetest consolation, our purest enjoyment, and highest zest of life, our friendships must become a source of mortification, chagrin, and discontent.

But are we, therefore, to say there is no such thing as friendship, or that it is not worth the seeking; morosely repel it, or suspiciously distrust it? If we do, we shall pay our folly's price in the forfeiture of that without which, however we may pretend, we never are or can be happy: preferring to go without the very greatest of all earthly good, because it is not what perhaps it may be in heaven. Rather than this, it would be wise so to moderate our expectation and adapt our conduct, as to gain of it a larger measure; or, as far as may be possible, to gather of its flowers without exposing ourselves to be wounded by the thorns it bears. This is only to be done by setting out in life with juster feelings and fairer expectations.

It is not true that friends are few and kindness rare. No one ever needed a friend and deserved one, and found them not: but we do not know them when we see them, or deal with them justly when we have them. We must allow others to be as variable, and imperfect, and faulty as ourselves. An old writer has most forcibly said—"To say nothing of our friends, will not the sinking of our own hearts below the generous tenor of friendship, blast the fruits of it to us? Did we use so little affection in making a friend, that we need none to keep him? Must not we be always upon the stretch in some minute cautions and industries, in order to content that tender affection we would have in our friend? Can we make our love to him visible amidst the reserve and abstraction of a pensive mind? In our sanguine hours do we not assume too much, and in our melancholy think ourselves despised?" Whether we feel it or not, this is the truth of ourselves, and if of ourselves, of others also. We do not wish our young readers to love their friends less, but to love them as what they are, rather than as what they wish them to be—and instead of the jealous pertinacity that is wounded by every appearance of change, and disgusted by every detection of a fault, and ready to distrust and cast away the kindest friend on every trifling difference of behaviour or feeling, to cultivate a moderation in their demands, a patient allowance for the effect of time and circumstance, an indulgence towards peculiarities of temper and character, and above all, such a close examination of what passes in their own hearts, as will teach them better to understand and excuse what they detect in the hearts of others; ever remembering that all things on earth are earthly, and therefore changeful, perishable, and uncertain.

No. X.

A FABLE.

Beside the several pieces of morality to be drawn out of this vision, I learned from it, never to repine at my own misfortunes, or to envy the happiness of another; since it is impossible for any man to form a right judgment of his neighbour's sufferings.

ADDISON.

I DO not know whether my readers ever felt a desire of the sort, but I have often thought it must be pleasant to listen in the days of Æsop, when every Thrush could offer counsel in a voice as sweet as that with which she bids farewell to the departing sun, and every butterfly could whisper a warning to the frivolous and vain, before the cold wind numbed her golden bosom. However remotely wandering from the walks of men, however much condemned to solitude and silence, he could hear something that was worth the listing; and worth the telling, too, as the world has seemed to think; since, for ages after, it is content to read what the Fabler has ceased to tell, and the birds and the beasts have so unkindly ceased to utter.

Perhaps my readers do not believe that it ever

has been so. That is a scepticism very unfavourable
to the reception of my story—but if it be so, I can
only say, that all I repeat, I did surely hear, and if
they listen they may hear it too—and perhaps they
will think with me, that since it cannot be the discourse of creatures rational, I do wisely to attribute
it to those we term irrational. Perhaps, could these
irrationals be heard in their own behalf, they would
say our fables do them much injustice. They have
shared our miseries, but not our sins. The wolf
devours the lamb because he is hungry, and the lamb
is the food that nature has appointed him : when he
no more is hungry, he will no more slay the lamb.
He obeys the hard necessity brought on him by man's
delinquency, and thinks and knows no wrong. But
the jealousy, and the pride, and the hard unkindness, and the restless discontent, and aimless mischief, is all reserved for bosoms rational—we have
put into the mouths of the viper and the lion, words
of wrong that amid all created things, perhaps, were
never heard but from our own. However this may
be, I must proceed with my tale ; and if my readers,
after a careful perusal, should be of opinion that I
was deceived, and that the creatures I saw and heard
were neither birds nor beasts, I willingly submit to
their decision.

One day—if it was not in the days of Æsop, it
must have been in some region not very commonly
known—I was wandering by myself in the fairest
of scenes, on the finest of days, and in the best of

humours—How could I be otherwise? It was a day
and a scene in which the spirit that delights in nature's charms feels almost a painful struggle to
enlarge its powers that it may enjoy them more—It
was not hot, for the fresh breeze blew from the sea,
bearing with it the perfume of the moss and herbage
over which it passed—It was not cold, for a bright
autumn sun wanted yet some hours of setting; and
if now and then a silver fleece passed over it as a
veil, it was but to change the tints and vary a prospect nothing could improve. Either my mind was
that day free from cares, or in the overwhelming
sense of gratitude for the bounty that with so much
beauty clothes this perishable world, the remembrance of them was for the time absorbed; could I
be dissatisfied where all besides was harmony and
peace? Every thing was beautiful, and every thing,
as I thought, seemed happy. A crowd of living
creatures gave animation to the scene, and each one
appeared, in my delighted vision, exactly formed to
be what it was, and to do what it was doing; and
could any one be other than itself, I thought it must
lose something of its fitness and its charms. Yonder
cold Worm, I said, that crawls in naked ugliness
upon the soil, and cannot rise from it, should I take
it up and lay it upon that rose, would thank me
little for my pains—it would pine on its beauty, and
starve upon its perfumes—and what would avail it, in
its earthy prison, the Beetle's golden wing, or the
velvet bosom of the fluttering Moth? From nature's

largest work, to the least insect that frets the leaf, each thing has organs, and feelings, and habits, exactly suited to the place it is to fill—were it other than it is, it could not fill its place—and being what it is, were it removed to any other, it would surely be less happy. The flower of the valley would die upon the mountain's top; and as surely would the hardy mountaineer, now flourishing on Alpine heights, languish and die if transplanted to the valley. The Maker of the world, then, has made no mistakes, has done no injustice—every thing, as he has arranged it, is what it should be, and is placed where it should be, and none can repine, and none complain.

I thought so, but I was mistaken—things are very different when you come to look into them, from what they appear on superficial observation. Viewed from a distance, the troubled ocean seems an unbroken surface; go closer, it becomes a scene of tumult and destruction. And I, alas! was not destined to carry home the delusion I had brought out, or had falsely gathered in the contemplation of nature's works, and the Creator's wisdom and munificence. Instead of all being fitness, beauty, and harmony serene, I had to learn that all was absolutely wrong, and nothing could be altered without being amended. First, from the tall summit of a rocking Fir-tree I heard the solitary raven thus bewail himself:— "It is surely hard that I am doomed to dwell for ever on the top of this tall tree, battered by every storm that blows, and chilled by every bitter blast. For many an age, my ancestors, they say, dwelt here before me—but why must one be born to a destiny not of one's own choosing? Yon tiny Linnet's nest, could I get into it, would suit my taste exactly, and I might spend my days in quietness and peace."

"This element," said a Trout to his fellow, as they glided down the stream, "is neither healthy nor agreeable. The sunbeam plays upon the surface but to mock us, and never comes beneath to warm our blood. There is no reason that ever I have heard, why fishes have not as much right to fly in the air as either birds or butterflies."—"True," replied his fellow, "and we would try it in despite of fortune, but that our lungs are so badly formed, I am not sure we could breathe when we came there."

"I am a contented creature," croaked out a Frog that sat crouching by the streamlet's side—"I like my condition well enough, nor ever wish to live but in this mud—yet I confess I see no reason why that gay pheasant should wear such brilliant feathers, while I have none. The gifts of Providence are very partially distributed, methinks."

A bulky Cabbage (for in those days vegetables as well as animals could speak), from an unweeded bed, where without much care it had grown full large and round, was just then looking through the window of a greenhouse, and with no small bitterness of tone exclaimed, "How blinded, how misjudging are mankind! While I, a most wholesome and useful vegetable, am left here to grow as I may, through summer heat and winter cold, these tawdry japonicas, fit for nothing but to look at, are to be nursed, and stoved, and watered. It is hard indeed to bear the world's injustice!"—"And I," rejoined an Ox, comfortably grazing in a field, who had, doubtless, overheard the last remark, "had I the management of this world's good, would have a very different arrangement, and if any did not labour, neither should they have food. I, who have toiled all day, am fed on grass, and sent forth to gather it for myself, while yonder idle spaniel is reared on dainties from his master's hand—but ere he be allowed to eat, he ought to be yoked as we are, and sent forth to plough."—"It is true," replied a team-Horse, his companion; "I see no reason why we, of animals the largest and the best, should be obliged to do the work for all. Why should not those idle blackbirds come down and prepare the ground for casting in the seed, while we go sit upon the tree and sing till it suits our appetite to come and pick up what others sow?"

"Alas! alas!" whistled a pretty, painted Goldfinch, with whom berries that day were rather scarce; "to what a hard destiny am I condemned! Were I yon ugly barn-door fowl, I should be fed and sheltered for the sake of my eggs and chickens—but in this sordid, selfish age, beautiful as I am, no one cares for me, because I can give them nothing in return."

And next there came buzzing by me a fine gilded Fly, fluttering and feasting itself upon every smaller insect it could catch, till I began to wonder where its appetite would be stayed—when, finely spun between the branches of a rose, a strong spider's web caught the gay reveller, and held him fast in chains. "So!" exclaimed the prisoner, "thus it is to live in a world of treachery and crime; placed by Providence at the mercy of every bloated spider; the innocent still the victim of the base!"

And so I went on and on, and listened and listened, and nothing could I hear throughout all the creation I thought so beautiful, but plaints of dissatisfaction, and charges of injustice: all were dissatisfied with what they were, and injured because they were not something else. My heart sunk within me at the hearing—I listened no more, but I had gained ample food for meditation.

Can it be then, I said within myself, that He, the Beginning and the End of all things, Creator, Lord, Disposer of the world, has done injustice to every creature he has placed in it? There are those, it is true, who have made it what He made it not, and have introduced for themselves sins and miseries, which he at first ordained not—but it is not of these we hear so much complaining—the cry perpetual is against the providential circumstances, of nature or of fortune, to which each is subjected. However infidelity deny, or carelessness forget it, these circumstances do, and ever will remain in the hand of

Him who is Lord of all: therefore, every complaint that is uttered against our fortunes, is a complaint against him, for He assigned it.

From the cold dust which was all alike before his spirit breathed on it, he moulded a world of creatures, so various as none but Deity could devise; but endlessly variable as they were, each one was in its formation minutely perfect; not one had a want that it had not the means of supplying; not one had a faculty without some purpose for which it was imparted. The more deeply we examine into the secrets of the natural world, the more certainly and surprisingly we find it so. Examine the minutest flower, and see with what wonderful forethought, as it were, it is supplied with organs, active, though to all appearance motionless, to feed itself, to grow, and to produce its fruit: not all alike, but each one differently. Had they been all alike, all must have grown on the same soil, in the same aspect—now, from the hardy Lichen that braves the rigour of the poles, to the tender offspring of a tropical sun, there are some that can thrive in all. There is no doubt that of two plants of certain descriptions placed near each other, each one from its different formation will imbibe the different juices suited to itself; on which its companion would have died, perhaps. It is certainly not without a reason, whether that reason can be traced or not, that one leaf is clothed with silken hairs, while another has a coat of glossy smoothness. Why has the Vine the long, winding

tendril that never grows upon the oak? Why are
the seeds of the Mistletoe denied the power of root-
ing in the earth, and yet have a quality no other
seed possesses, of adhering to the bark of trees on
which they take root and live? Why, but because
it is the place that God assigns them? More dis-
cernible still is the fitness of every thing in the
animal creation. Why has the Beetle rough harsh
scales upon its wings, when it could fly like the
Butterfly without them? Plainly because it was
meant to dwell in holes and crevices, where without
them its wings would be broken and destroyed.
Why is the bill of the Sparrow drawn to a sharp
straight point, while that of the Hawk is curved and
hooked? Because the Sparrow is to pick out the
minute seed from its hiding-place in the flower, and
the Hawk is to rend the flesh of the animals it feeds
upon. We know all this, and we admire it, and admit
the wisdom and beauty of the arrangement—it would
seem to us a thing most strange, perverse, and ludi-
crous, that the Frog, abiding in the muddy pool,
should sigh to be invested with the Pheasant's tail
—that the finned Trout should propose to be flying
through the air, and the Cabbage to be nursed and
stifled in the green-house. But, alas! bears it no
resemblance to the things we hear and see elsewhere,
to something that we feel and in our folly utter?

The same Being who created the animals and the
vegetable race, determined for us our powers, our
characters, and circumstances. So exactly right in

those, can it be here only he is wrong? Can he have placed one of us in a situation in which we ought not to be, denied us any natural advantages it would be desirable we should possess, or given us powers and faculties unsuited to the part he means us to perform? It is impossible. Our pride suggests it; our folly gives it utterance almost as often as we speak of ourselves or our affairs; scarcely any one among us thinks he is by nature and fortune where and what he should be. Yet not more absurd are the complaints and wishes we have imagined in the wiser brute, than those we hear from the lips of beings capable of knowing and reflecting on their absurdity—professing too to be aware from whom all things are, and by whose will all things are determined.

It is most true, indeed, that by man's defection confusion has been introduced into the Creator's perfect work, and that in one sense we are not and cannot be what we ought to be, and what we should desire to be. But while to this moral perversion we are sufficiently insensible, our murmurs and complainings are ever breathed against the natural and providential portion assigned us upon earth. To hear the language of society, one might suppose that every individual in it had been wronged, by not being or having something that he is not or has not. How unfitted he is for the station he is in, how unfortunate it is that he happens to be so placed, how happy and how useful he might have been under other circumstances, how hard is his portion, how unequal the distribution of things, how blind is fortune, how unjust is fate, how inequitable is the world in his behalf—what is all this but the language of creatures who think they could arrange the affairs of the world better than he who does it, and understand the nature and propensities of men better than he who made them?

But far from understanding what is best for each other, we may be assured we do not understand it even for ourselves. We come into the world very differently moulded and endowed, our minds as little resembling each other as our persons : and equally various are the portions to which we are born. The circumstances of after life, as much the arrangement of our Maker as our first introduction to it, make even more difference perhaps than our original constitution. The result is, that each one has character, talents, powers, habits, feelings, necessities, and capabilities, as peculiarly his own and distinct from others as his station in life, which, as we know, can be occupied but by one. Now, whatever these be, we may rest assured we have no right whatever to complain : no injustice has been done us, and no unfitness is imposed on us : where Providence has placed us is where we ought to be ; and except in so far as by our sin we may unfit ourselves, of which we have little right to complain, we are what for our situation it is best we should be. As much right has the Worm to complain that he has not the

Beetle's wings, or the Raven that he is not as small as the Linnet, as we to complain that we have not the talents, the beauty, or the fortune of another. As reasonable is it for the Ox to desire to sit upon the tree and sing, while the Blackbird tills the soil, as for men to envy and malign each other for being differently placed and differently accommodated. We cannot read, indeed, the fitness and propriety of things in the affairs of men as we can in the natural world—because we know not our own hearts, the cause and consequence, and eternal issues of God's dealings with us—but are we not bound to believe it? And if to believe it, to act, and speak, and feel as if we did so? Are we at liberty to suppose that we alone of all created things are misformed, mismanaged, and misplaced?

No. XI.

EMULATION.

Il faut rejeter non seulement ce faux éclat de l'esprit, mais encore la prudence humaine, qui paroît la plus sérieuse et la plus utile, pour entrer comme les petits enfants dans la simplicité de la foi, dans la candeur et dans l'innocence des mœurs, dans l'horreur de péché.

FÉNÉLON.

As in the hazy darkness of the scarcely-breaking twilight, every object is indistinct and uncertain, and the more the eye searches the more it is bewildered, and the foot moves uncertainly, unable to discern between the firm greensward and the darkening chasm—so obscured, so uncertain were the moral perceptions of mankind, ere the daystar of Christian truth rose upon our world. They who talked most of virtue, and professed to love it most, and would perhaps have loved it had they known what it was, mistook the nature of the good they sought, and took evil in its stead. When the great man of antiquity prepared the tissue of moral beauty with which to dress himself for popular applause, pride and selfishness were the thread with which he wove it, the flowers he wrought in it were the evanescent charms of time and sense. Examining the finest specimens of Greek and Roman virtue, what do we find them? The hero was one to whom the world was a plaything, and men's lives a toy. His hard bosom was forbidden every kindly emotion; every tender sympathy was imperiously sacrificed to a stern will determined on self-aggrandisement. He was a traitor, a tyrant, and a robber; yet he lived admired and beloved; and died, as he believed, the favourite of the gods—still looking to the laurel wreath as his eternal crown, and the tortures of his enemies as the amusement of his Elysium. The sage, the philosopher, though a more harmless, was a more self-deluded being still. He sought the applause of the world in affecting to despise it, and did but call off his senses, passions, and feelings from the things around him, to fix them solely and entirely on himself. He mistook for greatness the contempt with which he rejected all the good that God or man could offer, and for magnanimity the defiance with which he braved Heaven itself to subdue him. And these were the high standards of heathen virtue, by others admired at a distance, and at a distance imitated. A self-sufficing pride, an impatient susceptibility that would not suffer the slightest touch of wrong, a bitterness of revenge that never pardoned it—these were among the foremost of a heathen's virtues. In considering the institutions of Lycurgus and other ancient legislators for the education of youth, harsh and unnatural as they appear to us, we are struck with their fitness to effect the purpose designed in them, of rearing their children to what had been accepted as the standard of moral excellence. Having determined that there was more disgrace in the discovery of a theft, than in the theft itself, the Spartans pursued a consistent purpose in teaching their children to steal adroitly; and thus throughout, we find the institutions of the wisest of heathen nations admirably fitted to make their children what they considered that they ought to be—virtuous according to their dark perceptions—heroes and wise men, such as we have described.

Perhaps my readers are thinking, and my critics making ready to assert, that I am talking instead of listening; and lamenting what has been, rather than observing what is. But they are mistaken. Little connected as may seem the subjects, I never should have thought of Cato, or Lycurgus, or Cæsar, or Diogenes, if I had not listened one whole day in mute attention to the progress of education in a certain school-room, and following thence into the world its tutored inmates, traced in idea the results of all the lessons I had seen them learning. When they were taught music, it was expected they should play—when they were taught French, it was expected they should understand it—and except in some few unhappy instances, I suppose the results corresponded with the expectations. But some things I observed were taught them that it was not expected they should learn, or desired they should practise—and if, in after life, they evinced an un-expected proficiency in these studies, few, perhaps, of their instructors would recognise the fruit of their own labours, the produce of the seed their industry had sown.

Parents who brought their daughters to this school —at least I heard it of so many, that I am inclined to suppose it of the rest—had said, either that they were so stupid they could not, or so clever they would not, pursue their studies well at home ; and they thought that the emulation excited by rivalship with others would much tend to promote their progress. The governess who should venture to contradict this introductory clause would probably lose her school; added to which, it is an admitted rule, that what every one says must be true; by parity of reasoning, what one is always hearing one must believe ; and conscientiously, and in pure good faith, this lady undertook what was asked of her, and performed what she undertook—the young ladies were powerfully stimulated by the very means prescribed, and made a very rapid progress in every thing—Alas ! yes, in much that was unperceived and unsuspected by those who meant not to teach them any thing but good—unperceived by any one, perhaps, but myself, whose peculiar business there it was to look out for what was wrong; not maliciously, as I beg my readers to believe—but as the physician enquires for the symptoms of the disease he apprehends.

In the centre of a long and carpetless floor, around a coverless table — a cold and uncomfortable prospect, that I hope had not the same chilling influence on their faculties as it would have on mine — and in defiance of all consequent spine-complaints, placed upright upon a backless form, there sat a large circle of ladies, not many years apart in age, and considered, I suppose, from their being classed together, on something like a level of attainments. They were receiving, it appeared, a lesson of French from the master, and producing for his inspection the lessons conned or written in his absence. A pert-looking little creature, whose confidence bespoke a priority her size could not have claimed, handed up her exercise with all the air of certain and cheaply earned success, chattered through her lessons as if they had grown upon her tongue; and in a tone of carelessness withal, that seemed determined to show it cost her no pains. Monsieur, too happy to escape the murderous garbling of his native tongue, to which he was perpetually condemned, reiterated his "Bon, bon," "Brave, brave," with many a whispered and broken sentence — "Bien habile"—"tres petite "—"bonne fille "—the last being withal by no means proved. The little lady turned her black eyes round the circle with a look that said as plain as words, "Now, stupid girls, do the best you can, for you cannot help yourselves." This young lady was too well bred to laugh or mock; but as I watched her through the remaining lessons, a slight movement of the upper lip when any one made a blunder, a certain wriggle on her seat whenever their ignorance caused detention, betrayed sufficiently her impatience of their slowness, and triumph in her own superiority.

A pretty, pensive-looking girl, taller by half the head than her companions, in whose meek eye a sensitive timidity beamed almost distressingly, had the misfortune to be addressed with a preliminary exhortation to do as well as the demoiselle who had preceded her. The exordium was fatal—a lesson, very respectably done, and giving evident tokens of a great deal of pains, was begun and finished with a blush, that, to put the best construction on it, confessed a painful sense of inferiority, and a feeling of shame, that having done the best, it was not better. Many others followed — among the rest a heavy-looking girl, whose air of cowed despondency particularly took my attention — the helpless blockhead of her class, whose right to be hindmost had never been disputed since she came into it. Her ill-formed lips could no more pronounce the words than her memory could retain them. Yet this poor girl was urged, and upbraided, and reminded how much she was bigger than those who were less, and how little less than those who were bigger, and how absolutely inferior to them all; and the air of discouraging indifference with which the books were thrown back to her, was only equalled by the sullen acquiescence in disgrace with which they were received.

My attention was at this moment distracted by a voice behind me raised something above concert pitch, in reproaches against a child whose ruddy, vacant face, and large blue eyes, beamed any thing, at that moment, but a sister's feeling, for having allowed a younger sister to get so much before her; while the sister's swarthy countenance and deep-sunk eye, bespoke a power of intellect with which the little Hebe might have contended long enough. In this corner was a scene of excitation equal to any thing the most anxious mother could desire for the stimulus of her daughter's talents. The ladies here were all upon their feet in a circle round their teacher, answering questions made to them in succession, and taking places, as it is called, according to the correctness of the replies. It was not on their own proficiency only the victory now depended—all honours must be won upon a rival's blunders; and like the riders on a balanced plank, the uprising of the one was proportioned to the downgoing of the other. Never were pugilists met with looks of more determined contention than these gentle wrestlers for literary honour. I could not mark without a pang the look of disappointment in a child who knew the answer, when she found the one above her knew it too; and the eager delight with which another heard the blunder that gave scope for the display of her own proficiency. Envy, malice, jealousy, contempt, every evil passion of which their little bosoms were susceptible, played in succession on their features: their teacher, mean time, as if she took them all for virtues, went on adding fuel to the flame, in praises, taunts, and comparisons, without any regard to the passions she was exciting, or the feelings she was perverting.

I heard much more, but I have told enough for my purpose. This is the stimulant which, under the gentle name of Emulation, is thought indispensable to the successful education of children. The term itself is found in Scripture classed with no fair company—but we mind not the term, which we are aware in the original admits of a good as well as a bad sense. Is the thing itself good? It is asserted that children will not learn without it—that competition is essential to their progress. We doubt it much: we see not why the praise absolute may not be as enticing as the praise comparative. But let this point be conceded, if it must, and be it admitted that a girl will learn more in the hope of outshining, or the fear of being outshone, than she can do either from the desire of knowledge, or a wish to please her instructor, or any other motive. Still the question is not at rest.

The daystar of truth has risen upon our world, and opened to our view a standard of moral excellency such as heathens never dreamed of. Pride, the stronghold of a heathen's virtue, has been discovered to be a soul-destroying sin—the very sin that drove angels from Heaven, and man from paradise. Strife, resentment, ambition, rivalry, contention, envy, self-preference, have been determined to be sins—the eternal blessing has been pronounced by lips divine, not on the successful contender for this world's praise, but on the meek in spirit and the pure in heart. Our children are Christians, devoted in baptism, and, as every pious parent hopes, hereafter to be accepted as the servants and followers of Him, who, when he comes to acknowledge them as such, will not ask what they know, but what they are. Do we act as consistently as heathens did, teaching them that all the attainments and all the knowledge in the world were a dear-bought purchase at the expense of one right feeling, of one solid Christian virtue? I fear not. Let any one of my young readers but watch the movements of her own heart, and judge of the fact; for she is competent to do so, however young. What is her motive for the extraordinary exertions she is making in some particular study to-day? The wish to gain approbation and esteem, a desire to make the utmost use of the talents given her, perhaps the simple wish to excel in that particular study for her own gratification—or is it the fear that some one will do better, that some one she desires to surpass will come up to her? Suppose the point gained, and herself held up as an example and a shame to those who have done worse, she is delighted; but why? Would she have been equally delighted if every one else had done as well? Or suppose she has failed—why is she depressed? With regret that she did not make more exertion, and a resolve to repair it to-morrow; or with despite that others succeeded better, envy of their superior talents, and dissatisfaction with her own? If the former be the case in any of these supposed probabilities, the stimulus of rivalry was clearly unnecessary, for her feelings were independent of all comparison—if the latter, she gained improvement perhaps, she gained an accomplishment perhaps, and she went to bed satisfied that she had done well. But she had been proud, or jealous, or envious, or discontented. Pride, envy, jealousy, and discontent, are sins; by every indulgence of them God is offended; by every excitement of them an evil passion is fostered and strengthened.

The nature of this seed is but too well proved by the harvest it produces. In society, among women especially, a close observer might be astonished, if less inured to it, at the little idea of wrong attached to feelings of this description. There are few women, perhaps not one, who, if she knows herself, can say she was never pained by the praises of another, nor ever depreciated the merits of another to enhance her own. If we say this is natural, and cannot be prevented—yes, but it is hateful, it is sinful, it is diabolical. The Gospel has been sent to disclose to us our state of natural delusion, by the shedding on our bosoms of a purer light; and it has ranked these feelings in the catalogue of moral crimes, most offensive to God and man, and deserving of eternal condemnation. We, in our great wisdom, keep the opinions of our heathen ancestors; and, in our great madness, act upon them, teach them to our children, and say they cannot be educated without them. Then let them remain for ever ignorant. We strangely miscalculate, even for our happiness in this world, when we sacrifice character to acquirements of any kind. That is indeed to part from our decent and necessary clothing, for the purchase of some brilliant jewel with which to deck ourselves. I surely shall not be suspected of too lightly estimating the advantage of mental cultivation and polite accomplishments. By every proper motive, by every sinless incentive, we may provoke our pupils to exertion—to the gifted we may say, Make use by assiduity of what you have—to the less endowed, Make amends by assiduity for what you have not; and by praise or blame enforce the precept. But, if we must choose between the moral and the intellectual good—if the culture that is to raise the flower, must foster with it the poisonous weed, we hold the utmost acquisition of human intellect light indeed. Its future fruits will never allay the passions excited for its acquisition. When sin becomes the burden and the shame of a bosom struggling, and yet unable to repress it, learning and talent will not whisper peace. When the applause, and the triumph, and the approbation of men, are past and forgotten, the evil thought, the sinful emotion, will remain upon the conscience; and, unless mercy blot it thence, on Heaven's eternal records.

No. XII.

EVIL SPEAKING.

> ....'Tis slander,
> Whose edge is sharper than the sword; whose tongue
> Outvenoms all the worms of Nile; whose breath
> Rides on the posting winds, and doth belie
> All corners of the world.

One day—I suppose my readers do not exactly care what day, or what sort of a day, or at what hour, or whether in spring or autumn, in sunshine or in clouds—I tell these particulars sometimes, when I want to fill out my paper; but, on this occasion, I have enough to say without them. So it was one day—I had been walking a considerable distance through lanes where nature, unchecked by any interference on the part of man, brought forth together, in boundless luxuriance, her bitters and her sweets —the poisonous Nightshade twined her branches round the honeyed Woodbine—the Bindweed laid its head of pure and spotless white on the hard bosom of a neighbouring Thorn—the Thistle and the Harebell grew side by side. It was with difficulty, in some places, I had made my way through the midst of them; and sometimes the Brambles caught my dress, and sometimes I set my foot upon a Thistle—and when I attempted to gather a flower, the thorns pricked and the nettles stung me. But I do not remember that I felt any surprise, or any sort of resentment, that they did so. I neither wondered they should grow there, nor desired that they should be rooted out. I cannot recollect, indeed, that I had any thoughts upon the subject—it was so natural they should be there, and being there, that they should do what they did—all seemed too much of course to claim any observation.

Leaving these wild and lawless paths, I entered by a gateway into grounds, that, though scarcely extensive enough to claim the title of a park, were yet approaching to it in character, very beautiful, and of no inconsiderable extent. Though the house was not in sight, no one could doubt it was the paddock of some goodly mansion, on which the owner expended constant attention, and which it pleased him to adorn and beautify. The magnificent trees, feathered even to the ground, showed the care with which they had been protected from the browsing of the cattle. The flowering shrubs told, by their sunny looks, that they or their forefathers had been bred in something less than fifty-two degrees of latitude. A slender Leveret stole fleetly over the turf, scarcely bending under its steps; and a Squirrel, that looked as if he had been just combed and dressed, was leaping among the trees—but the Cur that should enter there was doomed to death, by notice written upon a board; and his owner too, unless the spring-guns could distinguish between the honest man and the thief. And now my path was broad and straight, and beaten very hard: having no more to force my road through narrow ways and paths uncertain, I began to walk freely and carelessly; occupied with the altered beauty of the scene around me, I did not look where I was treading. Nature was not displaced by art, for she was here in all her splendour, in the full-dress garb with which taste, and industry, and wealth, had clothed her, yet decked in no other beauties than her own. My mind became occupied with admiring, that He, who had made a world so beautiful that nothing could be wanting to it, had yet left to its inhabitants the means of improving it, and adding to its charms— for doubtless, even in Eden, it was the business of man to train and beautify what nature made: and now that it has become his harder task to humour the unwilling soil, and provide against a capricious climate, a mass of the most exquisite materials remain to him, and his toil and care are repaid by every combination of beauty taste can suggest, and skill accomplish. While I was thinking all this— one may think a great many wise things in less time than one can say them—and not regarding where I walked, I set my foot upon some low thistles, negligently left upon the path, and while it tingled from their thorns, felt very much inclined to upbraid the thistles that grew where thistles should not, and the gardener that did not dig them up, and the master that did not keep a better gardener. But why did that excite surprise, and almost indignation here, which a short time before did not awaken so much as a reflection?

The world is a wide wilderness. Things good and excellent are strangely mixed in it with corruptions the vilest and the basest. The most enormous crimes crowd round and stifle the most generous feelings. Natural virtues, the broken outlines of that image once impressed upon the heart of man, now indistinct, and faint, and almost gone, are found in such base company—it is true of nations as of individuals—that on the most brilliant character are marked the foulest spots. We have but to read the history of men in their natural state, to learn that this has been so—we have but to study the lives and characters of persons under no other influence than that of natural feeling, to be assured it is so still. But in this wilderness there is a garden, which He who made it surely takes pleasure in. He has fenced it round, he has gathered out the stones from it, he has planted it with the choicest vines. Separated from an idolatrous, self-adoring world, drawn round, as it were, with the compass of his most holy word, as far as the light of truth has in its spirit reached, the Redeemer has appropriated to himself a people under the appellation of Christians, to worship him, and love him, and, as far as in their weak humanity they can, to follow in his footsteps. He has left this fair garden under no ordinary culture: He knows that the soil he made it from is ever what it was, disposed to bear the brier and the thorn that choke the goodly produce of his care. But what could have been done more for it, that he has not done? The mid-day of Gospel truth shines on it: the most holy precepts and most sanctifying doctrines are shown forth in it—Like the light dues of the morning that fall, we see not whence, the Holy Spirit sheds its influence on the heart—the sweetest hopes and richest promises are whispered abroad for our encouragement. The result is, in some respects, what we might expect it to be. It is true that sin springs up every hour in the corrupted bosom, but it is not left to flourish there unchecked; a purer morality takes place of nature's blindness, a stronger principle comes in aid of nature's weakness. Have we not reason, then, to be more startled, and more concerned, if, in walking through this cultured ground, we meet with wrongs that should not flourish there? Is it there we must be cautious of the thistles and the briers that prick and entangle us at every step; and walk as insecurely as among those who know no better guide than their own perverted will?

It should not be; but it is so, in one respect at least; there is one evil to which Christianity puts no stop; even real, vital, spiritual religion, as far as I have seen, puts no stop to it; with some few, very few, individual exceptions.

So much I have said in introduction, the better to excuse the earnest offence I have taken against what is commonly treated as a jest. To say I listened is superfluous here; for whether you will hear, or whether you will forbear, it is impossible to escape the sound—Slander, Evil speaking,—what shall I call it, for it has many names? From one end of society to the other, among the grave and the gay, the wise and the foolish, where shall you escape? You might as well live on the ocean's edge, and say you will not list the breaking of the waters. We *must* hear it, and we have heard it so long, that I fear we have lost all idea of guilt attached to it. And most of all, I fear that our children cannot escape the infection, but must grow up with the same habits of doing, insensibly and without reflection, what their mothers and grandmothers have done before them. It is for their sakes, if not directly addressed to them, I have chosen the subject—the thistle may be eradicated when it first springs up; but let it root itself, let it get firm possession of the soil, and the task becomes difficult, if not impossible.

Evil speaking—I prefer that word to others, because it includes truth as well as falsehood—pervades every sort of society; the only variation is in the different sort of things people amuse themselves with saying of each other. In a frivolous fashionable, polite circle, I observe it has regard to things external — to the persons, fortunes, pedigree, and connexions of its subjects. Somebody's grandfather was something that he should not have been, or, at least, that he had rather not have been, if he could have helped it. Somebody has by no means so much fortune as they seem to have, and some are guilty of having lived more years than any body supposes. Those who sing cannot sing, and those who dance cannot dance, and somebody's nose is the wrong shape, and somebody's hair is the wrong colour, and one lady's diamonds are paste, and another lady's plate is borrowed—one is ostentatious because she talks too wisely, another is weak because she talks too foolishly. I am sure, and so do these—but it all amounts to nothing; and, saving the loss of time and words, I do not think there is much harm done; for no one charges the other with any wrong, precisely because they do not care whether she commits it or not—their estimate of evil makes their evil speaking idle rather than injurious.

In a society a little more rational, as if the rank weed flourished better the better were the soil, it is the character, the conduct, the vital interests of life, that are invaded. Every fault exposed, every luckless word repeated, thoughts, motives, and feelings ascribed, where the plain act was all that could be known—this is bad enough; for it loosens the bonds of kindness between man and man, it excites prejudices and suspicions, wounds the feelings, and affects the earthly interests—but this is not the worst. There is a sort of society we usually call religious, or serious society — company, that is, from which

the mention of God and our eternal interests is not
excluded as unpolite discourse, nor shunned as a
melancholy topic; where right and wrong are what
God approves and disapproves; where, when earth
is spoken of, Heaven is not forgotten, and when
wrong is mentioned, sin before God is meant. Is it
possible the weed can flourish here? Alas, it is here
it has its most bitter, its most cruel growth—for the
subjects of slander here are life and death — eternal
life and death eternal. The sinner whom God spares
and waits for, a fellow-sinner scoffs at and despises
—the stain that Jesus washes with his tears, a fellow-sinner eagerly exposes—the penitent bosom that
Heaven has comforted, has every wound made to
bleed afresh by the taunts and the whispers of his
fellows. They whom, for their Saviour's sake, the
Father has declared he will not judge, on earth are
more hardly judged than any, by those who stand
alike condemned and alike obtaining mercy. The
errors and inconsistencies the Almighty bears with
men pronounce at once to be decisive. The axe
which mercy has suspended yet another and another
year, and Jesus in Heaven, perhaps, is even now
entreating should be withheld another year to these,
man would lay instantly to the root of the unfruit-
ful tree. Do we say that no real Christian does
so? Real Christians — God forbid that I should
think them otherwise!—say it—and if their words
be so adverse to their meaning, as I hope they are,
is it not time they were better suited?

We are not here speaking of what those who say it know to be false—that is a crime that bears another name, and though under one false colouring and another, it veils its blackness oftener than it should, no one under its right name will venture to defend it. We have spoken of this elsewhere. Our subject is of that manner of evil speaking in which we believe what we say to be true. People are apt to think there is no harm in saying what we know to be true; but let them be aware that the things we know are very, very few—what we think, believe, conjecture, or hear, we can by no means be said to know. I may know that a person did such an act, or said such a word—in saying that he did so, therefore, I cannot risk a falsehood: but if I did add one thing more, if I ascribe a motive, a cause, an intention, a feeling, to that word or deed, I cannot know that what I say is truth, for these are things that can be certainly known but to God himself. And if I speak against another in their character and disposition — I may have very good grounds for my decision, and the best I can have; but it does not amount to knowledge. For instance —I hear a person say one thing to-day and the contrary to-morrow, and I presume myself justified in saying she is false and insincere. By no means—it may arise from an instability of character, a rapid transition of feeling, or uncertainty of judgment, which, though a great weakness, is not the vice with which I charged her. We know that the same disease will not show itself by the same symptoms in different constitutions, neither do resembling symptoms always imply a similar disease. So the act that with us would be the result of one feeling, in another mind may be the result of a very different one. And, alas! we do not even know our own hearts: we are deceived in every movement, in every motive and affection of our bosoms.—How then can we persuade ourselves we know what is passing in another?

But suppose our evil speaking be truth,—certain, indisputable truth. Are we justified? Say first, whether you have never done the thing you desire to conceal—never said the thing you would blush to hear repeated—never thought the thought you would not for worlds that any one should read. If never, then go and tell the worst you know, say the worst you think, of all around you. There is One in heaven who knows: He hath said, With what measure ye mete it shall be measured to you again — but never mind, zealous propagator of the truth— go on to tear away the veil with which your neighbour tries to hide his faults — the time is not quite come, when, if some one veils not yours, the rocks and mountains will not serve you for a covering, and truth will be sufficient to prove you deserving of everlasting misery.

Yet this is not all. God is taking account of something mortals overlook. What was your motive for that injurious truth you told this morning? For that remark you made to another's prejudice, too true to be disputed? You will say you had no bad motive: but did you consider before you spoke, whether you had or not? It will not do to run a risk in this: while you are keeping the register of others' faults with so much justice, there is One more just than you, who registers your thoughts and every secret motive of your heart. Jealousy is sin—envy is sin—strife is sin—unkindness, retaliation, anger, hatred, variance, all are sins—nay, evil speaking itself is declared in holy writ to be so. Will you risk the accumulation of sin upon your soul, and swell the dark catalogue that is against you, for the mere sake of setting the characters of men in their proper light, and undeceiving every body as to their neighbours' actions?

That those who make light of sin in themselves and sport of it in others, should do this, we need not so much wonder: but to return again to those who call themselves religious, distinctively from a careless and unbelieving world. You know, or pretend to know, the extent of your nature's corruption—you bewail before Heaven your inability to conquer it—you declare there is absolutely no good in you, and that the remembrance of your sins is an intolerable burden. How then can you venture to appoint yourselves the judges of your fellow-creatures, and take delight in exposing and talking of their faults? Do you not know the difficulty of conquering one native and deep-rooted sin? Do you not know the

tears a Christian sheds in secret for the sins he cannot conquer? Do you not know that the path of life
is dangerous, and full of temptations we have not in
ourselves the power to resist? And yet you go on
criticising, censuring, exposing one another; whispering from house to house of this person's inconsistencies, and that person's neglects, and one should
not do this, and another should not say that—Oh!
it is little, little indeed, with all your profession, you
know of your own heart, or it would surely find you
other work! If you think any one is more undeserving in the sight of God than you are, you have
a step downward yet to make, ere you reach the
place of safety at your Saviour's feet: and when you
come there, whatever God, who reads all hearts,
may think, you, who read only your own, will believe that it is worse than any other. And oh! if
you did really know, so well as you profess to do,
the agony of conscious sin to one who hates it, you
would not by your hard speeches add one feather's
weight to the intolerable burden. Would you have
mocked at Peter when he denied his Lord? When
Paul besought relief for the weakness that exposed
him to Satan's influence, and was denied, would you
have reproached him with it? Yes, you would—but
remember that your Saviour did not.

If such is the evil, where is the remedy? What
the best principle cannot exterminate, may seem to
admit of none. Take up the thistle before it has
taken root too deeply. Where there is not a mali-

cious love of mischief in the heart, which I trust is
very seldom, we speak evil because we always have
done so, and because we have always heard it done.
Let the young be watchful against the habit, and
resist the example.   To assist them in this, the first
thing is to induce a habit of thinking as well of
others as they can ; for those who think no evil will
say none.   You hear something you are disposed to
blame—but you may have misconstrued the words ;
the speaker may have used stronger expressions
than he was aware of; he may have regretted them
as soon as spoken.   Accustom yourself to such reflections as these.   You see, or are told of, an action
you disapprove—perhaps there was some reason for
it no one knows; some temptation that at least
extenuates it ; some mistake that led to it.   Try to
believe so.   You are shocked by defects and vices of
character in others—say to yourself, ere you condemn, Some neglect of education, some bad example,
some physical disorder, or mental imbecility, may
have caused all this—you will be in no hurry to
speak the worst while you are thus endeavouring to
think the best; and it will besides keep you in better humour with your fellow-creatures, and consequently more amiable in your deportment towards
them.   The next thing is to accustom yourself to
watch your own actions, and the secret movements
of your own heart, and to lay by the account of
them.   Then, when you are disposed to censure,
there will come the thought, I once felt that evil

passion too; I remember when I committed that same fault; I have not that wrong propensity, but then I have this other, which is as bad. This habit will make you humble; and whatever makes you humble, will make you lenient. Another preventive is, to store your mind with other matters, and provide yourself with better things to talk about; for it is the want of mental occupation that makes us so busy with other men's matters, and the want of something to say that makes us speak so much evil of each other. This is the reason women are more disposed to it than men; and would be a reason, if there were no other, for the solid and extensive cultivation of their minds beyond what their immediate duties may seem to require; and it is a reason why religious young women must not neglect their talents and give up their literary pursuits. And, lastly, —let those who would resist this habit, consider the difficulties, the dangers, the sorrows, that lie in the path of all to their eternal home — the secret pangs, the untold agonies, the hidden wrongs—thus the heart will grow soft with pity towards our kind. How can I tell what that person suffers? That fault will cost them dear enough without my aid. Thus you will fear, by a hard word, to add to that which is too much already, as we shrink from putting the finger on a sore. And, lastly, accustom yourselves to entreat Heaven for your fellow-creatures, asking pardon and forbearance of God towards what is wrong in them—then I am sure you will not be eager to expose, and hasty to condemn them. Strenuously accustom yourself to all these things from your childhood upward, and it may be that the disgraceful Thistle will not grow.

No. XIII.

PEGGY LUM.

> ....There are some
> Who look for nothing in the time to come,
> Nor good nor evil, neither hope nor fear,
> Nothing remains or cheerful or severe.
>
> *   *   *   *   *   *   *
>
> Leave her, and let us her distress explore;
> She heeds it not—she has been left before.
>
> CRABBE.

My young readers have often complained to me that I tell no stories. They might as well complain that the baker sells no sugar-plums, and the draper deals not in trinkets—all very good things in themselves; but of that of which there is enough—we have somewhere made bold to say, too much—there needs no supply of ours. Yet, lest my young friends should believe I think it wrong to write a story, or that I cannot write one, I intend, for once, to conciliate their favour, and compound a story, which, contrary to the ordinary practice of story-tellers, I beg to assure them, *is not true.* This is a bold assertion. Am I going to lay aside my office, and, ceasing to listen to the realities of life, take an imaginary flight among

things that neither are nor can be? Most surely not.
The skilful lapidary finds his jewels in the mine,
shapes them and sets them, and the work is his; but
still the stones are real, and on their reality depends
the value of his work. So have I sought in nature
the materials of my fiction; it is made up of truth,
though in itself not true—I tell nothing that I have
not heard and seen, though not in the form in which
I give it. I listened for my materials before I wove
my tale.

One of the hottest days of an English July, about
the hour at which it is usual to set out for a summer-
evening's walk; when the soil had been pulverised
by sixteen hours of sunshine, and the light breeze,
departing with the sun, had left the atmosphere
more suffocating than by day—excepting so far as a
sensation of dampness might persuade one it was cool
—I too went out to walk, because others did; though
I could not but observe in the dusty hue and drag-
ging gait of all I met, an intimation that all would
rather be at home, if they knew what to do with
themselves there. The grass was damp, and the
paths were dusty: and I was obliged at last to
betake myself to the sea-beach, which, as all men
know, is not the most easy walking in the world—so
that I was just beginning to consider how far it was
really agreeable to walk on a summer evening, when
my attention was withdrawn from myself by the
appearance of a filthy, squalid child at my side. It
is impossible to imagine an object more uninteresting

and loathsome. The vulgar ugliness of her features seemed rather the result of misery, starvation, and ill-humour than of natural deformity: her originally fair skin was burnt and freckled into fiery redness, and her once pale hair clotted into unequal shades of darkness by filth and exposure; her size bespoke her about seven years old; but her shrivelled form and the worn expression of her countenance gave to her person an unnatural appearance of age. I looked at her a few moments; she seemed to be doing nothing, thinking nothing, and feeling nothing; and questioning within myself what might be the use, or aim, or object of existence in such a brute-like form, I addressed her with the usual question of what was her name. She deigned me no reply, but sufficiently intimated by her looks that she took it to be no business of mine. I tried again, by asking where she lived. At this she impertinently laughed, but still returned no answer; and carelessly throwing a stone or two into the water, turned her back and walked off. My curiosity was now excited, and I determined to follow her. This was no easy matter to my patience, for she clung round every post she came to, paused to throw the gravel, or make faces, at every dirty child she met; and put her fist through the railing of every garden, to tear away the flowers, which she immediately scattered. At last she stopped at much such a dwelling as I might have expected— a miserable hovel close to the high-road, formed of the shattered remnant of a boat. The dwelling contained a single room, with a door standing open, a low mud chimney, and a small window without glass, of which the wooden shutter was already closed, or probably had not that day been opened.

My guide entered; and to her astonishment, and apparently no great satisfaction, so did I. In one corner, or rather one half of the hovel, was a sort of bedstead, without bed or mattrass, on which lay the figure of a woman, nothing beneath her but a threadbare blanket, or above her but a sort of ragged coverlid, of which it was impossible, through the dirt, to discern the colour or texture. There was in her features what had been, and that but recently, both youth and beauty—yet now they were haggard, harsh, and almost ghastly. She looked at me, but made no motion of surprise or pleasure, nor gave the least expression of civility. "You seem ill, good woman?" I said. "Yes," she replied, "and please God I shall soon be worse."

I was much struck with her manner of speaking these words, totally free from the coarse broad accent of the country people in these parts, yet strongly marked by a deathly hollowness of voice, and the reckless daring of a hardened heart. "Is death, then, desirable to you?" I said. "What cannot be worse may be better, they say," she answered.

"But may not your case be worse," I answered, "in the world of which you know not yet the "——

She interrupted me with a long "Ay!" that at once announced the carelessness and the impatience of one who listens to an old story of which the interest is past.

I scarce knew how to proceed; I took a seat that had not been offered me, and drawing it close to her bed, attempted to put as much kindness as I could into my voice and manner while I questioned her of her illness and condition. She showed no unwillingness to communicate, but still there was a hardened despondency in all her answers, that seemed to reject assistance or consolation; and, to my assurance that I would give her any thing she needed, she only replied with indifference, "Ay, I dare say you will; I shall not want any thing long."

She replies to me, I thought, as to one who has done her wrong—but that is impossible. Willing to try another point, I reverted to the child, and asked if it was her only one—"Ay, please God!" she answered again.

"My friend," I said, "that word is often in your mouth, but it does not seem to me that you hold it in much reverence."

"As much as others, belike," the woman answered. Again there was something in her tone, which implied that, however bad she might be, she did not consider me any better.

"Has that child of yours no employment? Does she not go to school?"

"She may do what she can when her mother is gone," said the wretched woman, with some emotion;

" and I suppose they will teach her what they taught me."

I was inexpressibly moved by this first symptom of feeling; I had observed, too, a delicacy of person and a correctness of expression, that belied the stern ruggedness of her voice and manner, and I was determined to know more. "It does not seem to me, good woman, that you have always been in this situation; have you been always so badly off?"

" Never till I deserved it," she answered, while an almost convulsive agony distorted every feature, and her eyes grew liquid with tears, which no mention of her sufferings or her wants had before extracted.

" I should like to know your story," I replied :— " There is One above who is the sinner's friend, and who "——

" He is not mine!" she eagerly subjoined, " nor ever has been since "——

" Since you neglected him and broke his laws? but perhaps now, if you "——

" Ay, ay!" said the woman, with her former sullen air, " you need not tell me about that—they taught me all that; but they did not mind it, and I did not mind it—and," looking steadfastly in my face, " you do not mind it, I dare say."

This woman, thought I, is neither ignorant, thoughtless, nor unfeeling. Some deep-rooted memory of wrong, some fatal impression from past events, remains upon her mind, and makes her what she is ;—and I determined to pursue my inquiry till I traced her story and her sufferings to their source. I visited her often, and gained her confidence, and by degrees extracted from her the following melancholy tale, which I give as in her own simple words, though not all at once, and, in exact order, received from her :—

"My name was Peggy Lum. My father kept a poulterer's shop at the corner of the High Street, and he had no child but me. The farthest I can remember is, that he taught me on the Sunday evening the Lord's Prayer and the Belief, which he·told me was my religion; and for what he called my learning — for having but one child, and being well to do in the world, he was determined I should have both—he sent me to a day-school in the next street, for which he paid sixpence a-week, being twopence more than the schools to which most of my acquaintance went; and this, of course, made me a greater person than they. But this was not my only distinction ; I had a clean coloured frock twice a-week, wore white stockings, and had my shoes blacked every morning ; for my father said his child should be always decent, though she wore no finery. There was not in the town of H—— so happy a child as Peggy Lum, nor one so envied. My sense of superiority gave me a feeling of high responsibility for my conduct. I would not, for the world, have been heard to use an evil word, or have been seen playing in the streets, neither should it be ever said that I tore my books or puckered my work; these were accidents that befell all beside, but never could be charged to Peggy Lum, the boast of the mistress, and the pride of the school.

"When I was twelve years old, my mother suggested that it was time I learned to be useful, and I was accordingly kept at home, to clean the house and pick the poultry: but that I might not lose my learning and my religion, I was allowed to attend a Sunday school, superintended by some excellent ladies in the parish. Here Peggy Lum was equally distinguished above her fellows. She never came too late, she never wore flowers in her bonnet, whispered at church, or forgot the text. Every lady took notice of my good manners, said kind things to me, and what was of more consequence, took extraordinary pains in instructing me. I could read my Bible well, but I had hitherto never understood its meaning, nor indeed had ever supposed it had a meaning. Those kind ladies explained it to me all, and especially the commandments, which I had been taught to repeat by heart; and some things they told me, I remembered, alas! when——but I shall come to it. And so I grew up, the neatest, quietest, and civilest girl, as they said, of all the school; and when at fifteen my parents said it was time I should go out to service, there was quite a dispute among the ladies who should have me. I was disposed of at last to a family of respectability in the town, of which some of the ladies had interested themselves about the school; and I was not a little satisfied with the persuasion that I should continue to be bettered by their precepts and example. It was my place to attend on the ladies, and sometimes help to wait at table, and answer the bell; and most happy still was Peggy Lnm in the approbation and kind treatment she met with; and every night when I went to bed —for I had been taught now from whom all good things come—I gave thanks to God for the fair portion he had allotted me on earth.

"While I was in this situation, there came one day a single rap at the door, which I opened; a woman presented herself, and with a mysterious air, and sort of undertone, drew from beneath her apron a bundle, which she gave me, and bade me take it to the ladies, but not let any body else see it. I hesitated, for I remembered that when I was at the Sunday school, the ladies taught me whatever needed concealment was likely to be wrong. The woman, seeing my hesitation, whispered, with a significant look, 'Some silks, ma'am, some silks—you'll please to show them to the ladies.' Not having any reason to give why I should not, I did as I was bidden, and conveyed the parcel up stairs, rather anticipating a reproof, though I knew not why. By no means. The ladies spread the contents of the bundle on the table, and eagerly descanted on their merits; and very soon the woman was desired to add her presence to the council. I now understood the matter—to every fault found to the texture or the price, the vender answered that they were French; though from the frequency of the question, it was evident the ladies did not themselves know whether they were or not. It just came once into my mind, that these ladies used to tell us it did not signify whether our gowns were coarse or fine, so they were neat and becoming our station: yet now it seemed of great importance to them whether the silk were French or English, though they could not tell which it was when they saw it—but then I recollected that to be sure they were ladies, and I was a servant, and that might make a great difference. At last some purchases were made, and the woman once more placed the bundle under her apron. The ladies asked if she was not afraid to carry it, and what she would do if she met any one. 'You'll be pleased, ma'am,' she said, 'to let this young woman put me out at the back-door, and just look that no one is about, and tell the other servants that I came about some old clothes from your ladyships, if they should see my bundle, just.' To my great surprise the ladies assented. Never before had I heard them assent to a falsehood, or connive at a deception—but then they knew best, and it was no business of mine. Happily no one seeing her, I escaped the falsehood I was desired to tell.

"I waited that day at table — there was some company, and the subject of the morning purchases was brought up. A gentleman asked the ladies if they felt no scruple upon the subject of smuggling.

They replied, that they did not see any harm in it.
'And pray, ma'am,' said the gentleman, 'do you see
any harm in stealing?' I thought of the eighth commandment. The lady smiled assent. 'And may I
ask you what is stealing?' I thought I could have
answered that, for they had told me often enough
in explanation, that it was taking that which belonged
to another; and now they replied something to the
same purpose. 'And may I further ask, is the duty
you evade, or the revenue you lessen, by the purchase of smuggled goods, your own or another's?'
The ladies replied, that defrauding the government
was not the same as defrauding an individual. The
gentleman asked in what part of the law of God such
a distinction was made or intimated. The ladies
could not point out such a passage, and I could not
myself think of one; but I supposed there might be,
since I was sure they knew the Scripture better than
I. Some one said she did not see why a portion of
the profit of manufactured goods should belong to
the government. 'You know, madam, probably,
why this house and grounds belong to you.'—'Because they belonged to my father, and therefore are
mine by natural right.'—'I beg your pardon—by
natural right every thing belonged to him who took
it first—and there are places, and have been times,
when your father's property would not be yours.'—
'But now it is mine by law.'—'Exactly so—and he
would commit theft who should deprive you of it.
By law the profits of the revenue are another's, and

not yours; and pardon me, you commit theft if you appropriate it to yourself, or in any way deprive the rightful claimant.'—'But these laws are oppressive and injurious, and ought to be abrogated.'—'That admits of difference of opinion—but at present it is law; and if every one may break the law that does not please him, there is not a malefactor in the kingdom but may say the law that condemns him is a bad one.' I did not understand any part of the reasoning—but I concluded that, as my ladies were so very good, they most likely were right, and that there could be no harm in smuggling. One of them said, that to be sure it might not be quite right, and that in the purchase of spirits, tea, &c., where it was only to save the duty, she should hesitate to smuggle —but in articles that could not lawfully be purchased at all, she was obliged to do it. 'Certainly,' replied the gentleman, 'if it is more necessary to you to wear French silk than to do right.' I opened my ears wide at this; for I remembered how many times I had been told, it never could be necessary to do wrong; that to do right was the most important of all things—and by the very lady, too, who now said she must do what she allowed was not quite right, because she wanted a certain sort of dress. But it was not for me to be wiser than my betters. The dinner was ended, and I left the room; and excepting when I repeated the eighth commandment, or saw French silk now and then by chance, I do not remember that I thought any more about

what I had heard, till the sad days that I am going
to tell of.

"Mean time my years went on. The ladies liked
me, and made me presents, and increased my wages :
and in all the house it was who but Peggy Lum.
And now I began to save a little money, besides
buying myself now and then a good book, such as my
mistress recommended me, over and above a prayer-
book with gilt edges, and a large-print Bible. And
when my mother fell sick and died, I was able to
buy for her many little comforts she had not got,
besides sitting often by her bed, and explaining the
Bible to her as it had been explained to me — and
many and many were the times she said it was a
comfort to her death-bed that her Peggy had turned
out so well—and sure it was a comfort to me to hear
her say it—and many times I gave thanks to God
for all his mercies ; for I knew it was He who had
, made me what I was ; and with all my heart I praised
him that I was Peggy Lum and nobody else ;—little
did I then think what I should come to !

"By this time I was twenty years of age, and as
comely a young woman, so they said, as any in the
parish. I had a great many suitors—but I always
consulted my ladies about them, and they generally
persuaded me not to marry, because, as they said, I
was better off. I thought so for a while ; but at last
I began to think the time was getting on, and I had
better settle myself; so I was married, one Mid-
summer day, to a young man who had been a gar-

dener in a gentleman's family, and having saved a
little money, was going to take some ground, and
raise fruit and vegetables for the market. To be
sure he had not quite so much learning as I had;
and having never been to a Sunday school, he did
not so well understand his Bible and Catechism;
but he was honest, sober, and industrious, and loved
his church, and bore a very good character; and my
mistresses said if I wished to marry, I could not do
better—and he was besides a very good-looking
young man : so we were married, and all the ladies
went to church with us, and we had great feastings,
and crowds of lookers on, and all the parish knew it
was Peggy Lum's wedding.

"And now I was surely happier than I had ever
been before; and I wondered how God should never
be tired of blessing me. I had a little cottage in the
garden which was all my own. It is true my kitchen
was not so good as that I had left at my mistresses',
nor my fire so bright, nor my bed so soft, nor my
table so plentifully spread—but then it was my own.
And it is true I worked harder, for I had more to do
than to walk up and down stairs and wait upon the
ladies—but then I worked for myself and those I
loved, and not for hire : and who does not know the
difference? And who ever looked back from the little
that is her own to the much that was not hers? The
rich leavings of my mistresses' table were never so
sweet to my taste as the pork I had salted for myself, and the cabbage that grew in my own husband's

garden. I had children—Ah! and brave children were they too, as ever mother's eyes have looked upon—as straight as beautiful; their white hair curled upon their heads; their eyes"——

Here the wretched woman's voice began to falter, the tears chased each other rapidly down her ghastly cheeks, her eyes wandered towards the corner where her unsightly offspring was skulking, as if to make a comparison between what she remembered and what she saw—but it was all too much: an agony of unutterable feeling convulsed her frame, and for that time closed her narrative.

As the unfortunate Peggy Lum was enabled from time to time to renew her story, the following was its melancholy purport :—

"My husband cultivated most industriously his little garden, and for a time it seemed to answer to his toil. The pease and beans he raised, I gathered and carried to market—I weeded his beds, and I watered his strawberries; and when he grumbled at the prospect of a bad crop, I told him the times and the seasons were with the Lord, and that we should be content—for so I had been taught while I was young. When Saturday night came, we reckoned up our gains, and saw what we had taken above what our rent and our expenses came to; and it was always enough, bating now and then a little, to live on for the next week. And light were our hearts, and glad were our bosoms, on the Sabbath day, that followed such a reckoning; what remained to us was our own—it was all we wanted for that week; and before the next the cherries would be ripe, or the potatoes would be fit for digging, or something would be sure to come in to supply our daily necessities. And so we went on, and so we prospered, for a year or two. But God was tired of us, or we were tired of him; or he knew, as well he might, that we only served him while he blessed us, and should disobey him as soon as things went wrong. Some way or other our fortune took a turn. My husband had a long illness, and was obliged to hire a man to keep his garden—and then, when the doctor's bill came in, we did not exactly know how to pay it, and sold off all the potatoes we were used to keep for winter, when they would fetch better prices —and when winter came we had not the potatoes to take to market, and so on Saturday night there were no profits, and we were obliged to live on credit all the week. And when summer came again, there was an old score to pay off—and it was a bad year for gooseberries, and my children had the measles— and the next· winter was worse than the last: the rent was behind hand—and to be sure it did grieve my foolish heart when Easter Sunday came, and my children could not have their new bonnets, as they were used to do, and their mother before them. But oh! I was happy then—happy when worse befell— when the rent could not be paid, and the garden was to be given up, and the furniture was to be sold : and my own little cottage, and the roses I had planted, and the honeysuckles I had trained, and all my fine things, were to pass over to another. Oh! I was happy even then, to what I was in the times that came after—for then it was no fault of mine.

"We got into a hut by the roadside; my husband went out to day-work, and I earned now and then a shilling at charring and one way or another; and when we might have wanted bread, there came often to my door a lady or so, that had known me in my better days, and give me a shilling for old friends' sake, bidding me trust to Providence. Thus even here we did not much amiss, if we had but been contented. But it happened one day—oh! luckless woman that should live to see that day!—we had been more short of money than usual—to spare my husband's meal at night, I had not eaten any thing myself that day—the children's frocks were getting very ragged, and I had not the means to buy them new ones— I was just folding them up, after putting the brats to bed, and my wicked heart was getting ready to murmur against God, when a handsome carriage stopped in the road before my door; two ladies, richly dressed, alighted from it, and, desiring the coachman to drive about, advanced to the door of my poor dwelling. I could not directly guess what they wanted, for they were strangers, and they looked about them more as if they came to do some harm than any good: so I curtsied, and waited till one of them, still looking behind her, asked if I did not sell gloves. I told her no, for that to be sure was a plain case. She still hesitated, as if she did not believe me, and said she had been directed to this cottage. I then recollected there was a cottage further up the row, where some people lived who were known to be smugglers; and though I had never had any acquaintance with them, I supposed they might sell gloves, and answered the lady accordingly, pointing out the house; but surely, as I yet held in my hands my children's ragged frocks, I did wish I had something to sell that they would like to buy. The ladies went away—and, alas! my foolish woman's heart went after them, and in my wicked curiosity I resolved to see what they were going about; so I followed under pretence of showing the way, and loitered about the casement to listen. Dozens by dozens the gloves were produced, and this pair and that pair were chosen, till there was quite a pile of them; and then out came the silks, and the shawls, and the stockings, and after all out came the money; and many a golden piece glittered on the table, and many a bank-note was unfolded. And whilst my eyes rested upon them wishfully—'One of those single bits of gold,' I thought, 'would serve my hungry babes with food for many and many a day, and replace the ragged frocks besides.' The ladies went away, and so did I,—they to their carriage, and I to my hovel—but if their hearts were at rest, mine was not; envy and discontent were awakened in my bosom; my children were asleep, and my husband was not come home;

I set about to get his scanty supper, and for the
first time in my life found no heart for the task—for
the first time since I came into it I left the floor of
my house unswept, and my children's tea-cups unwashed; and sat down to ruminate upon what had
passed. The silks and the gloves, and the gold and
the notes, were running in my head. 'It is no
wonder,' I said, 'that Dame Willum's children are
better dressed than mine, since money comes in so
fast. Yet Dame Willum never toils as I do; and
her husband is not sober and industrious as mine is;
and if the world says true, neither the one nor the
other is any better than they should be.' I knew
that Dame Willum's husband was a noted smuggler,
and a very bad man; and therefore I need not have
envied them their riches—but evil was in my heart,
and the tempter was surely at my elbow; I never
thought of this, but began to consider of the advantage of being a smuggler, and having plenty of money
to receive. Conscience was not altogether silent,
for I had always considered smugglers a bad set of
people; but then if there was no harm in smuggling,
they need not be more wicked than others. And
now, though it was many years agone, it came into
my head, as naturally enough it might, what I had
once heard and seen in my mistresses' house—in those
happy days, every moment and every circumstance
of which was written in my grateful recollection.
My ladies had said there was no harm in smuggling
—my ladies had bought smuggled goods—what was

I, that I should esteem myself wiser than they?
Had they not taught me to fear God and understand his commandments, and would they be doing
wrong?

"I had just settled this point to my satisfaction,
or rather to my inclination, when my husband came
in. He looked a little surprised at the disorder of
the house, and my sitting idle—but he was a quiet
man, so he said nothing, and sat down to his supper.
Having waited a little while in patience, he said,
'Peggy, where's the Bible?'—for ever since we
were married, and that was many a year now, I had
gone on as my ladies first persuaded me to begin,
with reading a chapter in the Bible to him every
night while he ate his supper. I took the book
down—but alas! though I was not conscious of it,
the Bible and I were no longer of a mind. What
wonder, then, I felt but ill-disposed to read it!—I
turned over the leaves—I could not find my place—
I lost it again as soon as I found it—at last I got
through a few verses, but it would not do: my
thoughts were elsewhere; and, closing the book—

"'Jem,' I said, 'Dame Willum's children have
food while mine are starving.' Jem looked amazed,
and well he might—for never in all my troubles was
he used to hear the language of complaint from me.
'Our children, Peggy, have eaten the bread of
honesty; and though it has been sometimes but a
hard morsel, they have thrived upon it, and no man
can say they have robbed him to come at it.'

" ' There are wiser in the world than we, Jem, who do not take smuggling to be so much a sin.'

" ' Belike there may,' said Jem, who was not much a man for arguing, ' but I have thanked God often that I am no smuggler: and I do not suppose any smuggler ever thanked God that he was one.'

" ' But our children are getting older, Jem, and they should have some schooling—and if the free trade is an honest one '——

" ' I pretend to no learning, Peggy—but a trade that brings men to the prison and the gallows is not apt to be an honest one.'

" ' But I know those that think the law has no right to take men up for such things, and '——

" ' 'Tis like enough it hasn't—but I do not see what good that would be to me, if I were in prison, and could not get out.'

" ' One might as well be in prison,' said I, ' as living in this hut with our poor children ragged and starved about us, and we without the means to feed and clothe them.'

" And so we left talking for that time, and went to bed. They who remember the first step into some wilful sin, may know how I went to sleep that night—and they who know what it is to have a wrong purpose in the bosom, with a determination to pursue it, may know how I felt when I awaked. In my dreams I saw a strange confusion of things: sometimes the golden pieces glittering on my table —sometimes the vessel tossed upon the waters, and my husband struggling with the waves—Gloves, silks, prisons, chains, coaches, king's officers, and fine-dressed ladies—all jumbled themselves together in my fancy. Never, never till then had I known such slumbers or such a wakening. And well they might be such—for my days of honesty and innocence were done!"

When the wretched woman reached this part of her narrative, her whole voice and manner changed· In telling the story of her better days, she seemed to have recalled the spirit of them. Her voice was gentle and subdued, her manner simple and affecting ; and the tears that fell from time to time might well have passed for those of chastened and penitential sorrow. It was but a passing impression, arising from the recollection of early happiness. Now her face resumed its sternness, her voice its bold and reckless daring—the tear no longer fell ; but in its place there was an agonised expression in her eye, too vivid almost to be looked on without a shudder.

With a view to still her increasing vehemence, "Peggy," I said, "your sin was doubtless great, but it was not wilful—you did not then know the wrong, or foresee the consequence of your advice."

"Ma'am," said the woman eagerly, "I did know, I did foresee. But for me, he had been now an honest man. He knew I had more learning than he, and always believed what I said—he knew how religiously I had been educated, and that I had known

God and the Bible before he thought of either, and
he did not think I should tell him wrong. It was I
who persuaded him—I sent him into the company
that corrupted him—I sent him to pass his nights
on the wild ocean—I sent him to his death—and
perhaps—but there at least I shall go too, and share
the mischief I have done him." I entreated the
woman to proceed calmly with her story; for I saw
it needed a stronger power than mine to whisper
peace to such a bosom. She proceeded—

"I did not accomplish my purpose all at once,
but from time to time I renewed the subject. Whenever we were short of food, I said I knew where it
was to be had! Whenever I saw Dame Willum's
brats, I said they were better off than mine, though
I knew the contrary. Sometimes, indeed, when the
wind blew loud all night, my heart misgave me —
and sometimes, when I was reading the Bible, my
conscience smote me—but I would not feel, I would
not hear, and at last I accomplished my purpose.
Jem was a strong and a brave man ; some way or
other my foolish talking was heard among the neighbours, and those engaged in the trade came and
persuaded and tempted him. In short—for why
need I prolong my miserable tale ?—Jem became a
smuggler, and from that hour the blessing of Heaven forsook our dwelling—the eye of God was
averted from us, sin took its course, and this is what
came of it. But you will hear.

"Things looked well at first : Jem was paid seven

or eight shillings a-night—my children were dressed,
my children were fed—we got a better house—but
what was I with all?—a miserable, miserable woman!
In the long dark nights, while the wind was blowing and the waves were raging, did I sleep soundly
on my comfortable bed, bought with the price of his
perils?   When the Sabbath day came, and the bells
rung, and I dressed my children in their nice neat
clothes, was my heart light as I went forth alone
where he was used to go with me?   No—from the
first I was a miserable woman, though no one knew
it but myself; and it rapidly grew worse.   Jem, un-
used to the fatigue and exposure of such a service,
was forced to take spirits to carry him through it:
necessity soon grew into choice; obliged to drink
when he was out, he chose to drink at home; the
coarse and blasphemous language he heard among his
desperate companions he repeated before his wife
and children; he laughed at his Bible now, and
when I remonstrated with him, he told me, if I had
believed it myself, I should not have wished him to
become a smuggler.   Oh! if this had not been so—
if he had died as I knew him once, as I once saw
him on a bed of sickness—oh, I could have borne it
then—but to die so!

"It was then my last child was born; she that is
yonder—look at her, for she was conceived in iniquity indeed—she was ugly as her father's and her
mother's sin, and she has been the torment of our
lives—her evil disposition has defeated all our efforts

to control it—she will learn nothing, do nothing, and does not seem to have wit enough to know good from bad; though she has enough, God knows! to get into all the mischief she can find. But the sin is on our heads—she was fed on the bread of iniquity, she heard nothing but oaths and curses from her father and his bad companions—from her mother but fretfulness and reproaches. I had children —but they are gone—my blessings are taken from me, and she is left to be my curse!

"Some years went on in this way: at times we had plenty of money; but as my husband drank and gamed, we were at other times much distressed. One day when he came home rather more sober than usual—'Peggy,' he said, 'the blood of a fellow-creature is on my hand!' I shuddered, and so I thought did he—for we had known, we had sometime felt, the commands of God; we had believed them once, and once had feared to disobey them; and, though we had contrived to persuade ourselves that smuggling did not break the eighth commandment, we could not well persuade ourselves that murder did not break the sixth. My husband had killed a man in a fray; and though he was never discovered, he was ever after that as one desperate and careless of what might follow.

"On one occasion my children were sick; we had spent all our money, and I was advised to go to some charitable lady in the town, and ask for nourishment for them. I went, and was conducted to the lady : but as soon as she heard my name, she said my husband was a bad character, my house was a notorious place of drinking and wickedness, and she could not by any means encourage me. I looked at her, for I thought I had seen her once before—but whether I had or not, I whispered, as I walked away uncomforted, ‘ If it had not been for you, or such as you, we had never been what we are :’ and I went home with my bosom hardened in sin and aggravated in wretchedness, by the repulse of those whom I considered as the cause of both. For think not that my first sin had been the only one—no, it is a road on which she who starts is driven forward as with stings and scourges. By degrees I had ceased to go to church or to read at home, because it reminded me of the days that were gone ; I could not bear the recollection ; and I could not bear to see the minister, who used to talk kindly with me, go by me now without notice. I also ceased to teach my children good ; for I feared lest they should compare it with the ill they saw, and I should but be teaching them to hate and despise their parents. Yet did my heart yearn over them as the destined prey of the Evil One, given by their own parents to destruction. In one of my better moments, as I looked upon that graceless girl, my heart was moved towards her with pity and with shame, for I had taught her nothing : and I resolved to make one effort to save her from destruction, by asking for her from others what I could no longer render her

myself. I knew the days on which a committee of
ladies were to meet for benevolent purposes, especially for the supporting of a school for the indigent,
and I knew that in this school the children were
carefully and religiously taught. I took my neglected offspring in my hand, and presented myself before
them to solicit admission for her into the school ; it
was the first right thing I had done for many a day,
and there was a peace in my bosom it had become
but little used to. When I had made my request,
I was asked my name, and the occupation of my
husband. O that the time should have come when
such questions would bring shame to the cheek of
Peggy Lum ! I equivocated a little on the latter
question, but the ladies understood my language,
and told me with some harsh expressions, that my
child could not be admitted, as they had many appli-
cations, and always gave the preference to those
whose parents followed an honest calling. My bosom
was ready to burst with grief and indignation—yes,
indignation—for, as I looked round the circle, I saw
the contraband articles about their persons ! I
knew well enough the gloves on the hands of one
and the handkerchief round the neck of the other—
and my child was rejected, cast off, left to ignorance
and vice, because her father pursued for subsistence
a trade that they encouraged for the ornament of
their persons ! With some show of impertinence,
which still more confirmed their rejection of me, I
was leaving the house, when a lady of a very kind

aspect whispered me, that she would call and talk to me about putting the child to school somewhere. But the last spark of good was extinguished in my bosom—the last good purpose I ever formed was repulsed in a way that completed the hardening of my heart—'No,' I said, as I walked along, scarce knowing where I went, 'she shall neither go to their schools, nor learn their learning. If she sin, as she will do, it shall be in ignorance and stupidity: they shall not teach her the will of God, only to make her more guilty when they afterwards teach her to disobey him. They taught me first the meaning of moral and religious honesty; then they told me by words and by example, that there was no harm in a secret and unlawful trade—and now that I come to them with the wretchedness in my heart, and the ruin on my head, which were brought on me by that trade, they reject my supplication, and put scorn upon my guiltless child, because I have pursued it. No—not a child of mine shall go : if she must follow in her mother's course, she shall go there without her feelings :' and when the kind lady did, in fact, come and offer to put the child to school at her own expense, I obstinately, and insolently, rejected the proposal ; and thus made myself guilty of my child's as well as of my husband's ruin.

"But the measure was full and the time was come, and my tale will soon be told. My eldest boy was now a lad of sixteen ; and never since he had come into the world had he made his mother's heart to ache. He was the birth of better days, for he was the first-born child I had. The good impressions of his early years had lasted him through worse ones—he had been to school, and since that he had been to sea in a collier; and in spite of all the ill he heard when he came home, he was ever a good and steady lad. It was some time now that he had been out of employ, and had got a sort of hankering to go out with his father; only, as he said, for a bit of sport, for he was a brave boy, and loved danger and the seas; but he loved his mother better, and he had ever till then yielded to her entreaties not to go. One night—yes, that night, that very night—there was rough work to be done, and they wanted hands—there was danger, and they offered high pay. My boy's spirit was roused, his father persuaded him, and when I would have retained him even with tears, my husband said that since I did not care about *his* being drowned or murdered, he did not see why I should make so much ado about the boy. They were the last words he ever spoke to me. They were not true—for in all his wickedness Jem had been kind and affectionate to me; and it was not for me to love him less for sins that I myself had driven him to. They were not true words—but, Oh! I remembered them when—Remembered! I remember them now—I hear them in my sleep, I hear them in my dreams, they are whispered about my bed, and about my pillow. Grant, Heaven, they come not after me to the grave!

"They went, and surely something in my heart misgave me of what was coming : for I felt I could not go to bed that night. It was already dark when they went away ; and many a time I opened the casement to look out upon the night. The wind howled frightfully. I heard the waves thundering upon the rocks, as if they would have rent the firm earth in pieces ; and so dark was it, that when, in my restlessness, I went out to try it, I could not find my way across the road. Not a star was there in all the heavens, nor a bit of moon to light them on their perilous way—'twas ever such nights as these they chose to do their boldest deeds. Hour after hour I listened, though I knew not for what, for they were miles away. I shuddered at the silence—I started even at the noise I made myself, as from time to time I threw on a log to keep the fire burning, that they might warm and dry them when they came. I saw my neglected Bible on the shelf, and remembered the time when it would have consoled me— but not now : I remembered when in times of fear and danger to those I loved, I should have betaken myself to prayer—but not now. I could but sit and watch the dial-plate, and long, and long for the hours of darkness to be gone. And when they were gone, and the daylight opened, I liked it no better. I looked out upon the damp, cold landscape, and thought it was like my desolated bosom ; the very light was hateful to me ; for surely the truth was in my heart, though yet I knew it not. The morning grew apace ;

the people in the surrounding cottages came forth to their honest labours. I saw one and another making ready the breakfast for her husband, and giving a parting word to her boys—but where were mine? Nine o'clock struck, ten, eleven, and still they came not. This was no uncommon thing, but there was a presentiment of evil in my bosom. The clock was just upon the point of twelve, when I heard a noise of voices—I went out, and saw a crowd about Dame Willum's door. I knew her husband had been out with the party, and guessed the rest: ' Where is Jem?' I said to the first who would hear me. ' He will be here presently,' said the man in a sullen tone. I had no more to ask—every body was talking, and every body was eager to tell the worst they could make of the fearful story. All murdered, all drowned, all prisoners! And soon there was not even need to listen, for my eyes beheld the worst— the dead body of my husband, borne upon the shoulders of ruffianly-looking men, whose downcast looks bespoke that even they felt pity for his fate. And where was my boy? Him the cold waters held, and would not give me back so much as his lifeless body! The smugglers had been attacked in endeavouring to remove their cargo; they resisted; some were slain on the spot, and the rest were drowned in attempting to escape. Who will tell out the story? Who will tell the wife's, the mother's agony, when she received of her husband no more but the disfigured corpse—of her son, not even so much as that!

Tell who may, I cannot. But you see me, what I am—I have told you what I was. Want and disease, and remorse and agony, have brought me to the grave. What is beyond, you may know; I do not— I believed once, now I dare not believe."

The story is finished—need I write the moral? If my readers believe I have drawn an exaggerated picture, let them inquire and know. They will not, perhaps, find Peggy Lum upon her death-bed, nor meet her squalid offspring in their evening walk— but they will find more misery resulting from this traffic than language of mine can picture. They may see, as we have done, the suspected fall under our windows. They may see, as we have done, three or four at a time, the murdered bodies borne into the churchyard—and they may hear, as we do daily, the thoughtless multitude, one moment repeating the melancholy story, the next moment creeping about the lanes and alleys, in search of the venders of forbidden goods. It is for such that I have told the story. The miserable victims of this traffic will not read our pages, nor is it for them that I have written. They are incapable of appreciating the moral wrong of the traffic itself; the only question to them is the gain and loss, the risk and the inducement— and in this, as in all other sorts of gambling, we know that men will put all they have on the stake, if the prize proposed be large enough. To these poor creatures the inducement is their daily sustenance, the support of their wives and children: that they ruin them eventually is beyond their calculation; for we know, that in exact proportion as the mind is uncultivated, its feelings and cares are limited to the present time. Much, therefore, is to be said in excuse for them. But what is to be said for us? It is the purchaser that makes the trade. Can we, without compunction, see the lives of our fellow-creatures put to venture, their families plunged into misery unspeakable, their morals corrupted, their souls, it may be, ruined eternally—and all for what? To save a few shillings, which we would freely give to any one who needed it, or to deck our persons with some prohibited article of dress? I fully believe, there is not a lady in Britain who would not take the costly shawl from her shoulders, and present it to the person whom she could thereby save from such misery as we have described, though the consequence were that she should never wear another— and yet we expose to such misery hundreds and thousands of our fellow-creatures, and when it is named to us, think it quite enough to say, " French goods are prohibited, and we must have them, because"—most sufficient reason—" because we like them best!"

No. XIV.

SOCIAL KINDNESS.

Vivre en soi ce n'est rien ; il faut vivre en autrui
A qui puis je être utile, agréable aujourd'hui ?
Voila chaque matin ce qu'il faut se dire ;
Et le soir, quand des cieux la clarté se retire,
Heureux à qui son cœur tout bas a répondu,
Ce jour qui va finir, je ne l'ai pas perdu ;
Grâce à mes soins, j'ai vu, sur une face humaine,
La trace d'un plaisir ou l'oubli d'une peine !
Que la société porterait de doux fruits,
Si par de telles pensées nous étions tous conduits !

THERE was somewhere—not in England, I should
suppose—a very extensive prison-house, in which
immense numbers of persons were confined under
suspicion, for they had not yet been tried, of manifold misdemeanours, some in the overt act, and
others in hidden disaffection towards a Government
to which they all owed allegiance. From the babbling
infant, who had come there for his father's crimes,
before himself could have committed any, to the hoary
head of age, bowing already to the grave that was
waiting to receive him—from the coarse, unthinking
peasant, who had followed where others led, to the
lofty and commanding spirit that must answer for

many a crime beside his own—every age was here, and sex and nation—every complexion and condition of mankind were assembled in this vast prison-house, to wait till it should please the sovereign—for in that country there was no Habeas Corpus Act—to come from his far distant court, and judge the prisoners for the crimes of which they stood accused.

Around this strange abode, there was a wall too high for any foot to scale, too thick for any eye to penetrate, in order to discover what might be beyond it. Within the limit, the imprisoned seemed to walk at large—there was space for all to live and move at ease, but not without perpetually crossing each other's way, and coming in near and frequent contact; and if any would have fled from his fellows, he could not, for the wall was round him and about him, and he might not pass it; there were paths many, and ways many, but the impervious barrier was the issue of them all, and "no further," was the fatal check upon their else unrestricted motions. Suspected of unequal crimes, but as yet untried and unconvicted, they were not distinguished from each other by any anticipatory punishments, seeming to suffer promiscuously the hardships inseparable from their state of durance and disgrace. And not few, indeed, were these. Famine, and want, and pain, and misery were there. Some eyes looked upwards in untold despair, as if still to demand of Heaven what to Heaven itself had become impossible to bestow—and some were on the ground in deep despondency, as if they loathed to meet the sunbeam that had shone on scenes now lost to them for ever. Their very pleasures, when they seemed to flourish most, were but as that baleful tree, very fair to look upon. that drops pestilence and death on all who venture to repose beneath its branches. For while the parent sat at ease, fondly administrating to the needs and pleasures of a beautiful family, one by one he saw them sink beneath the hardships of their condition, till there were none remaining. And the bosom that had brought with it all that was needful to its happiness, in sweet possession of which whatever was suffered was scarcely felt, and whatever was wanting was not missed, was doomed to see the pestilential vapour of the prison arise, and chill to death the frame of its beloved. Industry toiled hard and sowed its seed, and forgot in labour, as others in pleasure, the dangers of his state; and when he should have reaped the fruit, the winds of heaven, from which his prison-house was all unsheltered, had blighted it, and he was left to want. Some, who once had friends, and families, and homes, sat here apart from all, and laid claim to nothing, and found regard of none—and some, whom all caressed and all bowed down to, and who seemed to abound in every thing, fed secretly on the ashes of affliction, and fasted from all but tears, consumed by memory of something past, or dread of some half-seen future. The lofty and capacious intellect was there, working its own misery with its own greatness, to which there was nothing to respond, and which nothing in that small space could satisfy. And feebleness, and ignorance, and imbecility were there also, suffering contempt, neglect, and scorn, for deficiencies not of their own choosing. And though there were some on whose cheek the bloom was fresh, and in whose eye the beam of joy was bright, they were regarded by the more experienced, as but the less conscious victims of as sure a fate; for it was known they could not evade, though they might forget, the consequences of their suspected character. And to all, and to each, besides the unequal sufferings of their actual state, there remained the approaching judgment to which they were reserved, coming they knew not when, threatening they knew not what; more awful for its uncertainty, more appalling for the obscurity that hung upon the issue.

Does not the question forcibly suggest itself, How would these prisoners conduct themselves towards each other? Involved in one common calamity, standing in the same fearful predicament, compelled, willing or unwilling, to remain together, to take of the same scanty comforts, and abide the same but too sufficient ills—each one liable to whatever the other was enduring, and no one secure from succeeding to his neighbour's wo—how does it seem they would deport themselves to each other in this strange condition; which had brought them together without their leave, and forced them to abide each other's company, without any choice of theirs? Reason, and

common sense, and feeling, nay, and self-interest itself, are agreed upon the answer—kindness, courtesy,
and pity, would be the tone of such society. They
would not all love each other—dissimilar habits,
uncongenial tempers, varieties of intellect and condition, would make that impossible : they would not
all esteem each other—for defect of moral worth in
some, in others native imbecility or deformity of
character, would render them no objects of esteem.
But there would surely prevail in this society a tone
of benevolence and courtesy, the result of a participated destiny. The untried criminal would not begin
beforehand the punishment of his fellow criminals,
by treating them according to the measure of their
supposed, though yet undecided guilt. However
much unlike, no one could stand off from another as
a being with whom he had no feelings or interests in
common. The common misery, the common danger,
would create a fellowship between the most opposite
characters, that would claim a word, a look at least,
of kindness, as they went by each other, or sat down
together in the narrow limits of their prison-house.
It would seem that one could scarcely have a concern
in which the others felt no interest, a feeling that
the others would not wish to spare, a desire the others
would not wish to gratify—from sympathy if not for
love, from pity if not esteem. And least of all would
those who had most hope of pardon and favour from
the sovereign, when he came, look coldly on those
with whom it might fare worse—a sense of their own

danger would teach them pity, and conscious guilt would make them merciful. Here, in short, the wisest would see in the most simple, the noblest in the basest, a being whom, if nature had placed afar, suffering and danger had brought near of kin.

Some one has wisely said—our readers may have observed before now that we always think that saying wise which agrees with our own opinions—and beautifully as wisely said, " Courtesy is, strictly speaking, a Christian grace. It is a plant of heavenly origin. This present evil world, like the ground which the Lord hath cursed, is utterly incapable of yielding any thing so good and lovely. Courtesy cannot grow in selfish nature's soil. It is never found but in the garden of God." I had just been reading this very pretty sentence, as quoted for my observation in the letter of a friend, when passing into society, I happened to hear it boldly asserted that it is not desirable to make ourselves agreeable to those we do not like, and warmly contested that universal courtesy is almost a sin. " So, then," I said within myself, " here are opinions in most determined opposition— the plant that one would cherish as the very growth of Heaven, the other plucks up and casts away as a noxious and pernicious weed." I had dwelt with pleasure on the former sentiment as true, and just, and beautiful—but what then becomes of the other? They cannot both be just or both be true. Yet it seemed to me of some importance, that they who are beginning the business of life, should perceive

between the flower and the weed; and setting myself
to consider of the matter, it appeared to me that this
world of ours is no other than the prison-house described, and our condition in it that which we have
depicted. How then does it seem that we should
behave?

It has pleased God, for reasons wise since they
are his, to form the inhabitants of earth in moulds
so different, that each one cannot assimilate with
another—like ill-accorded instruments, well-tuned
perhaps, and perfect in themselves, but which yet
can make no harmony together, because the pitch of
one is higher than the other. It has pleased Him,
too, to endow our minds with feelings, known and
understood by all, though difficult to define, that draw
us towards some persons in preference to others,
and while we go by the mass with indifference, bind
us with indissoluble affection to some selected few;
for no reason that can be given, but a natural and
spontaneous preference; or perhaps some affinity of
taste, principles, and pursuits. These selected few,
for however many, they are few in the comparison,
are what we usually call our friends; and to these
our deportment may be left to other influence and
guided by other rules than those of general courtesy.
But these apart, the larger mass of those with whom
we are brought in contact, are persons for whom, to
use the common expression, we do not care—we
have no choice or preference for them. It is to these
that a habit of universal courtesy is or is not to be

cultivated—that we are or are not to take pains to render ourselves as agreeable and acceptable as circumstances and higher duty will permit.

We know there is a sinful conformity to the world that is forbidden; and whatever that may be defined to be, we beg not to be understood to desire that the line be broken; for God must not be offended that man be pleased, and sin must not be committed from any motive of expediency whatever. But civility, attention, regard to the tastes, and respect for the feelings of others, are not sins—on the contrary, they are the plant that has been asserted to be of Christian growth, a flower of the garden of God. We are aware, also, that it will be contested there is a degree of insincerity and deception in assuming an appearance of attention and complacency towards those for whom we have no regard, nor any kindly feelings. Be it admitted, however, that we ought to have kindly feelings towards every one. Criminals chained to the same galley, slaves fettered and toiling in the same mine, are not more closely conjoined in one common fate, have not more claim upon each other's sympathy, than men inhabiting together this prison-house of earth. We ought to have a feeling of benevolent interest for every one of mortal birth —our aversions, our contempt, our disunion, our animosity, all these things are defects, blemishes, symptoms of mental corruption and disease—and if they cannot be eradicated, we are obliged to any garb of decency that can contribute to conceal them.

Our Christian perfection would be to have no unkindly feelings towards any one—and the next best
thing to this is to be conscious of them and ashamed
of them, and endeavour to conceal them as we would
a loathsome and unsightly wound: the effort is a
self-sacrifice, and will go far to subdue the feeling.
It may be asserted again, that a universal desire to
please and to oblige, is dangerous to ourselves, as it
may be the offspring of vanity, too eager for the
approbation of men, and ever seeking its own gratification. It may be so: but in this case it is the
motive, not the conduct, that needs to be amended.
To pay a courteous attention to those who do not
particularly please us—to give satisfaction to those
who can give us none—is, as we have observed, a
sacrifice of our selfishness that may proceed from the
highest tone of Christian principle.

Are we, then, to be as courteous, and to attempt
to be as agreeable, to those whom we do not admire,
or perhaps do not approve, as those whose qualities
and principles claim our esteem and approbation?
We need not choose them for our companions, or
take them to the confidence of our bosoms—we need
not seek them or desire them—but our house is
narrow; the path we go on is strait; the way is
crowded, and we must be much in contact; the duties
and intercourse of life must bring us into connexion
with those whom we did not and could not choose.
And what are we, that we should feel contempt or
disregard for any one? If others have their pecu-

liarities, have we not ours? If they have their defects, have we not ours? nay, and our vices, too, for
which we are all hastening forward to an equal
judgment? And in this narrow house of our sojourn-
ing, surely every one has a claim to what every one
can do to make sweet the bitterness of life? For,
oh! there is enough for all to bear—the dwellers in
that prison-house were not so happy that there was
no need of each other's courtesy to soften their condition; there was not so much scarcity of suffering,
that the conduct of one should prejudge the other's
crimes, and aggravate the punishment prepared for
him. And who are those we think unworthy of our
attention and civility, unworthy the care to please?
beings, perhaps more worthy than ourselves, though
less externally endowed: they, perhaps, who, had
we been in need, would have cherished us in affliction, would have consoled us, though, needing them
not, we have never proved it—some, it may be, who,
though we perceive it not, have hearts so deeply
tried in sorrow, that, could we know all, our bosoms
would yearn with tender pity over what we igno-
rantly wound by neglect and incivility—and some,
it is more than probable, whatever be the cloud of
ignorance or sin that now hangs over them, with
whom we are destined to pass a long eternity in the
holy fellowship of heaven.

Upon Christian principles, then, we are prepared
to say, that it is our duty to be courteous; and, as
far as may be, agreeable, to all with whom Providence

bring us in connexion, whether we meet them for a day or an hour, or the whole compass of our lives. We are not to be idle to please the idle, or ignorant to please the ignorant. or vicious to please the vicious —and if we were, we should not succeed in pleasing them—but we are to laugh with those that laugh, to weep with those that weep—to contribute all we can, in small things as in great, to ameliorate the dark condition of our race, and scatter flowers on a thorny path. If we are in company with those whose tastes and habits are opposed to ours, we are to put some restraint upon our own, that theirs may not be offended : if with those whose manners are disgusting, or tempers uncongenial to us, we are bound to cast a veil over the disgust they undesignedly excite. We are bound to withhold a remark that will give pain, or an opinion that will offend, unless some essential purpose is to be answered by their expression. To say, this is deception or insincerity, is no other than to say, it is deception to restrain any evil passion, or suppress any angry thought or selfish feeling—nor is there any thing in manners and tempers we hold more selfish, unlovely, and unchristian, than that sort of self-indulgence which wounds every body's feelings, under pretext of candour and sincerity. I advise the lovers of so much honesty, to make clean the mansion, and put forth no few of its inhabitants, before they venture to set wide the gates, that all may be witness of what is passing within.

It appears to me, young people cannot go forth

into the world under a more false impression, than this persuasion,—that they owe no courtesy to any but those whom circumstances or preference happen to make their friends. They owe it to every individual without exception who has not forfeited it by offence against them—for every individual is their fellow, and their kindred, and their companion, in a destiny of which the beginning, and the purport, and the issue, are the same; and, therefore, each one is a claimant on their sympathy and benevolence. To say that we would do them any kindness in their need, or confer any substantial benefit in our power, but refuse to conciliate in our ordinary intercourse, is to offer that which we have not, in excuse for withholding that which we have—our benevolence may never have an occasion of exercise in substantial benefits—in complacency, kindness, and courtesy, and an accommodating spirit, we may always, and to every one, evince it.

We know that the devoted Christian has something more to say respecting the discountenance that should be given to folly and irreligion, the distinction to be made between those who serve God and those who serve him not. This distinction must exist in the feelings of all who sincerely love their Lord: but I cannot see in it an excuse for the cold, repulsive, harsh, unsocial, unconciliating manner, some pious people assume towards those whom they consider less religious than themselves. We are the fellow-criminals, not the judge: whatever be our penitence and hope of pardon, we are here the attainted rebels of our sovereign, not the administrators of his justice; and whatever be the present promise of his mercy towards us more than them, his pity takes not its limits from our judgment, and it may be they will enter into the kingdom of heaven before us.

But if still it does not appear that we ought to cultivate habits of kindness, attention, and civility, to all around us — behold, there was One who came into that crowded prison-house that did not belong to it—its attainted inhabitants were not to his mind —there was no spirit there congenial to his nature, or fitted to hold communion with him—their ways were not as his ways, nor their feelings as his feelings —day by day their discordant natures jarred on his holy bosom, and their impure pursuits revolted his celestial innocence. Yet He walked courteously in the midst of all, and stood not aloof from any. He wept over their ills, indeed, and he reproved their wrongs; but he kept none at a distance as unworthy his regard; he dwelt with them as a brother and a friend; took an interest in their lawful occupations, conformed to their habits, and adapted his benefits and his advice to their peculiar character and need of each. Is the subject greater than his King? Is the servant wiser than his Lord?

No. XV.

POLITENESS.

Politeness is the moral grace of life, if I may venture so to term it : the grace of the mind. What the world accounts graces are little more than the graces of the body.

Dr Brown.

WALKING one morning by myself—an unfavourable circumstance for a Listener—and in a lonely place, where, though I could not please myself as Rousseau did, with believing the foot of man had never trodden, I certainly could discern no traces of his despoiling hand—a fit of enthusiasm, such as poets, I suppose, are subject to, seized upon my brain in favour of nature's unassisted works ; and in most sublime soliloquy I began to decry the assassinations committed by man's sacrilegious hand upon her charms. I compared the briery path I was creeping through with difficulty, to the broad, beaten turnpike: the elegance and simplicity of the wild-flowers, half hiding, half showing themselves, upon their beds of green, to the trained, and trimmed, and methodically planted flowers of the garden ; trees whence no pruner had ever lopped a branch—grass whence the mower had not filled his scythe, nor the reaper his bosom —recesses, where for years the redbreast had returned to build his nest, and found it as he left it. "What a pity it is," I exclaimed, "that man should intermeddle with what God has made, and mar the beauties he can never mend! When all that avarice and vanity suggest has been tried, to torture our parks and gardens into form, are they to be compared to the wild, woody glade, that knows no training but from nature's hand, yearly returning to re-dress her work?" So I thought, and so have poets said and sung for ages past: and so sure was I growing that every thing should be as nature made it, that it is possible I might have gone on to say, as some have said, that rather than clear a wood for building houses and making turnpikes, it would be advisable to live like our forefathers, in the hollows of trees, and reach our habitation over sting-nettles—had I not, in the midst of my soliloquy, egressed from this same wood, and within ken of man's lamented depredations, found myself upon the beach. It chanced that there was walking there a man who seemed intent on finding something among the pebbles. Often he stooped down to pick them up, and after a little examination, threw them from him—once only I perceived, that having looked at one with attention, he retained it in his hands. "Why," said I, "do you prefer that stone to all the rest?"—"Because," he replied, "it is of value, and they are worth nothing."—"And yet," I answered, "I see

no beauty in that, more than in the others—it is a
rough, brown stone."—"It is so now, and there is
no beauty in it; but there is value: when I have
cut and polished it, and set it in a golden rim, its
beauty will be acknowledged, and rival purchasers
will contend for the possession. Come to my labo-
ratory, and I will show you the richest jewels of the
Eastern mine, and you will say they seem but inelegant and worthless stones: see them again upon
the brow of royalty, or on the neck of beauty, and
you will gaze upon them as nature's most exquisite
productions." This was true, but then my soliloquy was absolutely wasted—for here were nature's
most valuable, most inimitable, and probably most
tedious productions, not only improved by art, but
owing to it all their perceptible, though not their
real value. The gem was a gem while it lay neglected in the sand: but most would have passed it by
unheeded; or, finding, have rejected it as of little
value: and even when the worth was ascertained,
we doubt much if any lady would be ambitious to
string the unpolished jewels for her bosom, or bind
them in her hair.

There are things besides stones, that, valuable in
themselves, need the factitious aid of ornament to
make them lovely. All the polish in the world, it is
true, would not make of the worthless stone a dia-
mond; and whoever knew the value would take the
gem without it, and reject the other in its richest
brilliancy: but the rich jewel must be set and po-

lished, before its beauty is perceived; or with the unskilful, the glittering paste may be preferred before it. Is not this a truth too much forgotten by some who think it enough to be good, without remembering to be agreeable? With some parents, who, while they store the minds of their children with knowledge, and lead them forward in the paths of truth, fearful, perhaps, of fostering vanity, or over-looking the importance of recommending by exterior beauty the interior worth, totally neglect their manners, habits, and appearance? Is it not so with some young persons, who, earnestly desiring to please God, and loving their fellow-creatures for his sake, do yet misjudgingly despise, or carelessly neglect, those trifles, that, trifles as they are, make all the difference between an agreeable and a disagreeable woman: and though they affect not the moral or religious worth, will make that worth the more or the less acceptable and lovely? Such persons are surely doing wrong, and if professing to be religious, doubly wrong—for the blame will be cast upon their religion, not upon themselves; they render that un-lovely and unattractive which is in itself most beautiful; they revolt where they ought to win. There is no natural connexion, no possible affinity, between religion and awkwardness, coarseness and incivility, an unpolished manner or an ungraceful mind. This seems so impossible, that we should not think to speak of it, did we not see every-day instances of a mistaken, we could almost say, a proud neglect of

these attentions, in persons whose minds are truly
occupied with great matters ; and did we not every
day hear, without being able to contradict it, that
good people are disagreeable. To elder persons and
to parents, much might be said—but I listen for the
young, and will end my apostrophe with the tale that
gave rise to it.

I have heard, or read, of somebody, who, on visiting the magnificent fabrics of Italy, which they had
heard were of marble, was very much disappointed
to find them not polished from top to bottom, smooth,
and shining like a marble chimney-piece—for any
thing they say, the buildings might as well have been
of stone. Much such a dunce, I fear, did I prove
myself, when I accepted an invitation from a family of
whom I had heard so much good report, that I had
long been anxious to be admitted to their society.
The excellence of their education, the cultivation
bestowed on their minds, and the high religious principles that regulated their conduct, were things of
so much notoriety in the neighbourhood, I could not
but form the most pleasing anticipation of pleasure
in my intercourse with them, and the highest possible
estimate of their worth. If I was disappointed, the
fault undoubtedly was mine ; for their worth was
equal to the representation made of it : they were
all I have said, and all I had heard : what right had
I to expect more ? I had heard these young ladies
had both talent and principle, and I went prepared
to admire and love them. As I stayed some time in

the house, I had opportunities of observing them under different circumstances, at home and abroad, in company and alone : what I have to remark, therefore, must not be understood to have passed in one day, or in quite such rapid succession as I tell it ; neither did each thing happen once only—I describe their habitual deportment.

When I was first conducted into the house, two young ladies were sitting in the drawing-room, one engaged with her book, the other with her needle : whether each one had a task to perform, and feared the doom's-day clock might strike before it was completed, I cannot say ; but neither ceased their occupation when I entered, though, as a guest and a stranger, it might have been expected I should be in some manner received by them in their parents' absence. They answered when I spoke to them, it is true ; but they never made any attempt to address me. Miss Julia kept her elbow on the table, and her head on her hand, in such a position as almost to turn her back towards the sofa on which I was sitting : and even when she did speak, held her eyes as intently fixed on her book, as if some magic power held them in perpetual durance. Miss Emma, whose work was of a description I thought might as well have been done in her chamber, or at least removed on the entrance of a guest, was, I perceived, under the influence of some vow not to remove her nose above two inches from her thimble, though there was scarcely a passage between them for the few

words my importunity forced from her. The most
natural inference from such a reception would have
been, that my visit was unwelcome; but I had reason to know the contrary; and I had frequent occasion afterwards to observe that all persons, whether
friends or strangers, had to encounter, on their approach, the persevering industry of these ladies. Indeed, whoever desired the Miss B.'s civility, must
wait for it; for when, a few days after, I introduced
to them in our walk some young persons with whom
I knew they desired intimacy, they gave an inclination of the head with a look that might very well be
mistaken for a frown, turned their backs immediately,
and went on with their own conversation. Be it
not, however, supposed that the Miss B.'s could not
communicate, or would not—when it was perfectly
convenient to themselves. Julia was indeed of a
temper silent and reserved, though wanting neither
feeling nor affection; Emma was lively and animated
in the extreme. It was easy to perceive that the
same effects in each had resulted from different
causes: in Julia, from an indolent indifference to
things she considered not essential—in Emma, from
a contempt of what she believed beneath her.

There was company that evening, and having
found the young ladies so extremely agreeable alone,
I was curious to see what they might be in society.
They did not, however, think it necessary to be
ready for some time after they were expected in the
room. At length Miss Julia made her appearance

through the doorway—one might almost say through
the door—for she opened it but barely wide enough
to force her small person through the interstice.
Whether there was any one present she was glad to
see, remained a riddle ; so eager was she to get possession of the nearest corner of the nearest chair she
could find, seeming by no means aware that she
might sit as safely in the middle of it ; and having
reached the port, she took care to leave it no more
that night. Emma's approach was by no means so
peaceful : with the assistance of a gust of wind, she
contrived to startle every body from their seats by
the banging of the door, stumbled over two stools
and a work-table before she reached the upper end
of the room, and went down on the sofa with a bang,
that, had her specific gravity been greater, might
have endangered the fragile ornaments of the chimney. And this evening, though I could not hear the
subject of her discourse, or guess the cause of her
mirth, I had the first proof that Emma could both
laugh and talk ; for she continued during the whole
evening in half whispering discourse, accompanied by
frequent titter, with a young person of her own age ;
their hands fast locked in each other, to intimate, I
suppose, the inseparability of their affections. And
wo to the unlucky wight who attempted to be thirds
in the discourse ! I addressed them sometimes, and
so did others—but an immediate cessation of their
discourse, a monosyllable reply to our address, and a
look exchanged between them, sufficiently intimated

that we might spare ourselves the trouble. Certainly, had I been asked that night if the Miss B.'s were agreeable girls, my veracity or my friendship must have conceded in the reply.

The time did come, nevertheless, when I was allowed to hear these young ladies converse: but though to all appearance they spoke the vulgar tongue, the subject of their discourse was not much more intelligible than if it had been the vernacular language of Kamschatka or Peru. Neither persons nor things had the names by which I had been accustomed to hear them called: and then there was so profuse an admixture of "bywords," "family sayings," and "standing jokes," one needed to be provided with a glossary as long as the list of French idioms with which a modern traveller sets out on his first visit to Paris. That all this was very amusing, and very innocently so, to themselves, I make no doubt—but I had been accustomed to suppose that when we speak at table, or in company with others, good-breeding requires we should converse in some known tongue, that all may, if they please, take part in the conversation. So sure was I, however, of the talents and good sense of the ladies, I did not doubt their conversation would be very edifying, if ever I could gain a share of it, and I resolved to abide in patience some opportunities of addressing them in my own way. In pursuance of this resolve, I watched every occasion to draw them into conversation. Walking with Miss Julia,

I gathered a flower and made some remarks upon its properties; she knew nothing about flowers, and thought it a useless pursuit. I ventured to observe that since the Almighty had condescended to create them, it might possibly not be beneath his creatures to take notice of them. Thinking these subjects might be too light for the lady's wisdom, I next attempted something deeper—but her modesty here came in aid of her taciturnity; and she said the subject was too deep for her understanding : and so the conversation ended. Sitting with Miss Emma, I asked if she had finished any drawings lately. She answered that she had done several, but did not know where any of them were; a plain intimation that she drew for her own pleasure, not for mine. When assembled in the family circle, my attempts were equally fruitless : the young ladies never happened to hear what was passing in their presence. Julia seldom answered till she had been addressed three times; and Emma generally chimed in to the middle of somebody's speech, with remarks quite foreign to the subject—setting all right in the end by confessing they were thinking of something else—a compliment of which they were very prodigal in all companies. As these ladies were Christians, I would not suppose them to be more than usually selfish—nor in their dispositions were they; but in defiance of what is usually supposed to be a requisite of good breeding, they were invariably fond of talking of their own affairs. It has been said that, to be agreeable in conversation, we should never speak of ourselves; the Miss B.'s had no such maxim; however abstract might be the subject where it began, it always ended in, " *I* saw," " *I* said," " *I* did—*my* friends—*my* house—*my* studies—*my* family—*my* prospects." I had not long been acquainted with them, before I perceived that particular attention had been paid to the pronunciation of their words, and as their education had been something classical, it cannot be disputed that they were most technicall correct. There are those who think it more elegant, because more polite, to talk the language of the society in which we live, and allow words to keep the sound custom has assigned them—however this be, they had an invariable habit of repeating immediately, by accident of course, every word they supposed to be mispronounced by another : I never found an opportunity of telling them that I knew those who would spoil any speech they happen to be making, rather than repeat, in a different manner, a word they suppose to be mispronounced by another. I might not have observed upon this extraordinary accuracy, had it not been to contrast it with an inaccuracy of a very remarkable kind—for though so particular about the sound of words, these ladies evinced a marvellous disregard of their meaning. At the breakfast table we had tea *excruciatingly* hot, poured out of a *lovely* teapot, and accompanied by bread and butter of *infinite* excellence. In our walks—when the *vile* weather did not prevent walking—we saw the *sweetest* ships that ever sailed the waters, the most *exquisite* cows that ever ate grass; and returning *agonised* with cold, we not seldom found a *heavenly* fire, by which we sat down *enraptured*, comfortably bewailing the *cruel* shortness of the days, and the *eternal* length of the nights; particularly when we had an *immeasurable* quantity of chestnuts to roast, of which the ladies declared themselves to be *devotedly fond.*

My ears were not the only senses doomed to be *agonised,* to use the ladies' own word, by their incongruities. As there was no appearance of extraordinary economy in Mrs B.'s establishment, and I had no reason to suppose a want of means, I could not but be surprised at the ordinary adjustment of the young ladies' habiliments. The evenings I saw them in company, they were indeed expensively dressed—but, on all common occasions, it was difficult to say whether the sempstress or the washerwoman was most wanted: added to which, their clothes, being always too big or too little, were evidently made for somebody else; the outer and the inner garments could seldom agree to keep the same boundary —the buttons would not button, and the ties would not tie—if other people wore things one way, the Miss B.'s wore them in the opposite—not, as I found on inquiry, from affected singularity, but because they did not observe but what other people's were the same. After keeping us waiting half an hour for their presence at the dinner table, they made their appearance in their morning dress, not at all the cleaner for another day's service, excusing themselves that they had not had time to dress. Observing Miss Emma's locks one morning in all the simplicity of native straightness, I ventured to ask if she had been bathing. By no means; but she had been reading so late the night before, she had not time to curl her hair.

One thing must be acknowledged—if the Miss B.'s never thought it necessary to please in manner, person, or conversation, there was at least so much of fairness in their dealing, that they never thought it necessary to be pleased themselves. I had been in the habit of supposing that civility requires us to seem pleased with whatever is done to please us— and that without dissimulation; for if the thing itself is not acceptable, the motive of kindness that dictates it should be so. Nothing you could show them met their expectations—nothing you could give them was what they wanted—wherever you went with them, they wished themselves at home. If you talked to them they yawned—if you played to them, they chattered—if you read to them, they went to sleep. They were sufficiently attentive, at all times, to their own accommodation; some might think they were totally occupied with themselves, to the entire exclusion of every thing else. If their companions would walk, they were tired—if they would sit, they feared to take cold—the grass was wet, and they could not damp their feet—the bushes had thorns, and they should tear their clothes—the stiles were

high, and they could not get over—the hills were
steep, and they could not get up,—all great incon-
veniences, as every body knows—but as they were
strong and healthy, I was inclined to wish they
would sometimes wet their feet, rend their clothes,
and take cold into the bargain, rather than be always
consulting their body's welfare, to the impeding of
every body's purpose, and the interruption of every
body's pleasure.—But I fear my readers will be tired
of my friends—in truth, and so was I.

No. XVI.

THE TWO INVITATIONS.

Nothing can less contribute to vigour of action than protracted, anxious fluctuations, intermingled with resolutions decided and revoked: while yet nothing causes a greater expense of feeling. The heart is fretted and exhausted by being subjected to an alternation of contrary excitements, with the mortifying consciousness of their contributing to no end.

FOSTER.

SOME of my readers, I understand, wonder I contrive to hear so many things they never happen to have heard themselves—nay, some even go so far as to doubt if I really do hear all I tell. I would advise them, that hearing depends greatly upon listening; for many things pass under our eyes that we do not see, and under our ears that we do not hear, for want of attention and observation; and, what is far more extraordinary, these very things that we hear not and see not, are the things we are ourselves doing, or saying, or thinking, or feeling. If I could prevail on some of my incredulous friends to listen to themselves, to what is whispered in their bosoms. as well as to what finds louder utterance, for one whole year, I should be much surprised, if, at the end of it, they could not tell me some very marvellous stories; and some, perhaps, that, had I told them, they might not have taken to be truth. This preamble I should not have made, as having little to do with the subject of the paper, had I not been apprehensive that some of my readers will doubt whether I ever heard what I am going to relate.

The three daughters of Lady S. had received something more than a fashionable education; though it must be allowed, a fashionable education in the days of George IV. is nearer to being a good one, than at any time we know of in the annals of the world. I do not mean to speak particularly of her Ladyship's character, because my criticisms presume not to reach my elders; except so far as her character may disclose itself in the concerns of her family, and the conversations I was so fortunate as to hear. The outward seeming and circumstances of her condition I may mention, as being that with which the world is, doubtless, well acquainted already. A widow, while her children were yet babies, with more rank than she had fortune to support, this excellent mother had supplied, by most assiduous care, and many ingenious contrivances, the deficiency of income, as it might have affected her daughters' education. Withdrawn from a world that had lost its attraction for her, since the bosom's friend was gone who had been to her all its zest and interest, she had time to form and execute her plans of education, without interruption from other claims: and, whether

her plans were good or bad, or both, of which I mean to give no opinion, they were maturely considered, and very consistently executed. She knew her daughters were to move in a genteel, possibly an elevated station in life; and she resolved to omit nothing that could prepare them for it, and fit them to be admired and beloved. She knew they were to pass out of this sublunary sphere of action, into one in which neither the love nor the admiration they had gained in it would avail them any thing; and she resolved to prepare them for this too. The proportionate degree of importance she attached to these separate objects, or whether either had undue preponderance in her measures, remains a secret to me, and may as well remain so to the world; since He who judges from principles rather than from actions, who, while he looks closely to the motives of a conduct seemingly fair, judges leniently of the mistakes that supervene upon the best intentions, has alone to do with this decision.

The Miss S.'s had been taught, as all other ladies are, to do every thing; and they had been also taught, as all other ladies are not, to understand, reflect, and judge. Unlike those parents, who, by too much constraint, make their children passive machines up to a certain age, and then expect they should know how to move alone, Lady S. had rather guided than constrained their minds—she had accustomed them to deliberate, to reason, and to choose. Whether at their age she did right to let them take their choice when she herself thought it a wrong one, is not my business to determine—I have only to disclose the fact that it was so. If, in relating what I overhear, I should alter things to my own taste, my readers would have cause to complain of my want of veracity; therefore, whatever may be thought of this, I am not responsible; and can only say, so runs my story. Nothing had been omitted to give grace and beauty to the minds and persons of these young people—they had been taught to walk and to dance, and to lie down and to sit up, and to dress and to undress; but not more assiduously had they been tutored in all these things on a Saturday, than they had been taught to read and pray on a Sunday. I do not mean ostentatiously—far from it; they had been accustomed to spend the Sabbath properly; they had learned all the catechisms that ever were published, and read all the tracts that ever were written; and, better than this, they had been made intimately acquainted with the sacred language of Scripture, and pains had been taken to make them understand and feel their interest in it. And here, alas! so captious are our critics, I must again pause to make excuse for my story. I am aware that some will say the dancing and dressing should have been omitted—and others will say the catechisms and tracts should have been omitted—for who ever met with a lady that thought another lady's child had been properly brought up? I never did. But if any one says the statement is not consistent, I beg their pardon.

Every one who knows Lady S. knows it to be exactly correct ; and those who are not of her Ladyship's acquaintance, may find many among their friends, titled and untitled, who are pursuing very much the same plan.

Lady S.'s system of education had, in one respect, differed from that of some fashionable mothers, who think the best preparation for succeeding in the world, is to be kept in total ignorance of it till a certain age ; when the new claimant on its smiles, who has had intercourse only with her governess, her waiting-maid, and possibly, but not certainly, with her parents, comes forth, as at a signal, into the mid-day of its splendours, its allurements, its joys, its difficulties, and its crimes, to understand them if she can, and abide them if she may. What would become of the mazed and dazzled vision, that had for eighteen years been closed in impenetrable darkness, as a preparation for opening at once on the full blaze of a meridian sun? Lady S. had accustomed her girls to her own society and that of her friends, and without exactly taking them into public, had accustomed them to frequent and free communication with beings, among whom they were to find their future happiness, and perform their future duties. How the three daughters happened to come to maturity at the same time, is, I confess, a difficulty. I do not say they were all of the same age ; yet they could not be very far apart. If I were more used to telling stories, I should not be puzzled by these small difficulties, perhaps. A good novel-writer can have the moon at the full many times in a month; and what might seem equally difficult to a plain astronomer, can make a full moon rise in the middle of the night. Why, then, may I not make the three daughters of Lady S. *come out* at the same time? It remains only to be further understood, that I, listening, heard the succeeding conversation.

"My girls," said Lady S. to her daughters, as they sat round the tea-table one Sunday evening, "you have reached the age at which I have always promised you an introduction to the world, for which you have been so many years preparing yourselves. I have given you every advantage befitting your rank, that may enable you to enjoy its pleasures; and such principles as, I trust, may help you to avoid its dangers. I have prepared you for the world, because you must sojourn in it a little time; you must act in it the part assigned to you; society will lay its claim to you; and if I had neglected in your education any of its requirements, the world would have said, and you might sometime have said yourselves, that your mother had failed of her duty towards you, and suffered her own sorrows to blight the budding of your joys. But I have told you, too, that this world is not your abiding-place, nor its maxims your safest guide, nor its pleasures your best enjoyment. The higher importance of eternal things, the greater claim of Him who made you, on your affections, the better happiness his love prepares for you, are themes you have not now to hear of first. Knowledge of either world, as far as it can be communicated to you by another, you cannot want: the time is come when you are to take upon yourselves the character of women and of Christians on your own behalf, and personally to answer to God and man the claims that each may have on you, for which hitherto I have been in some measure your sponsor. I need scarcely remind you that you have, a fortnight since, after the manner of our church, renewed in confirmation your baptismal vows—you cannot be forgetful what they were; and that you promised by them, not only to believe the word of God, but to obey it; not only to devote yourselves to his service, but to renounce every thing that may stand in opposition to it, or interfere with it; whether it be the sinful suggestions of your own heart, prompted by the evil spirit to do his own dark works, or the allurements of the world, whose pomp, and fashion, and too vehement desires, you pledged yourselves neither to follow nor to be led by. I trust you are ready to fulfil your vows, and keep your faith with Heaven."

"I hope so, mamma," said Emma; "it was a solemn service; and when I had gone through it, I felt I had pledged myself to do I scarce know what, and certainly have but little power to perform, except as strength from above is promised to the wish and the endeavour."

"On the other hand, the world you have promised not to follow, awaits you and invites you: you have blessings to seek from it, and duties to perform in it—you can neither do without the one, nor are at liberty to evade the other :—these opposing duties "——

" But why, dear mother," said Maria, " should they stand opposed ? God made the world, and placed us in it ; surely, then, we may partake of it without offence to Him ? I do not see any difficulties in dividing our attention between our religious duties, and the concerns of life, and giving to each "——

" Its due proportion, you would say," interrupted Lady S., " and, it is true, you must ; but not to each an equal share ; and as they will too often clash, there must be in every such instance a preference to one above the other—my children surely know to which the preference is due."

" Of course, mamma," said Fanny ; " every body knows that God is to be preferred before the world, and we shall never think of doing otherwise. But I do long to go out, and taste the delights of society : it is so natural at our age to like pleasure, that it cannot possibly be wrong. When one is older, it may be different. When are we to begin to go out, mamma ? "

" That is exactly what I was preparing to tell you—I have two invitations for you this week."

" Two in one week ! O, that is delightful ! " cried Fanny.

" I should have preferred that it had happened otherwise ; for, as we are circumstanced, considerable preparation will be necessary for your appearance in public on such occasions, especially as it is the first time," said Lady S.

" But then, dear mamma, it is the more fortunate, because one preparation will do for both," answered Maria.

" Not exactly so, I fear : it rather appears to me that it will be desirable to put off one or the other— but I intend to leave this to your choice. You are invited to a ball on Friday, at Mrs Askall's, where all that is most distinguished in the country will be assembled together. Though there will be but few girls there whose rank is higher than your own, there will be none, perhaps, whose fortune is less ; therefore, to make an appearance equal to others, you must depend on your own industry and contrivance."

" O yes," cried Fanny, " we can make our own dresses and all that—there will be plenty of time before Friday—I should not mind sitting up all night if—But what a pity we did not begin before ! When did you get the invitations ?"

" On Saturday—but I had reasons for not communicating it till this evening. Could it be avoided, I had rather not see your time so spent ; but you know I cannot afford to purchase dresses for you, such as you will like to appear in, where all will be so gay and brilliant."

" Certainly," said Maria, " I should like to look like other people. I shall lie awake to-night thinking how we can contrive the prettiest dresses at the smallest cost. It will not signify about the time they take ; for once we can put off our other employments just for a single week. One, two, three, four, days, besides great part of Friday—for it will do if they are done by the time we want to dress ; but "——

"But, mamma, you have forgotten the other invitation," said Emma.

"The other, my love, was received this morning ; you heard it as well as myself, and cannot, I am sure, have forgotten it. You know that it is not usual for young persons in the Established Church to take the Sacrament till they have been confirmed ; but after that ceremony has been attended to, I should be sorry that there were reason longer to delay it, as I believe I have mentioned to you before : and the invitation was given this morning to all that are religiously and devoutly disposed."

"Well, but, mamma, what has that to do with Mrs Askall's ball ? " said Fanny.

"No more, my dear, than that I do not see how you can attend to both."

"I cannot see that at all—the Sacrament is on Sunday, not on Friday, and "——

"Stay, my child ; recollect the nature of the invitation before you decide on this matter. The feast you are invited to is at the table of the Lord. It is a joyful feast, indeed, for it is the commemoration of his love, and to us the sweet pledge and foretaste of eternal bliss : but it is also a serious one, setting forth, in lively emblems, a tale of agony and death that must ever fill our eyes with tears, and tinge our cheeks with shame. It is with good reason, therefore, that we are exhorted, ere we present ourselves at the feast, to consider the dignity of the ceremony, and examine deeply the state of our own hearts, that we may make such appearance there as may become the occasion. If you think a whole week's preparation scarcely enough to do honour to the invitation of an earthly friend, can you present yourselves before your heavenly benefactor, the Maker of heaven and earth, without any previous means bestowed, or time expended, to make ready for his presence? The dress is different, indeed, as is the occasion ; one is the outside trickery, of no importance in itself, for with it you are no other than without it, attended to in conformity to the *convenances* of society, by custom only rendered suitable or unsuitable to the occasion. The other—how shall I speak meetly of its importance ? You cannot, indeed, make yourselves fit to appear— no pains of yours can veil your unworthiness or lessen it ; nor any preparation be, as some mistake it, a ticket of admittance that gives you a right to come and claim the benefits of this holy feast. You come by invitation free and unmerited ; but there is a requisition plain and positive from Him who sends it, as to the manner of your appearing. The form of invitation used by our church is the lau-guage of Scripture, and those who do not use the same words, give it the same meaning. We are bidden to examine not only the state of our hearts, at the present moment, but the records of our past lives; that where we have been wrong, we may confess the wrong, lament it deeply, and determine to amend it, as far as may be, for the future: and it is not only the act, but the thought, and word, and deed, we are to examine. Nay, there may be something even to be done as well as determined—for we are expressly forbidden to approach with malice or envy in our hearts, or unforgiven wrong rankling in our bosoms, or injury on our heads, for which we are inclined to make no reparation. Scripture is very express in this—for even when we arrive at the altar, if we recollect any thing of wrong between us and our fellow-creatures, we are bidden to go away, and make no offering till we are in better mind. The reason of all this is very plain. We come to the feast as sinners, unworthy to gather up a crumb that falls from it, and seeking for our unworthiness an unconditional pardon. Ill would it become us to bring in our bosoms, envy, and jealousy, and resentment; the birth of pride, the workings of a mind that holds itself at higher price than others have had respect to. Ill, very ill, would it beseem us, to bring with us a reckoning of the unpaid dues we are determined on exacting from each other. We come to a banquet of love—love immutable, immeasurable, such as heaven wonders at, and earth can never comprehend. Ill-dressed guests, indeed, we must appear, if love be not the absorbing feeling of our souls, to the suspension, at least, of every other sentiment. And then we come for a purpose—we come for remission and a cure, as well as to make acknowledgment of deepest gratitude to Him, through whose death and passion we can alone receive them. How can this be, if we have taken no account beforehand of our debts or their amount; or if we have known nothing of the symptoms of the disease we come to be relieved of, nor have given ourselves the trouble to inquire how far we really need or desire any of these things? Our enjoyment at the feast will be proportioned to our sense of the benefit—our sense of the benefit will be proportioned to our sense of need—and our gratitude to both—and what can we know of this without examination of our hearts and lives? This preparation is called by our Church the marriage garment, and with reason, for the resemblance holds: the garment was not a cause of the invitation, nor an inducement to receive the guest, nor to a title to sit down at another's table, nor a payment made for the entertainment there—yet was it that, without which, none could be welcomed at a marriage-feast. And now, my children, you must decide for yourselves, whether you can, without preparation, accept this invitation for the first time in your lives."

"I think we cannot," replied Fanny; "and as we shall certainly not have time to think of it properly, it will be better to put it off: for the ball you know cannot be put off, and Mrs Askall gives but one in the year—it is a long promise that we should be there, and she is of so much consequence in the neighbourhood, it would not do to offend her; besides, we shall have so much pleasure; every body will be there, and it will be such an odd reason to give! The Sacrament will be repeated in a month or two, and then, perhaps, we shall have nothing to prevent our receiving it seriously, and as we ought."

" You are left to your own choice, Fanny; but be mindful of your profession and your vow. You are preferring what you esteem pleasure to what you know to be a duty—you are setting the opinions of men before the express command of God—you are offering to your heavenly Father an excuse that will not be accepted by an earthly friend. I fear that preference you were so sure just now would incline to the right side, has already fallen on the wrong. But what says my Maria ?"

" I am thinking very seriously what is to be done," answered Maria ; " I should be very sorry to neglect the Sacrament, which I anticipated with desire, besides the sense of duty. But, indeed, mamma, I do not see why it cannot be managed. We shall be busy, to be sure, till Friday—but while our fingers are employed for one purpose, our thoughts may be upon the other: and then, you know, there will be a day on Saturday that we can quite give our minds

to serious thought. I should not like to give up
either, if you leave it to my choice."

"You may try it, Maria—for I believe you sufficiently conscientious, when the Sunday comes, to
give up your purpose, if you find your mind unfit.
And, Emma?"——

"I cannot go to the ball, mamma—it is not possible."

"And why not, Emma?"

"Because, while you were speaking to me, my
mind took a hasty glance upon itself; and I saw
within it so much to think of, so much to reflect
upon; and I felt so much need of the medicine, and
so long a debt to reckon up, and so great a desire to
receive the offered pledge of my Redeemer's love;
and, after sixteen years of kindness and favour
lavished on me, to make my first public acknowledgment at his table—I cannot, mamma, do any
thing that will prevent this invitation, or unfit me
from accepting it."

"You have your choice, my children," answered Lady
S., "with liberty to change it, if you see occasion."

We left our story on the Sunday evening: I
would persuade myself it is not there we should
resume it. I would rather believe, and so I am sure
would my readers, that I was mistaken, when, after
a sermon had been read, and family prayers had
been offered, and the ladies had withdrawn to their
chambers, I heard through the walls that parted us,
certain words which might be construed into a com-

mencement of the week's preparation—such, for instance, as blond, and chenille, and gimp, and piping —all very innocent things in themselves; and if my imagination connected them with any thing not quite appropriate to the time and circumstance, my readers will say the fault is mine; that I have no right to suppose, still less to relate, any thing more than I did really hear. I would not, on any account, be thought censorious; therefore, I will leave it as a thing of course, that while the evening sermon was read, the invitations came not into the minds of the young ladies, and that while prayers were offered, no thought of dresses occurred: and that before they went to sleep they did not speak, and after they went to sleep they did not dream, of any thing connected with the subject. In which very probable case, the Miss S.'s stand acquitted of having commenced their preparations before Monday morning. I am quite certain they rose that morning at daybreak: and as getting up early, whether to do any thing or nothing, is an established proof of industry and activity, I beg I may not be understood to object to that circumstance.

As my curiosity had been considerably excited by the conversation of the evening, I felt some regret that I could hear nothing during these early hours, but the opening and shutting of drawers, the overturning of bandboxes, and certain other indistinct sounds to which I could not attach any meaning. The breakfast-table relieved my mind of this regret.

"Mamma," said Fanny, the moment she appeared, "we have been so busy trying on all the gowns we have, to find which pattern will fit us best; and then we could not determine upon the colour—we have been trying all colours to see which becomes us, and, I think, I look best in blue, and Maria is positive she looks best in pink, and so we almost quarrelled about it; for you know we must be dressed alike. At last, when we found it was impossible to agree, and we were only wasting time, we determined to refer it to you, to choose for us."

This at least proved a wise measure, and before the whole hour of breakfast had elapsed, the decision was made—as the young ladies were decidedly amiable, of course the lady of the rejected colour showed no signs of vexation. And now the plot thickened fast—for the mercer came, and his bale of goods came, and the yardwand came—and there was measuring of breadths, and measuring of lengths, and many very intricate calculations besides, to make the least possible quantity do the greatest possible service. In the issue, it appeared to me that the materials selected were simple, tasteful, and very little expensive.

It would be quite superfluous to describe the whole process of dressmaking—every lady, who has made her *entrée* into the gay world, without a long purse at her command, knows what ensues upon wanting a ball-dress in a hurry, and can picture to herself the state of the apartment, during the first stage of the proceeding—the various articles of apparel consigned to the backs of chairs—the piano converted into a measuring-board—the attendance of all the females in the house, except the cook, with thimbles on their middle finger—the trying on, and cutting out, and fitting in.   It was impossible not to admire the skill and ingenuity of the young ladies. I should have felt much interest in the scene, and made many a wise reflection on the beauty of domestic usefulness, and feminine industry; and, for any thing I know, might have written an essay on the advantages of ladies being early taught to help themselves in these indispensables of life, could I have forgotten as early as they had done, the conversation of the preceding evening: but lest it should ever seem that I neglect to commend what is in itself commendable, I beg my friends to remember that I was marking the progress of this week, with reference to its destined termination, and with the TWO INVITATIONS ever on my mind.

Dresses, as Miss Maria had previously observed, are made with hands—but excepting the housemaid, who did, or meant to do, only what she was bidden, and always had that to undo, because, as she said, she was thinking of something else, more probably because she was not thinking at all, the thoughts and tongues of the industrious group were fully employed during this first day.   And much I heard of the comparative merits of full fronts and plain fronts, and high backs and low backs, and circles and squares,

and vandykes and scollops, and straightways, and
crossways, and longways. It came once in my head
to wonder if, in the days of Grecian elegance and
classic taste, there were so many *ways* of making a
gown. Time, with its usual malevolence, sped the
quicker for the need there was of it—night came,
and the ladies stole some hour or two upon its wintry
length, and rose but the earlier to renew their
labours; and like to the first day was the second.

"I am very glad," said Maria, as they sat something more quietly at the work-table on the evening
of Tuesday—"I am very glad the bustle of choosing
and planning our dresses is over: now, though
we must work hard to get the trimming done, we
have nothing more to contrive, and therefore need
not talk or think about our work; I really shall
be glad to give my mind to better thoughts."

"I do not know what you can do, Maria," replied
Fanny; "but I never can attend to two things at
once. Any very serious subject would be so totally
out of harmony with my present thoughts and desires, which are all engrossed with the care of my
personal appearance, and the anticipation of pleasure, it would seem almost a profanation to introduce
any such. Solomon says, there is a time for all
things—but he does not say we can do all things at
the same time—therefore, till this week is over, I
can give my mind to nothing but this ball."

"If we were doing wrong," replied Maria, "I
should think with you; but we are employe l as pro-

priety and circumstances require, and certainly in a very innocent occupation. The last two days it has been indeed impossible to attend to any thing else; but to-morrow I shall try to complete my task without so much talking and thinking about it — and perhaps I can get Emma to read to me."

Emma had firmly held her purpose; but let it not be supposed that she had withdrawn herself to a cloister, or a hermit's cell, or even to her own chamber, during all this time. Sincerity is seldom ostentatious, and firmness is seldom boastful. Emma seemed to be going on with her ordinary occupations; she gave her opinion simply when asked it, and cheerfully offered occasional assistance to her sisters; but her mind was evidently otherwise engaged; she shared not the interest of the scene. It cannot be denied that she was less gay than they, and felt a frequent wish that she could share their pleasurable excitement, without the sacrifice of what she esteemed her duty.

"It is surely absurd in you," said Fanny to her, one day, "to give up this ball, on purpose to make yourself singular. It will have a very odd appearance in the eyes of the world. I cannot think it right in one so young to make such a public display of religion, by acting differently from the rest of her family. Singularity always wears the appearance of pride: to say nothing of the pleasure you needlessly throw away."

"It cannot be making any display at all," answered Emma; "for, as I am the youngest, it will naturally be supposed I do not yet go out; and in respect to singularity, mamma gave us our separate choice, and, I think, was by no means dissatisfied with mine. Then for the pleasure, dear Fanny, I confess I should like it, if I could share it: but never in my life could I find pleasure in any thing while my heart was heavy, and my conscience ill at ease. If I felt as you do, I would go; but feeling as I do, I should be miserable when I got there. You may be right in your determination, pursuing innocently a natural and unforbidden pleasure, while I am but indulging a needless scruple. I do not pretend to decide upon that point, or to be wiser than you. But of this I am certain—if wrong in my judgment, I am right in my conduct. I cannot be doing wrong in foregoing a pleasure that seems to me to interfere with my religious duties, and unfit me for the sacred ceremony in which I desire to participate. If my maturer judgment should discover it to have been a needless sacrifice, the memory of it will at least not lie heavy on my bosom, when it will probably have weight enough without it. I may sometimes smile at it as a childish weakness, but I shall never have to blush at it as a sin. The veriest fool that follows the will of God, as far as his weakness can discover it, will gather the reward of wisdom; while the wiser one, who pursues his own, will reap but the meed of folly."

Maria had hitherto said very little upon the subject, yet there was an air that seemed to say, I am wiser than either of you. The temptation of giving words to her wisdom now became too great to be withstood. "Nobody," she said, "can think it right to pursue their own will in opposition to the will of God; but it is the part of discretion and good sense to distinguish between a right principle and a needless singularity. We have been very religiously brought up, and accustomed to attend to all our duties: I therefore do not see why we should be so very ill-prepared for receiving the Sacrament, even if we have not time to think of it particularly this week; but, for my part, I shall find time. There is no harm in dancing, and there is no harm in dressing, and there is no harm in mixing with other people for a few hours' recreation: if we make a sin of what in itself is not so, the fault must be our own. I can be just as religious in a ball-room as in my own chamber, if I please. God has nowhere bidden us to withdraw from the ordinary occupations of life, and become nuns and hermits, that we may be more meet to serve him. We should rather learn to resist temptation in the world, than fly from it. I do not mean to suppose those who act thus conscientiously are absolutely wrong; but it is to be regretted that good people have not better judgment, but must be running into extremes. I should not exactly say that Emma does wrong; but I think it would be more proof of sense to do as other people do, at least till she is older."

"Indeed," answered Emma, "I had rather act than talk about it; and I would rather prove my want of sense by acting against the opinions of the world, than my want of principle by acting against my own conscience. I am not sure enough to like to argue: but I am sure enough to know what to do. There is a world, that, in my baptism, I have promised neither to follow nor be led by. Now, I do not know what that can be, unless it be the doing what others do, when in my conscience I feel and believe I should do otherwise."

"Well, well," said Maria, "I do not wish to persuade you. If we all do what we think right, we shall all do well, because nothing more is required of us. If I thought as you do, I would act as you do; for I am as much determined as yourself to go to the Sacrament on Sunday; and I dare say, when Sunday comes, I, who have been innocently enjoying myself, shall be just as fit as you, who have condemned yourself to a week of thoughtfulness and self-denial. We shall see.—Will you read to me something serious, while I work the silver into this bit of gauze? It does not need any thought, and I am quite at liberty to listen."

"That I will do with pleasure," said Emma; and the conversation was for that time superseded by the reading of Hawes's Communicant's Companion. I cannot be very exact in the chronology, but I think this conversation passed some time in the Wednesday evening. Mean while the preparation advanced rapidly. Fanny's spirits grew lighter as the day approached—all her walk became dance, and all her speech became song, so light seemed her heart and so gay. It appeared to me that Maria's was not so. She frequently kept silence while Emma read, and seemed to listen attentively; but it had rather the appearance of depressing than of soothing her spirits. She grew pettish, found fault with her thread, broke her needle, wished she could afford to buy her dresses, complained of the misery of being born without fortune, said the ribbons did not match, and the gloves did not fit. One moment Fanny's high spirits fatigued her—it was quite silly in her to be so elated about a foolish ball; the next moment Emma's gloomy silence depressed her—why did she spoil every body's pleasure? there was no amusement in going and leaving her at home.

"To-morrow night at this time!" cried Fanny, as she danced gaily round the room. "I wonder whom I shall dance with first. I won't dance at all unless I get a good partner—it makes one look so foolish. I should like to know how the Miss Dashoffs will be dressed—they are such pert, silly girls; it would be provoking to appear in worse style than they do."

"O, as to that," answered Maria, "I am not at all anxious. I should be very sorry to be jealous of any body. I am sure I do not go to the ball to show myself, but merely for the pleasure of dancing. Indeed I shall be quite glad when it is over, that I may return to more rational pursuits. One must do as other people do, but really it is a great sacrifice of time. I would much rather stay at home."

"Then why, dear Maria, do you not stay at home? I am quite sure mamma would be content to hear such a determination, and would not press your going even now," said Emma.

"Or rather," exclaimed Fanny, "why do you try to sit on two stools at once, to the manifest danger of going to the ground between them? Whether it will be more rational to go or to stay at home, I really have not time to consider; but I am sure it must be right to do one or the other; and you do not seem in the humour for either. I think it is quite wicked to be reading and talking of sacred things, as you and Emma have been doing all this day, in the midst of such occupations. It has served no purpose but to put you out of humour with yourself, and make you disagreeable to every body. It would be much better to give yourself up to pleasure this week, and put off those subjects till a more proper season. There's a time for all things. Come, let me just put these wreaths round your hair, to see which looks best. O, how sweetly!—I wish to-morrow was come."

Maria rose, and went to the glass. "Well, but, Fanny, I cannot wear this; It does not become me. I wish you would let me"——

"Well, but, Maria, that does not signify, as you do not go to show yourself, you know; and"——

I am sorry, that having forgotten to observe the timepiece, I cannot inform my readers how long it took the ladies to settle the difference of opinion respecting these same ornaments—but I dare say the vender knows how long he stood in the cold hall, waiting the restoration of his goods.

The date of the first invitation had now arrived. When the dressing began, I am at some loss to decide—I might allege arguments to prove it commenced over night—or probably there might be a sort of rehearsal—it is impossible to know exactly what one only hears through a wall. It does not signify, for certainly the ladies were *not* dressed in the morning. The time came, however, that they were dressed, and, as I believed, extremely well; and if the flush of pleasure on the cheek, and the sparkling of expectation in the eye, be proofs of happiness, I never looked upon a happier pair.

"Does my Emma repent her choice?" said Lady S. to the youngest girl, as she sat in her plain morning dress before the fire, between her gay and happy sisters; one hand drooping, the half-closed book upon her knee, the other hand pressed upon her lips, in the attitude of one who is not quite so happy as she meant to be.

"I am not sure, mamma, whether I do or not—I shall be glad when you come back."

"Well, never mind, dear," said the good-natured Fanny, "you will be wiser another time. I wish the carriage would come. The Miss Dashoffs will go in their own carriage, of course —I suppose almost every one will have their own carriage but ourselves. That is not particularly pleasant, I must confess—but it will be dark, and perhaps no one will observe what we come in."

"And it does not signify if they do," replied Maria; "I should be ashamed to feel any of that sort of pride. We are of higher birth than they are, though not so rich."

"And, pray, dear Maria," said Lady S., "what may be the difference between the pride that is mortified at being poorer, and the pride that is gratified at being greater than others?"

"Pride is a sin, I know," answered Maria, "however excited, and by whatever fed—and yet it does not exactly seem to me the same thing. If I should blush at being seen in a hack carriage, where other girls are in their own, it must be an emotion of mortified pride, and therefore is sinful emotion— whereas, if I should feel pleasure in hearing you announced as My Lady, while their mothers are introduced as plain Mistress, it would be "———

"An emotion of gratified pride; and, therefore, as sinful as the other, because the offspring of the self-same passion."

"But, mamma, it is impossible to keep off all such thoughts from our minds, when we come in competition with other people, on occasions in which every one is valued according to their exterior advantages."

"And therefore it is, that such occasions are unfavourable to that subjugation of sinful passion which is the Christian's aim.   But I hear the carriage."

A look of thoughtfulness passed over Maria's brow, as if she recollected something—but the desired moment had arrived, and they all stepped into the hired carriage.   I thought Fanny looked at it with more than common observance, but this might be fancy.

I now find myself under very considerable difficulty.   Most story-tellers know what passes in their absence, and can relate, without either seeing or hearing, even to the most secret thoughts and feelings of their characters; I am prohibited from telling any thing but what I hear.   What is to be done ?   The carriage drove off—and I remained at home—how, then, could I hear what followed?

The hired carriage had driven off, the large hall door had been closed by the housemaid, for the footman of course was gone—the same inelegant substitute brought up two solitary-looking tea-cups, in company with the undress tea-pot, and a kettle of water, that, in the universal hubbub, had neglected to boil itself; and in silent thoughtfulness, Miss Emma and myself sat·down to what is commonly called an uncomfortable tea.   What she was thinking of I cannot determine—my thoughts had gone to Mrs Askall's by a nearer road, and saw the carriage stop at the door ; after much contention of wheels, horses, and coachmen, whose sense of proprietorship made them dispute precedence with the hack. I saw the ladies ascend the stairs into the large uncarpeted room, of which the present coldness was only made tolerable by anticipation of future warmth. I saw—what they who are familiar with it need not to be told; and they who are not, will not perceive the merit of my description.

Mean time the tea hour had passed, and we prepared to amuse ourselves; I took my drawing, and Emma proposed to read to me. The book proved interesting, and gave rise to much animated conversation, in which the carriages, and their contents, and the ball-room into which they had been emptied, were alike forgotten. Emma grew gay and playful, the hours passed quickly, and when she took leave of me for the night, there was upon her countenance a look of such serene enjoyment, as bespake a spirit satisfied, and a mind at peace.

I had a task to perform, and therefore sat out the lingering hours of night, till, far upon the advance of morning, the revellers returned. The first question, of course, was respecting the pleasantness of the fête; to which exclamations of delight were the quick response! more there was not need to ask; all were in too much hurry to give the answers, to pay any regard to the questions. As they all talked at once, it would be impossible to repeat the conversation; but on most points of discussion I perceived considerable difference of opinion. Maria, who had by far the most attractive person, thought the gentlemen extremely polite and attentive —

Fanny denounced them all as bears and boobies. Fanny wondered the Miss Dashoffs should be so much admired, when they were decidedly plain—Maria was satisfied that they were not admired, but courted only because they were rich. Maria thought it quite impertinent in the Miss Somebodies to be more plainly dressed than others, when they were known to be rich—Fanny thought it equally impertinent in the Miss Nobodies to be better dressed than others, when they were known to be poor. Fanny complained of the rudeness of some one in attempting to stand above her in the dance—Maria complained that some one else had complained of her rudeness in attempting to stand above them, and both were resolved to retaliate another time. Fanny was vexed because she did not dance with the persons she wished to dance with — and Maria was vexed, because, when she had danced with the persons she wished to dance with, they thought proper to dance with somebody else that she desired they should not dance with.

On the whole, as far as by listening I could learn, every body had done something they had better not have done, or worn something they would have been better without, or said something not quite within the pale of good-breeding and good-sense. But these were specks upon the evening's brightness—the gratifications were exquisite, and the pleasures out of number. Fanny never was so happy in her life, as when Mr C. left Miss Dashoff to sit with

her; though, but to tease Miss D., she would rather
have been rid of him. Maria was enchanted to hear
Lady W. say the Miss S.'s were the best dressed
girls in the room, and wonder whom they employed.
Both ladies were delighted they had chosen to wear
pink, when they saw the vulgar Miss Thompsons
were in blue. In short, time would fail to tell out
the list of pleasures; and declaring they never were
so happy or so tired in their lives, to which last
assertion their pallid cheeks and rayless eyes sufficiently subscribed, the young ladies retired to their
room. I listened, for now the deeper secrets of the
fête were to be disclosed—it was here that, restraint thrown off, the compliments were all repeated,
the excited passions all exposed, the jealousies and
mortifications confessed, the triumphs acted over
again, and the satire repeated with redoubled zest;
but far be it from me to betray the truths disclosed,
and the secrets laid open, in the careless confidence
of private converse and sisterly trust. If any one of
my readers has been a partner in any conversation
carried on under similar circumstances, she has but
to recall it, to be perfectly in the secret of this.

The breakfast stood long in patient order on the
table the ensuing morning. The sun was mid-way
in his short wintry course before the slumberers
awakened, or, I should rather say, arose—for wake
they surely did not. These young people had not
yet been long enough practised in the hard service
of dissipation, to feel no morning consequence of

the night's exertion; and they came forth at length with looks as well as words of weariness, languor, and exhaustion; experiencing, though they probably neither understood the feeling, nor made the reflection, that, as there are more ways than one of being intoxicated, so there are others besides the wine-drinker who are doomed to experience all the misery of getting sober. During the remainder of the morning, of which the remainder was not much, they dozed upon the chair, or lounged upon the sofa, the discussion of the night being occasionally renewed; but neither the pleasures, nor the pains, nor the flattery, nor the neglects, were so fully appreciated as they had been — distance and the mists of lassitude had something lessened the distinctness of these receding objects. After dinner, Fanny gave herself up freely to the weariness she felt—Maria kept up an ineffectual struggle to read a book that seemed equally determined not to be read, if I might judge from the propensity it showed to close itself in her hands. Whether thinking, dreaming, or reading, however, the mind's occupation was one and the same, as was clearly proved by the occasional remarks that came from the lips of each, evincing that the intermediate aberrations of the mind had extended no farther than from coaches to complexions, from bracelets to quadrille tunes.

In the evening Lady S. requested some conversation with her daughters respecting their intentions for the morrow; observing that as, in conformity with her intention declared on the preceding Sabbath, she had neither spoken to them on the subject, nor interfered with their wishes during the week, so it now became necessary to renew the question; the second invitation yet remaining to be attended to, and the hour being near at hand: she desired to know which of her daughters intended to accompany her to the altar on the following morning.

The young people had too much right feeling to make any attempt to avert the subject, or show unwillingness towards it: but there was something in their looks and manner that plainly said the subject was ill-timed—that would have asked, if it might be, a more convenient season. But this could not be—Lady S. was patiently looking towards Fanny, as the eldest, for reply. Fanny rubbed her eyes, and stretched her limbs, and seemed to be looking about for the senses that were not immediately forthcoming: at length she said—

" I have never had but one intention, mamma; it is that I declared at first, and I have seen little cause to change it. I knew that whatever occupies my mind strongly, engrosses it fully. I knew very well, that besides being so much occupied with the actual employments of the week, my spirits would be too much elated for any thing like serious reflection—in short, that the thing would be too much in my head to admit of graver matters; and I knew equally well, that when the ball was over, I should be tired and asleep as I am now; and that the same images would remain on my imagination, though receding now, as they were before advancing. And, if I thought this at first, I am now but the more convinced of it —I have not had a thought of any thing but pleasure the whole week ; except to feel impatient at Maria's interruption of our occupations with subjects, that, at another time, I should have liked as well as herself. And now that all is over, there needs no examination to teach me that I am not prepared for receiving the Sacrament. I have not felt a feeling, nor thought a thought, nor spoken a word to-day, but those of vanity, rivalship, and folly. I am not so insensible of the sacredness of heavenly things, as to intrude myself on a rite so holy in such a dress as this : and besides that I do not feel ready, I have no inclination to it—it is not in unison with my present feeling—I am not in the humour—I never can presume to offer to God heartless and unwilling service. But you know, mamma, I never meant to go to the Sacrament to-morrow. I shall wait another opportunity."

" Do you know that you shall have one, Fanny ? "

" Yes—that is—no, mamma, I do not exactly know it. But I may fairly presume so—I have no reason to think otherwise—in all probability—I am young and well."

" I will not make trite remarks upon the uncertainty of life, and the deceptiveness of health, Fanny : we all know it, and we none of us believe it ; and when any one dies before they expect—and who,

with some few exceptions, does not die before they
expect ?—there is as much surprise as if it had never
happened before. But, my child, allowing it probable, would you stake your eternal welfare on a
probability ?"

"Nay, but, mamma, you have always taught me
that my salvation does not, cannot depend upon an
outward ceremony; my taking the Sacrament can
no more make me fit to die, than my not taking it
can exclude me from the realms of bliss."

"That is true, my love—and you are neither the
more nor the less prepared to die, for having par-
taken of the Lord's Supper. It is not, as some suppose, the make-weight of our insufficient merit, nor
the sponge that wipes out the record of our sins.
But what then is it ? If not the preparation for the
feasts of heaven, it is the emblem, the earnest, the
beginning of them ; you come to the one to profess
yourself an aspirant to the other; the same claim
that is pleaded here, must be pleaded there ; the same
emblem of the marriage garment has been used for
both, and the thing which it pictures is in both the
same. If you are not fitted for the one, you are not
fitted for the other—if you have put it out of your
power conscientiously to present yourself at the
Lord's table upon earth, could you expect admittance
to his presence above ?—if this his invitation be refused, how could you receive the messenger that
should bid you to his marriage feast in heaven ?—
'I pray thee have me excused ; I have been engaged

in other matters.' The plea has served you now; you are excused: you were free to choose whether you would accept his gracious bidding; you have chosen, and it seems that all is well. You have deliberately unfitted yourself for serious thought, and, by your own confession, made yourself at once incapable and indisposed to the commemoration of his love, and the participation of his blessings: and, in this state of conscious unfitness, you mean to go to rest to-night; and you will lie down to sleep in peace and confidence, as if nothing were the matter. But, my child, there is a feast in heaven prepared for them that love Him—what if the messenger be sped to-night to say that all is ready, and your hour of admission or rejection is at hand—that the decisive moment is arrived for you, which must determine your doom through all eternity! 'I have been engaged in other matters'—will the plea serve you then? Yes, then, as now, you will be excused, indeed—but the door will be closed and made fast for ever, and she who was not ready must remain without. Is it not so, Fanny?"

"Undoubtedly, mamma, it is; and I should hold myself unfit indeed to die to-night: I can scarcely suppose myself prepared to appear before the throne of God in heaven, when I cannot venture to present myself at his table upon earth."

"Then did I say amiss, Fanny, when I said, you were willing to stake your eternal welfare on a probability—a probability, as far as you can see, or know, or calculate? With God there are no probabilities, because there are no uncertainties : but in human language, and in earthly seeming, you say it is not probable you shall die to-night ; and with this you can content yourself—and on this you can go happily to rest—and with this you will wake cheerfully to-morrow, and the next day and the next you will remain the same perhaps—deferring, postponing, putting aside the invitations, the commands of Him to whom you have professed to devote yourselves, for the sake of those things you promised in your baptism to renounce. Whether you go to the Sacrament to-morrow or not, is, indeed, of no consequence to your salvation. It is not because you do not receive it, that you are unprepared to die—it is because you are unprepared to receive it, unfit to receive it, indisposed to receive it. Consider seriously how long it is wise to remain so, in a state of being where the youngest and the strongest is as the brief herbage of the field, that grows up to-day, and to-morrow is cut down and withered.—And what does Maria intend ?"

Maria hesitated—her tone of confidence was something lowered, and her wisdom seemed not quite so eager to express itself as it had been : yet still she kept her purpose, and said she saw no reason for declining to accompany Lady S. to the Sacrament on the morrow, if she herself saw none.

"What I see is a small matter, dear Maria—but do you feel none ?"

Maria again hesitated and stammered, but still said, "No."

Lady S. seemed surprised, and for a moment embarrassed, as if not knowing how to reply to an answer she had not expected : she then said, "Have you examined your own heart, Maria, after the manner enjoined you, to see if there be reason or not ?"

"I cannot pretend," answered Maria, "that I have made any special examination, or any particular preparation for this holy ceremony—I meant it, but I have not had time : I was not aware that I should be too much elated yesterday, and too much exhausted to-day, to apply my mind to any thing ; but, after all, there is something very pharisaical in the idea of preparing ourselves, as if the formality of a week's preparation, as it is called, a few prayers and a little reading, could be of any value in the sight of God, or by any means recommend us to his favour. We ought always to be prepared ; and therefore I conclude I am so without"——

"You have come to the conclusion by a short road, Maria ; but our church, which only echoes the language of Scripture, has ventured to make a doubt of this, and sends neither invitation, nor permission, nor a welcome to any one who, without examination, takes this for granted. But, since you are so confident of your own state, I must suppose you have some grounds for being so. To use the language of our catechism (not because I would rest on the authority of man, but because I know none better or more simply scriptural,) I would ask you first, whether you do truly repent you of your former sins ? "

" Of course I do."

" But have you inquired of yourself what they are ? "

" Not particularly. I know I must have sinned frequently, and of course am sorry to have done so."

" To be sorry is to feel pain—to repent is to be grieved, ashamed, distressed. Can you have felt this without knowing for what? And another part of repentance is, that you determine to lead a new life. Have you made any such determination?"

" I do not know, mamma, in what I am to amend."

" And how can you know, my child, if you have not inquired? And if you can perceive nothing in which you can amend, how can you repent of any thing? It is sufficiently plain that these are but empty words to you. Yet these things you will profess when you approach the table! The next requisition is that you have a lively faith in God's mercy through Christ, with a thankful remembrance of his death. A lively faith, to take no more than the common meaning of the word, must be an active, animated, conscious thing, something that gives signs of life. It cannot be a vague belief laid up in the bosom so closely, that even to yourself it makes no difference of sensation whether it be there or not. A thankful remembrance of Christ's death cannot, in common sense, be a total forgetfulness of it. Now, my dear girl, cast back your thoughts upon the transactions of the last week, up to this very hour, and say, have you believed, have you remembered, have you been grateful ? "

"Mamma, I am sure I believe these things to be true, for it never came into my mind to doubt them. I hope I am grateful, as I surely must be, for such great mercies: and as to remembering, my mind, as I confessed before, has been too full of other matters to think much upon the subject this week; but I suppose "——

" My dear Maria, you speak as if you did not know the meaning of words. You suppose you have a grateful remembrance of things of which you never think—you are sure you believe what it never came into your head to doubt, and, of course, not to examine. And these things you so certainly believe, and are so certainly grateful for, are nothing less than the eternal interests of your immortal spirit, the mercy that has pardoned, the sacrifice that has redeemed, the love that has suffered for you: and other matters can so engross your mind as to exclude the thought of them entirely. And what matters? The vainest and emptiest pursuits of a vain and empty world—the merest trifles of a life whose most important concerns are themselves but trifles, in comparison with these things so easily displaced. This, Maria, is neither to believe, nor remember, nor be grateful. It is to forget at once

the mercies of God, and your own need of them; to
put Him most ungratefully out of mind, and virtu-
ally to disbelieve the consequences of doing so. And
then the remaining clause, 'And be in charity with
all men,' I explained to you last Sunday what this
means. Is there no anger in your heart for others'
wrong—no pride seeking to gratify itself at others'
expense—nor envy of one who has the advantage,
nor contempt for one whom you surpass—no rivalship, contention, nor ill-nature? Are love and charity
the feelings of your heart towards all: and are they
the feelings you have endeavoured to deserve of all?
Have you been as careful to avoid every thing that
might excite unholy passions in the bosom of others
towards you, as in your own towards them? Have
you tried to excite envy, jealousy, and pride, or to
prevent it? Excited, was it pain or pleasure to
you to see others so suffer and so sin? Examine
your feelings for the last few days, nay, your words
only during the last twenty-four hours, by the beautiful description of charity in the 13th of Corinthi-
ans, and say, if it be true that you are in love and
charity with all men."

"By such an interpretation I certainly am not;
but I wish no harm to any one."

"It is God's interpretation, not mine; and it appears that of all you take for granted, nothing is the
fact."

"You advise me, then, not to go to the Sacrament to-morrow?"

"That I would still leave to yourself. I would not lead you superstitiously to suppose, that, by going in this state to the Sacrament, you place yourself in a worse condition than you are in if you stay away. For whether when bidden you refuse to come, or whether coming you refuse to wear the dress appointed for the guests, the act of disobedience is pretty much the same. But, as the case appears with you at this time, I would rather see you, self-convicted and ashamed, retiring from the table as an unmeet guest, than, in bold self-confidence, coming forward to offer to God the little remnant of your heart that the world has not engrossed, the refuse of time and spirits you have been able to snatch from the exhaustion of pleasure, professing things you do not mean, and asking blessings you cannot in conscience expect to receive. He to whom it was said, 'Friend, how camest thou in hither?' had no better portion in the feast than they who sent excuses. I need scarcely ask my Emma's determination."

"Indeed, mamma," answered Emma, "you have much need to ask, or rather to tell me: for I am much in doubt. I have given a large portion of time this week to the examination of my own heart, and I find little in it that encourages me to go. I have been listening attentively to all you have said to my sisters, and have heard much that condemns me also to absence from this holy ceremony. With all my endeavours to keep in mind my Saviour's mercies, I am perpetually forgetting them; with all the warmth of gratitude I at some times fancy that I feel, I am oftener disobedient, cold, neglectful; and though I should say I believe in Christ, when it appears how little consistent with that belief my actions are, it makes me doubtful if I do so or not. If sorrow for sin be repentance, I have repented; but if, as you say, amendment be a part, I am not sure; for, perhaps, I shall not amend; and with respect to the state of my passions, as it regards my fellow-creatures, all I have learned by the close examination of every word and feeling is, that my heart is full of selfishness and insubordination. I am certainly as little worthy to intrude myself as my sisters."

"My dear Emma, it was not to the worthy the invitation was sent, but to the sincere and contrite. You are right when you say you are no more worthy than your sisters to appear; but there is this difference,—When two things were held out to you, you gave the preference to the invitation of your Lord; when you saw what occupations were likely to interfere with your devotions, you put them aside: when you perceived of what unhallowed passions your mind was susceptible, you avoided the occasions of exciting them: so far you proved an honest desire to partake worthily of the benefits of this holy communion. The result of all your examination, and all your preparation, is, that you find yourself absolutely unworthy as to the past, and absolutely helpless as to the future. Such the result should be, and such it must be. But has this discovery made you feel less disposed or less desirous to go to the Sacrament?"

"On the contrary, mamma, it makes me more so; for the deeper grows the consciousness of my ill-deserts, the more precious becomes every emblem of redeeming mercy, the more welcome every record and remembrance of Jesus' love. If I before thought it desirable for me to be a partaker of the body and blood of Christ, and of the benefits received by them, I now know it to be necessary; for I cannot do without it. Ill-dressed, unclothed, unfitted as I am, I should like to go and try if the Master of the feast will admit me, and help me to provide myself a better garment; for I believe that none but He can weave it."

"Then, my dearest Emma, though I do not tell you you are better than your sisters, or that your conduct this week is sufficient to prove the reality of your faith, or the sincerity of your professions—for that is known only to Him who reads the heart—I do not hesitate to advise you to do as you desire; in humble confidence, that He who has invited you to his feast, will graciously receive you, and enable you to be what he requires."

The Sabbath morning dawned with more than usual brightness. The three sisters went together to their parish church; fancy might say the step of one was lighter than the rest: certain it is, that one only accepted the INVITATION.

No. XVII.

LENT.

Ce n'est rien, que le jeûne des viandes grossières qui nourrissent le corps, si on ne jeûne aussi de tout ce que sert d'aliment à l'amour propre.

FENELON.

THE eye that has long been accustomed to look upon the scene around us, has become familiar with its minutest peculiarities, reconciled to its deformities, and sated with its charms, can form but a very imperfect idea of the effect of that same scene on one who has never looked on it before. It is thus in every thing—we lose the general effect, in too close intimacy with the minute particulars. The painter feels this, when he has sat hour by hour over the laboured canvass, retouching every feature, measuring every line, till the effect as a whole is so entirely lost to him, he is obliged to remove it for a time out of his sight, or have recourse to the judgment of another. The poet feels it, when, having selected word by word the materials of his composition, and fitted them to the measure of his verse, he knows that to his ear they harmonise, to his perceptions they express the idea and excite the feeling he intends; but can very inadequately judge of the impression they will make on the mind of a reader who, for the first time, comes to their perusal.

And such is the difficulty I often feel, when I go about to listen for others to what I can only hear for myself; especially when it passes over my mind, that I am listening for those to whom nothing can appear under the same aspect in which it appears to me. Features of society that I have looked upon, till they seem to me too little prominent to excite attention, a young person, to whom the world is new, will likely fix upon as objects of inquiry and surprise : while those that, in minuter intimacy, I have discovered to be curious and important, they, in their hasty and unpractised glance, will either not perceive, or feel but little interest in. And thus, while I am carefully, and, as I think, very interestingly, telling stories and multiplying words about things that, for what they know, may have happened in the moon, they are wishing, wondering, and not altogether pleased, that I never happen to see, or see under so different a shape, the objects that most puzzle and surprise them. It was under the burden of this very disturbing apprehension, I bethought myself for once to have recourse to memory for my tale, and relate what happened when I was as much a novice as my readers, and liable to as much mistake as they possibly can be, respecting the things I saw. But then my readers must needs be forewarned, that my observations in this paper are not required to be correct ; what I thought wrong was, in all probability, very right—what I thought inconsistent, might be most beautifully systematic, if I had but had the sense to perceive the due connexion of things. And as all wonder is the offspring of ignorance—ignorance of what things are, if not of what they ought to be—any surprise that I may express, is to be, of course, attributed to my own inexperience at the time.

It happened once—that is the genuine way of beginning an account of things that never happened, but my readers may depend upon it this did happen some time, though I find it inconvenient to say when. It was when the habits and practices of the world were known to me only through the newspapers that reported them, or the moral essays that abused them, or the novels that misrepresented them —the world in which I had grown up being no wider than the walls of the paternal dwelling, and no more populous than the family that dwelt in it. What ideas or expectations I had formed through the medium of these informers of the busy scene of life in which I have since so largely wandered, is not of importance to be told—my readers may be satisfied to know they were in every way mistaken. Some time about the middle of March I was invited to spend a few weeks in London, where, with all my ignorance and all my prejudices full upon me, I found myself arrived at the given period. I was a

Listener then as well as now: then for myself, as now for others: and, among an infinite variety of things, the following circumstances are in memory's record as something that I heard.

"It is rather a dull time to bring a stranger to London," said Mrs Thoroughgood; "because in Lent we see less company, and our public amusements are for the most part suspended. But after Easter we shall be particularly gay, and able to show you every thing."

"I should like to know, mamma," answered young Selina T., "why we may not as well live in Lent as we live all the rest of the year; for I suppose we do not live irreligiously at any time?"

"I am surprised to hear you speak thus, Selina," said her mother; "I thought you had been taught to read your Bible, and attend your religious duties strictly; I did not expect from you so ignorant a remark—I thought you knew"——I was considering of the probability that Mrs T. had neglected to teach her daughter what she was surprised to find she did not know, when the lively Selina rejoined—

"O yes! dear mamma, I do know that in Lent we have no balls or plays, never ask more than twelve to dinner at once, eat salt-fish and pancakes, and go to church on the week-days. But I wanted to know the reason of it all; I am sure there is nothing about it in the Bible, and I could not find it this morning in the Prayer-book."

"Again, my dear, I must say you are very ignorant, if you do not know that the forty days preceding Easter are kept in commemoration of our Saviour's fast of forty days in the lonely wilderness, where, for our sakes, and for our example, he hungered and thirsted, and "——

"O, dearest mamma! I know all that, of course, —but I want to be told what that has to do with balls and dinner parties, and pancakes, and plays?" answered Selina, impatiently.

"I should think that too obvious to need explanation, my love," said Mrs T.—I thought so too; and, seeing her hesitate, I had almost a mind to propound the matter myself, so simple and so certain seemed to me the mode of explanation, and so clear to myself was my own understanding of it. I soon had reason to rejoice that I refrained my lips, when I perceived not only the difficulty of the exposition, but my own mistakes upon the subject.

Mrs T. took off her thimble, primmed her pleasant face into the length of gravity, bade her daughter to be serious, and she would explain to her what she ought to have known long ago. I thought she ought—little suspecting that I did not know myself.

There were not wanting symptoms in the old lady's manner which might have excited suspicion that she did not know—but that was impossible; the appearance must, of course, have proceeded from my want of knowledge of the world. Still there was a long pause: the old lady drew towards her

the large Bible and the little Prayer-book that lay
on the table, and put them carefully one upon the
other, the latter at the top, ready for action.   If so
much preparation should seem extraordinary, be it
remembered that Mrs T. had grown up at a period,
when, however much ladies might think upon religion, they were very little accustomed to talk about
it ; and few persons in the parish, except the parson,
were expected to have an opinion upon the subject,
much less to explain it.   Mrs T.'s exordium proved
nothing the worse for the delay.   She began by
commenting, with feeling and simplicity, on the
narration of our Saviour's sufferings, the object of
his mission upon earth, the awful consummation of
his errand that is at this season celebrated, and all
the heart-affecting circumstances with which the
season stands associated in the mind of a believer.

"And does not my Selina see," she added, "why
such a period should be marked, and kept by those
so deeply interested in its events?"

"Assuredly, mamma, I see it should be kept.
We commemorate the deeds of earthly greatness—
we celebrate the era of our country's freedom—we
remember the birth-time and the death of those we
love—if good or ill betide us, we grave, as it were,
the date upon our hearts, to be no more erased, and
thought recurs to it as duly as the day returns.   It
would seem strange, indeed, if of all important eras,
the most important was alone forgotten—if of all
great events, the greatest remained without appro-

priate celebration. Assuredly, mamma, it should be kept—but how?"

"By means appropriate to itself. Now, what does it seem to you that they would be?"

Selina hesitated; yet her countenance betrayed an emotion that said she knew; nature and feeling were in this instance better prompters than the wisdom of the schools. She had not reflected on it before, but she felt what she had not learned, and replied—

"In common sense, mamma, it surely should be this. Jesus suffered for our sins, died for our sins, rose again to free us from our sins. We were the cause of his suffering, and, therefore, should be sad at the remembrance — we were the gainers by it, and, therefore, should be glad and grateful. But as sin was the mischief, and pardon of sin the gain, it is natural that our joy, and our sorrow too, should express itself by abstaining from whatever is sinful, or can by any means be offensive to Him whose passion we at this time celebrate; and I would add, that we should keep it as a season of humiliation for our past sin, and of prayer and preparation for future amendment."

"You could not have spoken better, my child. And besides this purpose of preparation for Easter, it is required of us to follow the footsteps of our Lord; and, as he fasted forty days in the wilderness, so we have an equal period of self-denial appointed us in imitation of his. Do you not, then, see the wisdom of our church in setting apart the forty days preceding Easter for this good purpose?"

" Yes—but I do not exactly see how the purpose is answered by it—unless the ball and the theatre be the sins from which we are to abstain; and dining with twelve people instead of twenty be the self-denial, and "— Selina's vivacity was fast getting the better of her previous earnestness; but, recollecting herself, she gravely added, " But that, mamma, is confessing that these are sinful practices, which you know they are not."

" The innocent amusements of the world cannot be so: but "—Mrs T. hesitated—moved the Prayer-book off the Bible—turned it the other side upwards, and seemed at a loss for words — I thought I could have helped her, but I did not. " In the first place, these engagements occupy our time, and consequently leave us less for devotional duties: then they occupy our mind, and consequently interfere with the serious thought that becomes the season; and then it cannot be denied, that, though innocent amusements on the whole, there is an awful inconsistency in the gaiety and forgetfulness of such pursuits, when brought in near contact with the events at this season recalled and pictured out afresh to our imagination. You cannot, in the excitation of the theatre, think of your Saviour's dying groan—you cannot, in the hubbub of a crowded room, be in the steps of Him, who, as He sat at meat with those He loved, was ever teaching them his

Father's law, or speaking with them of his approaching expiation. Therefore it is not hard to understand, that, at a season when you desire to remember these things and to feel them, you must in some measure change your occupations."

I was considering how far the above ingredients might, if properly compounded, make a sin, when Selina ended at once my doubts and the conversation, of which she was manifestly tired, by the following exclamation :—

"O, yes! mamma—I am perfectly satisfied of what you mean, and beg your pardon for teasing you with such foolish questions—I see exactly, that things which are perfectly proper during the three hundred and twenty-five days in which we forget our Saviour's sufferings, would be very inconsistent during the forty days in which we desire to remember them; and since Jesus for our sakes at this time debarred himself of nature's first necessities, and endured a sufferance from which nature shrinks, we should, in imitation of Him, refrain from what we most delight in, and submit to what is most disagreeable to us—that is, we should give no balls, eat salt-fish and pancakes, and go to church."

Mrs T. smiled at her daughter's mirth, and possibly felt her satire, but contented herself with saying she was too giddy.

I was a thinker then as well as a listener, though not much of a talker, as may have been perceived. Reflecting, after I retired, upon this conversation, I felt angry with Selina's ridicule of her mother's sensible remarks. The truth of what had been said respecting Easter, the propriety of keeping it, and the manner of keeping it, had deeply impressed my mind. I felt ashamed that I had never before so seriously considered it; and a feeling of pious joy animated my bosom, that, for the first time in my life, I had come into a family where I should see it observed so consistently and so devoutly. How could Selina, I thought, who had been brought up in the constant observance of so excellent a principle, have remained till this time without a perception of its suitability?

I arose the next morning in a mood of more seriousness than I remember to have ever felt before, prepared, as I thought, and willing, to make any sacrifice required of me by religion and the church at such a season.

After the usual breakfast the carriage came to take us to morning prayers, and we rolled off to a fashionable chapel at the west end of the town. A few carriages brought a few people on the same errand—the chapel was so warm, and the seats were so well lined, and the hassocks were so near the elevation of the knees, and the reader made such admirable haste, that, contrary to my previous prejudice, I found there was very little trouble in a week-day service, and so we rolled back again, and went about our usual occupations.

"Selina, dear, you must not be idle," said Mrs

T.; "you know what a deal you have to do, and this is the last leisure week; there is scarcely a day in which we are not engaged after Easter, and our mornings will be occupied in showing our friend about London. If you do not make use of this idle time to prepare your things, you will be sadly bustled."

"O, dear me! I am bustled enough as it is," said Selina. "I have saved such a quantity of things to do this week, that I never shall get through them. It is a comfort, at least, that there are a few weeks in the year in which one has time to one's self. But did you not want me to write those cards this morning?"

"O, yes! indeed you must," answered her mother. "For to-morrow the dressmaker will be here all the morning, measuring and taking orders for your spring dresses; and next day I have appointed the upholsterer about the furniture, and all the house will be in confusion—on Saturday you must go to the dentist—I must get all these things done this week, for I shall have no time after Easter."

"But for what days are the cards to be sent out, mamma?"

"That I must think of, if I can find time to think. There is the 1st, the 6th, the 10th. Having no parties in Lent makes them come so thick afterwards, it is scarcely possible to find days enough."

The conversation was interrupted by the entrance of a lady dressed in black—she made a visit of the

usual length, during which she made a great many
ill-natured remarks, repeated several slanderous anec-
dotes, and expressed herself with much bitterness
against some persons who had offended her. As
soon as she was gone, Selina said—"Mamma, what
is Miss Tibbs in mourning for?"

" It used to be the custom, my dear, and it is still
retained by some persons who are particular, to wear
mourning in Lent."

"Nay," said Selina, "if Miss Tibbs is so particular in keeping Lent, she had better abstain from
speaking ill of her neighbours, which is the thing
she most delights in, and forgive her enemies, which
is the thing she is least disposed to."

The days passed on—every body ate and every
body drank, and every body enjoyed themselves as
usual. Two or three people came some days to dinner, and the entertainment was the same, and the
conversation was the same, for any thing I could see,
as if there had been twenty—and on the days we
dined alone, the objects that occupied our attention
were still the same. We talked of the things we
did not do, and arranged plans for doing them as
soon as we might. I heard no more of Jesus, of his
sufferings, or his death ; of sin, or its consequences,
or its pardon; nor, as far as I could perceive, was
any one thinking about them. This probably proceeded from my own inexperience and want of
knowledge of the world. It could not really be, as
it seemed, that the season, *so properly set apart by*

our church, as Mrs T. had said, for meditation, penitence, and prayer, should be passed over without
any extra-serious thoughts, of any kind whatever,
upon the events at this period commemorated. Certain it is, that no more allusion was made to them in
word or deed, except that some one now and then
took occasion to say, it was very unlucky it happened
to be Lent.

"Mamma, which night are we going to the Oratorio?" said Selina, on Friday morning.

"I believe, my dear, we shall have a box to-night;
but you will know when your papa returns."

On this subject I felt myself quite well informed.
I had learned by the newspaper that the theatres are
always closed during this season, except on Wed-
nesdays and Fridays, when they are opened for the
Oratorio, a sort of religious festival, as I conceived,
by the names affixed to the performance, and by its
being held on the same day of the week as the church
prayers; days, I was aware, to which custom had
affixed a peculiar sacredness. I was well pleased
with what I heard—for as this amusement was not
only allowed in Lent, but confined to it by peculiar
appropriation, I certainly might there expect to find
something of the devotion with which I had heard
the season was to be hallowed.

The box was secured, the hour came, we were
duly adorned, and set off, as I supposed, to our devotions. My thoughts by the way were serious—they
had not been used to be so; but what I had heard

from Mrs T. had made a strong impression on me; though I was effectually puzzled that it seemed to have so little affected any body else. I tried to compose my mind to feelings suitable to the occasion, though no one else in the carriage appeared to be doing so. But then they had been used to spend the Lent properly; I had hitherto neglected it; and the reflection caused me some feelings of regret and shame.

Shame, regret, and devotion, however, had no tickets of admission. I parted at the door with all of them, and became absorbed with such sense of pleasure as was likely to possess a youthful mind on tasting, for the first time, of such an amusement. The splendour of the house, the brilliancy of the lights, the music of the full choir, so unlike to any thing I had heard before; the gay appearance of the audience, where all without was prosperity and smiles, whatever might be beneath them—thoughts of sadness would have seemed to me a sacrilege; within the compass of these walls, at least, there was a world all joy; my reflections and feelings were absorbed in sensations of unmingled pleasure. I could not discern where vice and misery hid itself in that gay crowd; or, I should rather say, presented their unblushing front, as if by acknowledged right they presided there. I could not guess how the hundreds of immortal beings were employed, who, to support a useless existence, and fill up the measure of their crimes, were doing the drudgery of such an establishment. I knew nothing of all this—but ignorant as I was, and thoughtless as I was, I was startled from my delirium of enjoyment, when, accompanied by tones from the orchestra that might seem to be the music angels sing, I heard these words, "He was despised and rejected of men, a man of sorrows, and acquainted with grief. He gave his back to the smiters"—I need not pursue the words, we know where they are, we know what they mean—those deep mysterious words, at which patriarchs and prophets wondered, which sinners treasure in their bosoms as the criminal the signet that is to stay his execution—which the penitent weeps while he listens to, and triumphs while he weeps—the words of God himself, the prophetic picture of the Saviour's sufferings for a ruined, miserable world, for the world that at this season professed to commemorate his mercy and its own degradation — for the world at that moment assembled within those walls. I looked at the person by whom the words were uttered—I looked at the audience by whom they were listened to—I marked the dazzling accompaniments of the scene. Nature and reason spake within me—for, bribed, corrupted, spell-bound as they are, they will speak sometimes, if we will let them. The bold, unblushing front, the unshrinking eye, the immodest attire, the unhallowed air, on the one part—on the other, the expression of indifference or of emotions simply pleasurable, were so contrasted with the images those words brought like unwelcome spectres

to my imagination, that at no moment of my life do
I remember to have felt so involuntarily persuaded
that these things were indeed but the fiction that
they seemed — the tragic stories with which men
amuse themselves. The beings before me and around
me, could they believe themselves the creatures for
whom the Messiah had thus suffered? Was it they
had done it, they had caused it, they, at this very
time, professing to keep a fast in imitation of his
sufferings, and humble themselves before Him for
their share in it? It was nonsense, it was absurdity,
—it was imposition that could not be passed upon
a child—to suppose that they who sang, or they who
listened, felt themselves to be the sinners that had
been so redeemed; had there been any bosom there
to which the realising sense had come, they would
have drooped their heads for shame, and gone away.
No — I am bold to say, that whatever it was before
or after, the Messiah's sorrows were, at the moment,
to every bosom there, a fiction—enhanced by the
exquisite pathos of the music—a beautiful, exciting,
heart-affecting fiction, represented by the most degraded of mankind for the amusement of the gayest
and most profligate. Yet hither we had presumed
to bring the word of God. Here we addressed Him
with the cry for mercy, here we had his name re-
sounded from unhallowed lips, reverberating on un-
adoring hearts; succeeded as quickly as the scene
could change, by a heathen madrigal, sung by the
same performers, in the characters of Ceres and

Proserpine, in which Pluto received the orisons so lately offered in mockery to the God of Heaven; uttered in the same spirit, heard with the same feelings. We drop the picture. Satire grows grave when she touches on things like these; and our readers will say we preach. If there be meaning in words, or sense in any thing, God's commandment was that night broken, and his name profaned; and Christians were there to hear it, and were well pleased.

But to resume my story. A few days more, and the days of Lent were ended. The *imitation* of the Messiah's fast in the wilderness was completed, the season of *humiliation* was accomplished, and we were all *prepared* for the approaching festival of Easter. The day of the Redeemer's death that ended our days of *mourning*, was decently observed in Mrs T.'s family, as was also the Sunday, the commencement of our joy for his resurrection to eternal life, and our own in his. And what it before behoved us to remember, it now behoved us as quickly as possible to forget; what was sin the week before the expiation was offered, was no sin as soon as it was accomplished—there needed, indeed, the utmost ingenuity to make up for the time that had been lost. Miss Tibbs put off her mourning; Mrs Thoroughgood would have thought it quite Methodistical to go to church in the week; Selina honestly rejoiced that Lent came but once a-year; and I—I remembered, what I hope my readers may not have forgotten, the

beginning of my story. I remembered Selina's ignorance, and no longer wondered; for neither could I
perceive the connexion between the season and its
observances. I remembered Mrs Thoroughgood's
pious observations, and wondered what they could
have meant—for I had not seen a single illustration
of them in the practices or occupations of the family
in the interval. One good effect, however, came of
my meditations—they put me on good terms again
with myself: for whatever might be the intention of
our Church in instituting this fast—whether, that in
order to our being made conformable to our Lord in
his life, it was judged necessary that we should have
a season of self-denial and abstraction from the ordinary occupations and innocent delights of life—or
whether, He having fulfilled for us the law, and by
his sufferings done away the need of a similar penance
on our part, this was rather meant as a time of
grateful remembrance than of imitation, a time of
humiliation before God, and pious commemoration
of his love—in either or in any case, it appeared to
me that the intentions of the Church had been as
well fulfilled by my forgetfulness as by their observance of the season. Whatever mistakes may be in
this comparative estimate of wrong, I beg may be
attributed to my inexperience and ignorance of the
world.

No. XVIII.

THE CHILDREN OF ABRAHAM.

And where shall Israel lave her bleeding feet?
And where shall Zion's songs again seem sweet?
And Judah's melody once more rejoice
The hearts that leap'd before its heavenly voice?

Hebrew Melodies.

I WAS travelling once over a distant land—a land
it had been, by the way I travelled, of bleakness, and
barrenness, and danger.   If sometimes I had loitered
where there were flowers budding, fair as the first
and fairest of our Spring, while I yet waited in expectation of their blowing, I saw them wither in the
sunshine, fade, and pass away. If ever, amid the
parched and thirsty soil, I had looked upon the
bursting of a pure, clear spring, quickly there came
to it some unclean thing, and mudded and polluted
what had risen so pure.   And often, as, beneath some
shadowing tree, I had lain down to rest, before I had
shod myself again to hasten forward, the cold north
wind had come and stripped that tree, and robbed it
of its beauty and its shade.   It was a wretched land,
and they that dwelt in it were like the land they

dwelt in. Their well-seeming virtues rarely bore the bloom they promised, but failed at the moment of expected fruition—their wisdom, however rife it seemed to flow, flowed not far before it became mixed with error and empoisoned—their enjoyments were the evanescent verdure that could not outstand the first cold touch of sorrow. And surely I had felt pity for them as I passed, and mourned that they had not a better land to dwell in.

Having travelled thus some considerable way, I reached a spot, seeming more fair for the rude path that led to it, and beautiful in the contrast of its fertility with the coldness and barrenness of the land I had passed over. There was no barrier, that I perceived, between them; and yet were they distinct as the darkness of night from the broad light of noon. Why the inhabitants of the adjacent country did not pass on to it, I perceived not: but I concluded it was appropriated property—the hereditary possession, probably, of a people too powerful to need a landmark, or an armed outwork, against the encroachments of their neighbours. Certainly I saw that no desire was manifested on either part, to take possession of the other's land: and, unequal as seemed to me the destiny of each, each appeared contented to abide their portion. I entered with delight on the rich scenery of this pleasant land. I do not know that I need particularly to describe it: it was like the best spots in our native country—those that industry has toiled to cultivate, and some tasteful

hand has taken pleasure to adorn. It was like to
those wide estates, that, being appropriated to some
powerful and rich possessor, who finds pleasure in
them, and does with them what he will, manifest in
every part the influence of his interference. It was
no fairy land I speak of, where magic suns gave
birth to golden fruits, or necromantic power charmed
the elements to stillness. But it was one where
forethought had provided every thing, caution had
secured every thing, and whatever were the natural
ills to which it lay exposed, some defence against
their influence, or remedy for their mischiefs, had
carefully been provided. The blossoms of their
gardens died like others—but their departing beauty
left the fruit to ripen richly on the stem. The sun
of their daytime went down like others, and often
went down in clouds—but the damps of their night
were like the waters of affliction to the bosom of submission, the better for its tears. When the tree that
adorned it withered in the blast and passed away,
there came a friendly watcher and planted another
as lovely in its place. The menacing weeds sometimes came up, indeed; but quickly the eye of the
inspector marked them, and put in his keen-edged
tools to their destruction. Like our most highly
cultured grounds, its paths were made straight, and
its rough places were made smooth—the threatening
tempest passed over it harmless, and the winds that
rocked its habitations to their base, found them too

strongly founded for destruction—the dwellers in them slept secure in danger.

The inhabitants of this happy region, I observed, were many; and they seemed to know the value of their estates. They did not live on them in idle luxury, waiting the productions of a soil, that, rich as it was, would surely so have disappointed them: but they cultivated it in cheerful expectation of no uncertain harvest. Though they enjoyed its good in common, it was not in wild misrule, the lawlessness of promiscuous possession. Each one had his place, and each one had his task; and if the proportion of each was not the same, it showed a fair adjustment to his powers, his industry, or his deserts; it was enough to suffice him till time and circumstance should bring him elevation in the scale; there was enough for all; and all were secure they should not be deprived of the possession, unless they willingly departed to some other residence.

When I had staid some time with this people, I found that they too had a character something in conformity to the features of their country. They evinced the infirmities and dispositions of other nations; and this appeared to be the chief taint that sullied the lustre of their state, and marred their happiness. Yet even this was not without a palliative and a corrective remedy: the laws were so good, and the administration of them so good, the punishment ensued so quickly on misconduct, and the pardon so quickly on the effectual repression of the wrong, that order and peace were the general characters of the kingdom, notwithstanding the peccability of its subjects, and the frequent interruptions of their enjoyment by the obtrusion of their faults. I became, after a time, very anxious to know who these people were, and how they came to be in possession of so beautiful a territory, while all around it and about it, as I have told, remained so bleak, so bare.

"Tell me," I said to one I thought could inform me, "from what great line of ancestry these people are descended; the children, doubtless, of some pristine hero, who conquered for them this pleasant land, or perhaps the generation of its first possessors, who, when the inhabitants of earth were few, found it and took possession, and by their industry and wisdom, made it what it is, and bequeathed it, with all its blessings, to their posterity?"

"This land," he answered, "was not originally theirs who hold it now—their fathers did not conquer it, their progenitors did not possess it. They dwelt yonder, in the lands you passed through."

"Indeed!" I said; "most happy are they, then, in the exchange. But by what rich purchase is it theirs?"

He answered, "It came not into their hands by purchase, but was the gift of our Sovereign Lord the King, who gave it to them and their heirs for ever."

"In reward for some service to the crown?" I asked.

"None that I ever heard of," he replied; "it was confiscated property, and he gave it where he pleased."

"But who then, and where, are the original possessors of these lands? Do they who planted yonder vines not gather of their fruits?"

"No," he rejoined, "nor they who built those palaces may dwell in them—nor they who raised those altars may longer worship there. They were faithless ungrateful traitors; they broke their pledged allegiance to the king, their persons were outlawed and attainted, their estates forfeited to the crown—and what the fathers made themselves, the children have continued."

"What were the fathers before this happened?"

"The favourites of their Prince—the best and best-beloved of all his realm. The highest in dignity, and the most happy in estate, they came, every one of them, of royal blood, and could trace their ancestors by name to a period when ours were unheard of. Here, amid the blessings surrounding us, they lived secure, no man disputing their possession; for they had been its first possessors, the sole inheritors from remotest ages."

"And what are the children now?"

"Did you not see them," he replied, "loitering in helpless indigence on the confines of our territory? Come, and I will show you them."

We walked towards the way opposite to that by which I had entered; and I observed amid surrounding dreariness, a few miserable hovels, the abodes of the wretched, as their appearance told—humanity was glad to see they were not more.

"Are these all that remain?" I said.

"No," answered my companion, "but they are all that reside in this part of the kingdom, wandering round the dwellings that were once their own, where now they enter not."

I looked upon those miserable ruins of departed greatness, and saw, or fancied I saw, some traces of nobility in their features—but it was so mixed with an expression of sordid wretchedness, and abject acquiescence in disgrace, I could liken it only to the fallen statue, which the elements have discoloured, and the rank herbage overgrown. till we know not if we really perceive, or do but persuade ourselves of its former beauty. Misery, guilt, and deep-written melancholy, there certainly were upon their sallow brows—in some, I could have believed it the melancholy of penitence and shame.

"The children of royalty," I uttered, as I looked at them, "the certain claimants of that remote ancestry of which we are all so proud! And do they want for any thing?"

"It is likely they want for every thing." my guide replied; "for they have no possessions here or any where; they dwell upon the waste; they have no country, and no friends, and scarce a home—none but those miserable huts."

I entered one of them. An aged man was sitting; older, I judged, in misery than in years—and yet his head was grey, as sorrow's often is before its time. The scanty hair upon his half-bared head was strikingly contrasted with the abundant fulness of the beard. His features were harsh; there was vice in them, and there was misery—but it was vice and misery that had done its work and gathered its reward; and purposed no more, and feared no more, of either; poverty, abandonment, and despair, were the predominant characters of every thing in him and about him; excepting that there lay about his feet a group of children, whose sunny foreheads and deep hazel eyes glowed with the vigour of fresh existence, as yet unquestioning of weal or woe. And even to these, the long, falling line of the nose and forehead, and the shadowing eyelid that half veiled the oblong eye, gave such an expression of pensive melancholy, one might have fancied they borrowed their features from their fate.

I spoke to the old man softly, and said his store appeared a spare one; and something I said about the condition of his house, and the contrast with their former greatness, when in possession of the adjoining lands, which, as I was told, had been his fathers'.

"They tell me so," he said, "but they were

never mine; and I do not want them; for I am
going to my fathers, from whom the rapacity of
those strangers stole them."

"But I have heard that you forfeited them by
rebellion, and were lawfully ejected?"

"It may be so—but I know nothing about it.
Whatever happened, happened before I was born.
Compelled to toil my life through for my bread,
sometimes to beg it, ay, and sometimes to steal it
or forego it, I have had no time to inquire, and no
one has cared to tell me."

"You do not seem so much concerned as I expected. Would you not like to enter again upon
that pleasant land, and look at the dwelling of your
fathers?"

"No one has invited me. Concerned! Is the
loathed spider, think you, concerned when you wipe
it from your gilded cornices, and cast it out as a
pollution? Is the hated reptile concerned when
you put your foot upon it, as too vile to be sheltered even in your dust? What matters our concern?"

"But your children—perhaps the time may come
—do you not wish"——

The old man raised himself from his seat, placed
his back against the humid wall, his clenched hands
resting upon the staff before him. "My children!"
he interrupted me—"I have said I did not know—
you say I do not care—but this I know—I love my

children, miserable villain as I may be, and they
are suffering, outcast, and despised. The land they
dwell upon produces nothing—the returning seasons
bear them nothing—look at them, unwashed, un-
shod, and starving. Perhaps if they knew what
they are, and what they might have been, they
would try some means to be reconciled to their
King—but who is to instruct them? Where are
they to find him? They are born to misery, and
they will die in ignorance, the innocent victims of
their fathers' deeds, and no man comes to help
them." He paused a moment—then, with increasing mournfulness, resumed—"The boastful inhabitants of yonder place talk much of their abundance.
Proudly exulting in their unbought possessions,
they cast our forlorn condition in our teeth, and
weighing our wretchedness against their bliss, bid
us behold in it the issue of our fathers' crimes. I
have said I do not know if it be true. I do not
know if their land be as abundant as they say.
How should I? They have never imparted to me
of its fruits. I do not know if they are really the
happy creatures they profess to be. How should
I? They have never bidden me to their hearths.
But if it be that their halls are so wide, and their
harvests so rich, and their government so benefi-
cent as they say—ah! surely there should be room
enough for these few poor children. But none will
fetch them in." The father's voice grew hoarse

with deepened emotion—the dark eyes of the children moistened with a tear; they knew not why, but that their father wept.

I could have wept too—but I replied, "Perhaps the Prince your fathers so much offended, forbade your re-entrance on those lands—perhaps its new incumbents hold it on condition never to admit you—or surely they had not so long left you here unfriended?"

"It may be so," the old man answered, fixing a look of lorn despair upon his children, paused a moment—then, as if a hopeful doubt had broken in upon his sadness, added, "I never heard it. I have heard he loved our fathers—they who love the fathers are not used to hate the children. It may be so—but when you go back again to yonder halls, if you see that there is any thing to spare—if there be room enough in their chambers and food enough on their board, ask if they are forbidden to take in my few poor children."

Readers, I have fulfilled my commission. If you were the possessors of some rich tenement, given by the sovereign, as in former times it often has been in our country, the forfeited property of his traitor subjects to those he makes his friends—while you enjoy the gain of their disloyalty, should you feel no pity for their need? Should you leave their children to perish at your gates? I believe you would not. There is nothing more moving to our natural feelings, than to look on the residue of fallen greatness: if a suffering pauper be pointed out to us as the child of one who was of rank and birth superior to our own, a stronger emotion of pity is excited for his degradation; for we contrast his fortunes with our own, and measure his fall as what ours might be. Still more, if you were the gainers by that change, and held the property that was once his fathers', would you not hold out to the deprived and degraded offspring, some portion of your well-spared abundance? You would go out of those pleasant lands to the bleak forest I have described, to look for those poor children that were perishing on the waste, and bring them in to live on your estates, and be at least your servants? Now, believe me, it is no fiction I have told. Jehovah has a garden that he cultures with especial care, as unlike the heathen lands that lie around it, as the dwelling I have pictured to the country that was about it. He cast out in anger the original inhabitants, and put you in unearned possession of what once was theirs. A few of their outcast children, innocent of their fathers' sin, ignorant of the real cause of their degradation, and not knowing by what means to be reconciled to their offended Maker, are lying about your streets, and lurking round your doors, and you have taken no notice of them. You have not gone to their dwellings to offer them a portion of the word of eternal truth, on which you feed so richly. And you have not sought out their children to separate them from their miseries, and rear them to a better state, before habit has confirmed them in their errors and reconciled them to destruction. You know their high original—you trace with lively interest their distant pedigree, and are proud to call yourselves by the name of their fathers—it is your boast and glory to observe the law of Moses their legislator, and Christ who was born of them. And yet you hold these ancient people in contempt, individually, if not as a people; and feel no emotion when you see them perishing without those moral and religious advantages you possess in such rich abundance, and have never been forbidden to communicate. On the contrary, you know there would be joy in heaven itself to see the offspring of a Hebrew become a spiritual Christian. The only way in which an inhumanity not natural to our hearts can be accounted for, is thoughtlessness of the circumstances in which we stand respecting these people, or ignorance of the means by which we can amend their condition.

These thoughts were suggested to me when, on a late occasion, I went to listen where the holders of the rich blessings of the gospel were assembled to consider of the claims of these poor children; and deeply was my mind struck with the contrast I beheld. They were not indeed unfed and naked in their land of barrenness, for pity had fetched them in—but they were sitting there the suppliants for a small share of that which once was all their own—the children of Abraham were in the dress of charity—their little eyes cast down and often filled with tears, while their wants and claims were urged by those who spoke on their behalf, to wring a poor pittance from the gay Gentile crowd before them—gay in the ornaments of superfluous wealth, that, spared to them, had not been missed— and gay in the consciousness of moral dignity and enjoyment of spiritual good, that, divided with them, had surely not been lessened. The sight was to me the argument—the scene was its own sufficient illustration. Who are those? Who are these? Abraham, four thousand years ago, worshipping God on the only altar he had upon the earth, the temple of Jerusalem in all its splendour, his own presence shining in the midst, while our unknown forefathers were wandering somewhere in the wilds of uncultured ignorance, rose to my imagination with such impressive reality, every thing that was said, or could be said, came short of the spontaneous emotion of my bosom, that had already run through the world's history for an explanation of the scene before me.

In determining to represent to Christians the duty of instructing Jews in general, and Jewish children in particular, I have left the grounds on which more has been said than I can find to say— they are in better hands than mine—I have left to others the strength of Scripture language, and the mysterious voice of prophecy, and put in the plea of feeling, justice, and humanity; because I am writing for some who may not understand those, but must be accessible to these. I do not wish to suggest any particular measures or means; but merely to awaken in the bosoms of my readers some share of the shame I feel, that I have never given any of my time, or talents, or superfluous expenditure, towards the children of Abraham—that I have not yet, even by a word of persuasion, sent a messenger out from our Christian halls, to ask one of those few poor children to come in to the habitations of their fathers.

No. XIX.

INCONSISTENCIES.

Dieu nous développe peu à peu notre fond qui nous étoit inconnu ; et nous sommes tous éttonés de découvrir, dans nos vertus mêmes, des défauts dont nous nous étions crus incapables. C'est comme une grotte qui paroit sèche de tous cotés, et d'ou l'eau rejaillit tout a coup par les endroits dont on se défioit le moins.

FÉNÉLON.

A FRIEND requested me, a short time since, to write a paper on CONSISTENCY. I was well pleased with the suggestion ; it is a pleasant thing to have a subject given, when every body writes so much, that subjects are growing scarce; I thought I would quickly set about it, and indite a paper describing the beauty, and loveliness, and excellence of CONSISTENCY. But when I would have gone to work to paint the portrait, I found myself in no small difficulty—for where was the original ? Had I any acquaintance with it ? Had I ever seen it ? Imagination may make a drawing, but a portrait it cannot make—and what would it avail me to describe an imaginary being, whose features none would recognise, when I profess to draw always

from the life, and describe only what I hear and
see? What was to be done? I could think of but
one way of emerging from this great difficulty, without breaking the promise I had given to touch the
subject. If there were such a thing as Consistency—and I had never heard it doubted—it must
be somewhere to be found; why not look after it?
I must, of course, have seen it often, and my ignorance of its exact features, and the contour of the
countenance altogether, must be the result of inattention or forgetfulness? This might be repaired,
as ignorance mostly may, by diligent research—and
I resolved that it should be so. I resolved to listen
every where, and look at every thing, and inquire
of every body, till I should find my subject, and so
have no more to do but to paint the resemblance of
it. I put my pencil in my pocket—and my Indian-
rubber, lest I should sketch a feature wrong—and
patiently resolved to delay the portrait till I had
seen the individual, whom I did not doubt to meet
in some of the ordinary walks of society, now that I
had seriously set myself to watch for her. The progress of my researches is what I wish to disclose to
my readers.

It happened, a short time after, that I was stay-
ing in a house where, without that sort of profusion
that intimates abundant wealth, there was an air of
ease and liberality that spoke poverty equally distant. As many servants were kept as could do the
required service well; but not so many as usually

prevent its being done at all. As much ornament was about the house, as gave a tone of elegance and comfort to the apartments; but not so much that everything must be bundled up in sacks of brown Holland, till somebody is expected worthy to look upon it. The dress of the family was genteel, perhaps a little *recherché*; but not so as to convey the idea that the great essential of their happiness, the cardinal virtue of their character, was to have their clothes becoming and well made. In short, the whole air of the mansion seemed to say, We have not enough to squander, but we have enough to enjoy.

It befell on an occasion, that we—that is, myself and the ladies of the family—sate pleasantly engaged in our morning occupations, about as important as such occupations usually are—that is, one was making a frill, and another was unpicking a frill that somebody else had made—one was making match-boxes for the chimney, and another was making matches to put into the match-boxes, and so on. A person was announced who came to solicit a contribution to some charitable efforts making in the neighbourhood for the relief of indigence, or suffering of some kind, I do not exactly remember what. The lady of the house listened with much civility to the application; fully approved of the object and the proposed means; wished all manner of success, and greatly lamented that her very limited income did not allow of her doing so much good as she desired! They had contributed already to so many things, the objects of private charity that presented themselves were so numerous, it was quite impossible to assist in any new efforts. The applicant, who, as an intimate friend of the family, used the liberty of persuasion, again pointed out the necessity of the case, and the Christian duty of dispensing what we hold of providential bounty. The lady replied extremely well—spoke fairly of the beauty and the duty of charity—admitted that she did not give so much as she should feel to be right, and as she should be inclined to, but that she actually had no more to spare—her income was only sufficient for the proprieties of her condition—she never expended any thing unnecessarily—she wished she had a few hundreds a-year more, and she would give a guinea to this undertaking most willingly—there was nothing for which she so much desired wealth. Then turning to her daughters, she said, "I do not know how the girls' allowance stands—they are always anxious to give, and I am sure this is a case in which they would feel deeply interested—but they, like myself, cannot do all they wish."

"I really am sorry," said the elder daughter, "but I have given away every farthing I can possibly spare—if I had a shilling left that I could do without, I should think it my duty to give it on such an occasion."

"I have no money," said one of the younger girls, "but I am thinking whether I can assist the charity in any other way—whether I can take any part in the trouble of providing—of visiting the"——

"I am sure, Julia, you cannot," interrupted her sister; "you know you have more to do already than you can get through. Our time is taken up with so many things—it is impossible you can undertake any thing more."

"Well, I believe it is," answered Julia; "but this is so plainly a case of urgent necessity—a duty so obvious, that we certainly ought to aid it in some way."

"We ought, if we could, my dear," said her mamma; "but no one is required to do more than they can. As it has not pleased Providence to give us any superfluity of wealth, much is not required of us. It cannot be our duty to give more than we can spare with propriety, and in justice to ourselves and our families—I am really sorry, because I think it a proper case."

The contribution was declined, and the visitor departed. I held my tongue, because I always hold my tongue; but I had been thinking all the time. I thought it was a pity people so charitably disposed had so limited an income—I thought how painful it must be to them to feel that there was no way in which they could make their circumstances yield to the claims of their suffering fellow-creatures, without trespassing on the expenditure imperiously demanded of them by the proprieties of life. And, as my secret reflections are apt to excurse very widely from the point where they begin, and no one spoke to interrupt me, I went on to think what is the real extent of charity that Christian principle may demand of any one. It is immediately perceptible that it cannot be to do away with the distinctions Providence has made, and throw from us the advantages and indulgences Providence has given, and disenable ourselves to support the expenditure required by our station, itself a means of dispersing wealth, and averting poverty from the industrious. A limit, therefore, there must be to every one's liberality. But can that limit be within the point where a case of real want presents itself, and the possessor of wealth *can* command, without injustice or injury to any one, something to bestow? I was just entering in thought upon this wide field of rumination, when the servant announced the arrival of a vender of certain rare articles of dress and curious wares from abroad —things as pleasant to the eye of taste as to that of vanity. The vender was willingly admitted. Every thing was examined, many things were wished for, a few things were purchased. Mamma bought some ornaments for the table—the eldest girl bought some ivory winders for her thread, much prettier than the wooden ones she had in use before — Julia bought a gilded buckle to fasten her waistband. These things were all very pretty—not very extravagant in price—harmless indulgences of taste—the produce of some one's industry—the superfluity the Creator has provided means for, and therefore cannot disapprove. But they were all unnecessary. The one lady had added nothing to her influence or respectability by the ornaments for her table—the second lady had added nothing to her comfort or happiness by exchanging wooden winders for ivory ones—the third lady had added nothing to her grace or beauty by a new buckle for her waistband. "Therefore," I said within myself, "their words and their actions do not consist. They said there was nothing for which they so much valued wealth as to distribute it to the necessitous. That was not true—they preferred to spend it on themselves. They said they had not any money to spare, though they felt strongly the claim that was made on them. That was not true—they could spare money the first time they felt inclined. Had these people said they had given in charity as large a portion of their income as they thought it their duty to deprive themselves of, and wished to give no more, it had been well; and, whether right or wrong, they had spoken honestly; but inasmuch as they said they wished to give, and regretted that they could not, their words and their deeds were not consistent."

"Good morning, dear," said Mrs White to her cousin Mrs Grey, as I chanced to hear one morning on the Parade at Brighton; "I have a favour to ask of you—our girls are going to have a quadrille party next week—I wish you would let your young people come."

"You know I do not like my girls to enter into those things"——

"Not when it takes them into public, and leads to habitual dissipation—but in private parties, and when you know what company they mix with, and when you are sure they will neither hear nor see any thing calculated to pervert their principles or corrupt their minds, it is impossible you can imagine any harm in a party merely because they dance. We shall not have above thirty people."

"No, certainly not because they dance. To dance, literally, is only to move in a certain measured step, and jump a certain number of inches from the ground, and go about the room in a prescribed figure, instead of the irregular figure and unmeasured pace they would observe were they running upon the hills. I am not so absurd as to suppose there can be any harm in this motion more than in any other motion. Therefore that my girls do not come, is not merely because you have dancing, but I do not like that sort of party for them at any rate. It is a scene of display—an exhibition of the person and excitation of the mind, that they are better and happier without, and I should be sorry they acquired a taste for it."

"I cannot think why you should fear their having a taste for an innocent amusement that all young people enjoy—you are not bringing them up for the cloister, I suppose?"

"By no means: I bring them up to be agreeable and useful in society, and therefore would not wish to unfit them for it—but you cannot pretend to say there is any real enjoyment of society, any mental improvement to be expected, or benevolent feeling to be cultivated, in these parties?"

"Perhaps not—I cannot say there is—but at least there is no harm."

"That is not so certain—I apprehend a great deal of harm may be done. A great many wrong feelings are excited—if they are much noticed, and have the best partners, vanity and self-esteem are excited—if they see others succeeding better, jealousy is excited: jealousy, and vanity, and self-esteem, are sins, and in all sin there is harm. Then there is so much thought and care about what they are to wear, and how they shall look, and what will be thought of them by strangers—a set of people, in whose approbation or affections they can never find credit or advantage, whom they care nothing about, and to whom, therefore, I would not have them feel anxious to commend themselves by such factitious means. They are contented now with pleasing those who know and love them, and in whose society they find advantage—I would rather they did not come to you to acquire new desires, and divert their minds from more rational pursuits."

"I would not persuade you against your wishes—I know your sort of religion forbids you to conform to what you call the practices of the world—but I do not perfectly understand to which of its practices you do, and to which you do not, object."

The ladies parted. Mrs Grey and myself walked home to find the young ladies, to whom their mamma mentioned what had passed. They gave entire assent to her opinions; spoke with more vehemence and less moderation against the vanity and wickedness of such amusements — pitied their cousins' corrupt propensities, and detailed half-a-dozen instances of the spirit of emulation, and contention, and display, exercised in parties of the kind; and then they talked about renouncing the world, and its pomps, and its delusions—and the spirit of self-renunciation, meekness, and humility, that could only be maintained away from scenes of dissipation, rivalry, and display —and so on, and so on—and I thought they talked uncommonly well, only rather too fast; particularly as nobody was disposed to contradict them.

I observed, however, that they were remarkably busy all the time, as if in the act of preparing for something.

"Mamma," said Charlotte, "have you brought the flowers for our bonnets?"

"No, my dear, but we will send for them."

"Well, but we must make haste — the meeting begins in an hour or two, and we shall not be ready—ring the bell." The bell was not answered. " Ring again." The bell broke—that was the bell-hanger's fault. " Where is John?"—"John is gone out, ma'am."—"How tiresome! then Betty must go."—" Betty is about Miss Charlotte's pelisse that must be done to put on this morning."—" Was ever

any thing so provoking!—then, cook, you mus go."
—"I am just putting down the meat, miss, and can't
leave it."

"My dear," said Mrs Grey, "you can wear your
bonnets as they are."

"No, mamma, that is impossible—we had better
not go at all."

"Then you must fetch them yourselves."

"Yes, and how are we to be ready? Every body
will be there before us. Things always happen so
contrarily!"

And now a certain quantity of ill-humour, and a
considerable quantity of impatience, were manifested
on all sides. Mamma blamed the girls, first for
thinking about their dress at all, and then for not
having thought of it sooner. The girls wondered
their mamma had not brought in the flowers. John
was blamed for not being at home when he had
been sent out — Betty was blamed for being busy
when she had been set to work — the cook was
blamed for dressing the meat, though no one, as
I believe, meant to go without their dinner. The
ladies were what, in domestic phraseology, is called
put out; and, when that takes place in a family,
it does not signify who is to blame, or what the
matter is—every body must submit to be in the
wrong.

Time mends all things. The young ladies went
to the anniversary of some charitable society in the
town—and the young ladies came home again.

"Well, my dears," said Mrs Grey, "how have you been pleased?"

"Tolerably," replied Ann; "but we were so late, and got such bad seats—I could not enjoy it at all. Do you know that there were those Miss Browns in the High Street, sitting before us in the best seats —and they would not make room for us, though they knew very well who we were. A great many people put themselves forward who have not done half so much for the charity as we have."—"Dear, yes," said Charlotte, "and I had such a vulgar woman next me—she would speak to me, and I was quite afraid lest people should think I knew her."— "And, mamma, the three Miss Blacks were there— their servants were in such gay liveries—it made me feel ashamed of John's old clothes. Julia Black was very rude to me—but I took care to be quite as rude to her—for I think myself of as much consequence as she is."—"Lady Buff was there—I wish we could have gotten up to speak to her—people must have thought we belonged to nobody."

"Those who knew you, had no occasion to think, my dear: and those who did not, are not of much consequence to you. But you have not told me what you heard."

"O, we heard a great deal of good—I wonder my cousin Whites were not there—much better for them than going to balls—it was a very interesting meeting; but there were not so many people of consequence there as last year—these things always go off. There were some excellent speeches—it vexed me to hear that disagreeable man who was so rude to us once at the committee, so very much applauded—I quite hate that man; but he made by far the most sensible and religious speech."

To that connexion of ideas, which, on the repetition of a single word, brings back to memory all with which it has sometime been associated, it was, doubtless, owing, that I, at this moment, thought of pomps, and delusions, and inconformities — and self-subjection, and meekness, and humility—and love of approbation, and fear of opinion, and rivalry, and contention; and a great many other things that had not much to do with the dinner we were eating, or the meeting we were talking of. Had Mrs White been there, a part of her doubts had been solved at least—for though she had not learned what it was of the world the Miss Greys' religion taught them to renounce, she had certainly discovered what it was not. Is it the practice of the world, or its spirit, that stands most opposed to religion? Avails it any thing to renounce the one and keep the other? I saw no CONSISTENCY between the morning's discourse and the evening's, except in volubility of speech.

I was visiting lately a friend in the country; a rational good sort of woman; the queen, by long established courtesy, of a populous village, where nobody thought themselves of more consequence

than herself. She had been a very happy woman
all her life, and might have continued so to the end
of it, had she not been disturbed by the conduct
of her neighbours, and certain disorders that had
broken out in the village. All Lady Betty Ball's
sorrows grew out of her warm attachment to the
Church of England, and very susceptible aversion
to every thing that looked like a departure from its
rules, or a dissent from its opinions. Some of her
neighbours, and even the curate of the parish himself, were beginning to disturb her peace by mani-
festing most dangerous symptoms of dissent. The
former, in spite of her opposition, persisted in teaching grown people to read, and collecting children
into Sunday Schools — means directly tending to
make sectarians of them. Some had even gone so
far as to read the Bible to the sick and dying poor,
and draw their attention to the eternal world — a
dangerous encroachment on the rights of the established ministry. Nay, such was the spirit of dissent amongst them, it was becoming a common
thing to hear religion spoken of in society, and
theological subjects discussed at table. But what
could stay the infection, when the minister himself
had caught it, and actually took part in a Bible
Society, refused to go to the Assembly-rooms, and
administered the sacramental emblems to three or
four people at a time, without reading the appointed
words to each one separately? Then the poor—
the very poor—had come into the work of subver-

sion: she had heard with her own ears a day-labourer singing Toplady's hymns as he sat at dinner under a haystack: and she had seen with her own eyes a washerwoman reading a tract, as she paused to rest her bundle on a milestone by the roadside. The ringing of the church-bells on a Thursday evening totally suspended her appetite—on a Wednesday or Friday, provided it were at eleven o'clock, and there were no sermon, it was not observed to have the same effect. Lady Betty had great respect for the authorised version of the Scriptures in proper time and place: for instance—any part of it on the Sunday, or the Proper Lessons on any day—but if she chanced to see a Bible in the kitchen window that looked as if it had moved since Sunday, or in her children's hands after their lesson had been said, the spectre of dissent rose immediately to her afflicted vision, and her concern for the Establishment took no rest till she had suppressed the innovation. To hum a psalm-tune on a week day, to like an extempore sermon, to refuse a game of cards, or to be shocked at the use of an accidental oath, were things she held especially, and about equally, dangerous to the Church—the friend who was convicted of either lost her esteem, and the servant who was suspected of either lost her confidence.

Partly from participation in her love of the Church, and partly from the tenderness I always have for the honest zeal that takes fright even at the bugbears of its own imagination when they seem

to endanger the thing it loves, I should have felt a
great deal for Lady Betty's sorrows, had I not observed there were times and circumstances in which
her respect for the Church, and its decisions, and
its wisdom, was considerably abated. The established religion has appointed the celebration of the
Sabbath, and enjoins on its members to attend those
appointments strictly—it orders all secular affairs to
be suspended—the sale of the necessaries of life to
be forborne—the unnecessary labour of man and
beast dispensed with—the amusements of the idle,
as well as the toils of the industrious, to be superseded by public manifestations of religious reverence, and private exercise of devotion. Lady Betty
was of another mind : she could make a better use
of this day than that to which the Church has assigned it. It was the best day of the seven for
travelling, because there were fewer things on the
road, and there was not much else to be done—except the occupations to which the Church devoted it,
and they were of no consequence. She would go
to the morning service, and so might her children,
if there was nothing to prevent—that is, if there
had not fallen a shower in the night to make it
damp ; or there was not a cloud in the heavens that
might produce a shower by and by ; or she had not
slept too late to be ready within ten minutes after
the bells had done ringing. Two services are or-
dered ; but she held the second altogether superfluous—the carriage, and of course the horses, and of
course the servants, were always required at three

o'clock for her customary drive. She liked orthodox religion in inferior people, provided always it
did not interfere with the orthodox irreligion—that
is to say, the convenience of their superiors. She
did not disapprove of her servants going to church—
but it was seldom convenient to spare them. Articles
were purchased from her tradespeople on Sunday—
the law is otherwise, but it was convenient. Persons
were employed to fetch things, and carry things,
and do things, on the Sabbath, in direct opposition
to the law's command that they should be at church:
but this too was convenient. The Church has
issued a Catechism for the instruction and guidance
of the young, and Lady Betty's children were most
carefully taught it, and made to repeat it—but they
were not taught, nor indeed allowed, to follow or
believe it. Their mother would have thought them
very superstitious had they feared the influence of
an evil spirit, and very methodistical had they expected the influence of a good spirit; she would
have been much vexed had they grown up with a
contempt for the vanities of life to which she reared
them, or a distaste for the pomps and splendours
she taught them to aspire to. The articles of the
Christian faith, as explained by the Church, she
would not allow to be so much as named before
them, lest it should put odd notions into their
heads; and in respect to the keeping of all God's
commandments—that might be very well, according
to her own interpretation of them, but not according to that of the Church, given in the Catechism:

for they were by precept and example taught to consider their own advantage first, their neighbour's benefit second, and God's requirements last. They were to obey lawful authorities when it was dangerous or disreputable to do otherwise—but to circumvent the law, to evade it, or furtively to defraud the revenue, were daily practices. They might not tell a lie, so called ; but they were taught to tell as many indirect ones, by false representations, false excuses, false politeness, as might suit their purpose : and in respect to slander, evil-speaking, unkind and malevolent feelings, if they were ever checked in these, it was only because children should not be encouraged in them : daily proof was before their eyes. that when they ceased to be children, there would be no harm in these things. The Church has appointed certain times for the celebration of the Lord's Supper, and earnestly exhorts her members to be present there, and duly to receive it. Here Lady Betty dissents again — she can only attend once a-year, or when she happens to have a leisure week—that is, a week free from common engagements, to prepare herself for the ceremony. In opinions it were endless to trace out the differences—the Church teaches her perpetually to repeat in public, that she is a ruined and corrupted creature, needing the interference of divine grace to reconcile her to God, and make her meet for eternity—but she insists in private that she is a good sort of a person, and that her acquaintance are very good, and nobody is in need of conversion but papists and pagans, and nobody in need of repentance but drunkards and pickpockets.   In short, I could not be long with Lady Betty, without perceiving that she dissents from the Established Church in opinion, in practice, in every thing : and therefore is not consistent in her fears for it.

"Mamma," said little Julia to her mother, one of my intimate friends, " what is the reason you would not let us play at cards last night, when we wanted to amuse our little party—you let the boys play at marbles—I should like to understand the difference?"

" The difference," replied my friend, " is almost too nice for you to perceive—yet there is a difference, and perhaps I can make you understand it. Marbles is the game of our childhood, and in no danger of becoming the passion of our later years. It is also a game of skill and not of chance; what we win, therefore, is in some sense earned, and consequently ours ; which it is not honestly, when we come into possession by the chances of the game.   I should, however, object to playing at marbles, or any thing else, for money, lest it should induce a love of gambling that would soon transfer itself to other ventures. Cards are generally played for money.   They might be a most innocent amusement in childhood, were there no danger of their becoming the taste of the woman, and were there nothing to be won or lost by the game."

"But what, mamma," said the little girl, "is the harm of winning or losing?"

"If you win, what you gain is not honestly yours—you neither earn it, nor deserve it, nor receive it as a voluntary gift—it is not therefore a lawful possession. The law of man does not consider it so, since the gamester is not obliged to pay his debts; and the law of God, I believe, would still less consider it so. This appears a small matter, while the sum is small—but there is no limit to a moral maxim of this sort—a little and a little added, and the sum becomes a large one. The yet greater evil is the feeling excited while you play—the eagerness, the anxiety, the temper, the impatience, and the ultimate vexation—it is impossible to see a party of children play at cards for money, and not perceive these effects, even more obviously than among elder people, because they have less control over their emotions to suppress or conceal them. All these unnatural stimulants to passions, these morbid stirrings of the spirits, are destructive to the simple, calm, and innocent delights of childhood, and creative of a desire for excitation, which the duties and ordinary enjoyments of after life are scarcely likely to supply. I had the same reason for not allowing you to put your money into the raffle. I considered that the feeling of pleasure which would attend your winning, or of pain in losing, would be equally injurious to the mind it acted on, as arising from no legitimate cause of pain and pleasure: besides that the desire of winning—and if there were no desire to win, there would be no pleasure in playing—must be gratified at the cost of your antagonist. A most dangerous taste to cultivate, is the desire of succeeding at another's cost, and that without any superior merit or exertion of our own."

Here the conversation ended. I thought the mother's remarks very sensible and just, and indisputably applicable to the years of childhood, whatever they might be later: but a surprise awaited me. I had been invited by my friend to accompany her the following day to the school at which her elder daughters were educating, to be present at the distribution of prizes. As some of my readers have inferred, from my former remarks on the subject, that I disapprove of prizes altogether, I may take this opportunity of assuring them I do not. Reward is the natural fruit of merit, and I would have it ever be its attendant. In a school or elsewhere, I would have each one rewarded according to their merit. But it should be their abstract, not their comparative success—a prize for reaching some given point, not for outstripping, without effort, a less competent but as willing competitor. This by the way—for what I went to see is by no means to the point.

When we had passed the stone wall and iron gate by which the corruptions of the world are supposed to be excluded from minds not sufficiently matured to resist them, we were shown into the hall of this mansion of education, already crowded with the young

candidates for honour or reward—as yet I know
not which. They wore their gayest dress, and the
apartment was decked as for festivity; but it did
not strike me that the countenances, as I examined
them successively, wore exactly a festive aspect—
there was an expression of painful anxiety in most,
and in those that had an air of confident gaiety, it
did not seem to sit altogether easy. There was not
one among them I could have selected as the picture
of conscious merit waiting its reward. I began to
apprehend that, by some strange mischance, not
one among them thought she could make good her
claim. The ceremony began, and the names of many
were called in succession. As each young lady heard
her own, a vivid expression of pleasure passed over
her features, but they soon resumed the previous
expression of anxiety: while those who did not hear
their names, changed their air of doubt to one of
sullen despondency. I begged to know the meaning
of this proceeding, and was informed that those
whose names were not called, had, on previous examination, been found undeserving to be admitted as
competitors for reward. Nothing could be more
just than that those who had merited no recompense
should expect none, and receive none—though I did
not perceive why they should have been kept to this
time in ignorance of their exclusion; the harassment
of uncertainty and suspense not being considered
particularly good for the susceptible spirits of childhood. The more deserving competitors were now

numbered, and an equal number of ornamented cards
were put into a most portentous bag of bright blue
satin.   Now again I was a little puzzled : there were
fifteen ladies of this non-excluded class—they were
of different ages, and most likely of very different
attainments—but to all appearance they must be of
exactly equal merit, for the same bag received all
the cards, and the cards that went into the bag were
all alike.   As my old trick of listening could avail
me nothing, where the most profound and suspensive
silence prevailed, I was obliged to betake myself to
guessing how this could be.   My best conjecture was,
that to avoid all rivalship, every deserving pupil was
to have a prize proportioned to her individual merit,
and that, though my eye could not perceive it, there
must be written on each card the name of a lady,
and the prize adjudged to her.   It is true I did not
exactly see how these decrees of justice were to find
their way out of the blue satin bag into the fingers
of the rightful possessor ; unless Merlin, or Kater-
felto, or some other of the conjuring tribe, were
hidden at the bottom of it, while each in succession
thrust in her little hand.   What was my surprise
when, out of fifteen ladies who had been pronounced deserving of reward for their improvement in
music, the occasion of this first lottery, one only
gained the prize—not by merit, or talent, or industry,
superior to her competitors, but by the accident of
putting her fingers on the right card—while all the
rest, though judged deserving of reward, were to

suffer the disappointment of excited expectation, and see another enjoy the recompense to which their own claim had been admitted equal, and perhaps was known to be superior! I need not describe the repeated ceremony—one after another the lotteries went on—for each different branch of education. I turned to my friend when the ceremony concluded, and asked her how she could suffer the minds of her children to be thus acted upon—their feelings thus senselessly excited—the very spirit and essence of gaming thus instilled? She said it was the custom of the school; and she had never thought of any harm there could be in it. I reminded her of the conversation of the preceding evening with her little Julia, and remarked on the inconsistency of her keen perception of danger in the one case, with her blind insensibility to it in the other. For my own part, this system seemed to me such an outrage upon common sense, that on any evidence but fact, I could not have believed any rational governess could invent, or any careful parent suffer, such a practice. When all was over, I made especial inquiry into the results ; and I found one girl, whom I knew to be by no means the best, laden with prizes, exultingly setting off to her home to exhibit proofs of an advancement she had not made, and display her triumph over companions she had by no means equalled. I saw another, an industrious, clever girl, going off, with tearful eyes and saddened spirits, without a single testimony of good conduct or recompense of exertion; though she had been worthy of drawing for every prize, and of all the school had best deserved to be so.

We contemn the wisdom of our ancestors, who, when they could not decide the merits of a cause, referred it to the decision of Heaven by some superstitious ordeal. Do the ladies who superintend these schools really believe that fortune will respect the merits of their pupils, and do they so intend to teach them? Or—more probable result, and yet more dangerous lesson for their after-life—do they mean to teach them that success goes by hap, and not by merit; that it is *better to be lucky than wise;* that to win a prize is easier than to earn it? We doubt not that many of our readers who are not in these secrets, will think the practice so strange a one, we need not to have spoken so much about it. I should have thought so too, did I not know that it is practised by some governesses, and suffered by many parents, who, I believe, act under the influence of the best moral feeling, and the purest religious principle, in the management of the children committed to their care, and would by no means suffer them to receive such impressions under any other form.

No. XX

MORE INCONSISTENCIES.

Qu'attendons nous des hommes? Ils sont foibles, inconstants, aveugles : les uns ne veulent pas ce qu'ils peuvent, les autres ne peuvent pas ce qu'ils veulent. La nature est un roseau cassé; si on veut appuyer dessus, le roseau plie, ne peut nous soutenir, et nous perce la main.

Fénélon.

Mr Listener,

Having observed with much concern the ill success of your researches after Consistency, and felt a growing impatience that the portrait was not produced, it came into my mind that I might assist you in the search, happening to be intimate with a family who are continually speaking of it, and that after the manner of a familiar acquaintance. The word being perpetually on their lips, I could not doubt but they were well acquainted with the thing, and perhaps could afford the very information you had sought so far in vain. Anxious now as ever to assist you, I proposed myself a short residence among them, not liking to expose my ignorance by directly asking for the information I wanted. Nothing could be more promising than the first aspect of things. With the first breath I drew in their abode, I seemed to inhale a love of this unknown— and so contagious is example, that before many days had elapsed, I found it impossible to express myself on any subject without using the word. It is a delightful word—it will do for any thing—with the help of a small negation it will stand for sin, or folly, or falsehood, or treachery, or caprice, or infidelity, or any thing within the whole compass of moral defectibility. Whenever a fool committed folly, we said he was not consistent—when the false-hearted did one thing and professed another, we said they were not consistent—when the selfish betrayed their friends to serve themselves, we said they were not consistent—in short, whenever a sinner, under any form, committed sin, we said he was not consistent. I was delighted—for, in all the languages I had learned, I never found a word so universally applicable. But most of all was it valuable to designate those nameless discrepancies in our friends which all are quick to perceive, but no one can readily describe. We were no slanderers, and would not for worlds have said those who did not please were false, or ignorant, or disagreeable, or any thing that perhaps they might not be—but we could always say they were Inconsistent, without danger of contradiction: and we did say so of every one who had the misfortune to come within our observation. In one respect, at least, we obeyed the spirit of the Christian precept—for we treated our enemies in this matter to the full as well as our friends. Among the abundant examples and countless uses of this term, I know not where to select for your information—any instance I may give you can be but one of thousands.

We were just rid of some evening visitors with whom we had spent several hours in the rapid interchange of most polite discourse. They had said every thing that language can express, in praise of all that was in the house, or about the house, or within ken of any of the windows—and the ladies, my companions, had given back to the full, the measure they had meted. If they said our drawings or fancy works were beautiful, we said they were nothing in comparison with theirs: if they praised our music, we were surprised that they, who were used to so much better, should be so very kind as to listen to it. We said their children were the largest, and their dogs the smallest, and their jewels the brightest, and their words the wisest, in the known world—for any thing I knew, it might be so, for they were strangers to me. As soon as they were gone, Miss Sarah said, with a sigh, "What dreadful flatterers those people are—and they swallow it as willingly as they bestow it! There is no way of pleasing them, but by the grossest compliments. They are very false: I know exactly what they mean when they admire any thing—they only want you to say that something of theirs is better. I make a point of saying so directly, because I know they will be disappointed if I do not."

"Are they very superior people?" I asked

"Oh, by no means: they understand nothing: they praise every thing and every body alike: they think flattery must please others because it pleases them, and they bestow it as liberally as they desire it."

"There is, at least, good-nature in the intention."

"If they were more consistent in their good-nature; but they will not continue to praise us in our absence, I doubt."

"If they do," thought I, "we shall have better than requital at their hands:" but we were quite agreed that it was inconsistent to flatter people in their presence, and speak ill of them the moment they were gone.

"I wish," said Matilda, one morning, with reference to a lady who had just made her first visit at the house—"I wish Miss N.'s conduct were more consistent. If I knew nothing of her, I should be greatly taken with her manner and conversation this morning: I should really think her very sensible and serious "——

"And how do you know she is not?" I asked, interrupting her.

"One can only judge the tree by its fruits; and her conduct is so very inconsistent."

"In what way do you mean?"

"I really do not exactly know; I have very little acquaintance with her; I have avoided it, because I think such people dangerous: but I have heard many things of her, not at all consistent with a religious character. It is very easy to talk and profess, but when one knows she does not mean what she says, there is danger in having the form of godliness without the power."

I admitted the justness of this remark, but still desired to know wherein Miss N. stood more exposed than others to this danger: for I had been much pleased with her conversation in the short visit she made us. Urged again, Matilda said Miss N. wore feathers, which she thought not consistent with the sobriety of dress that becomes a Christian —then she had heard she went into gay company; she did not know if it was true, but she supposed it was; she often saw her speaking to people of that sort—the Scriptures had required us not to be conformed to the fashions of the world. I thought the Scriptures had also commanded us not to speak evil one of another, nor to judge one another; but I did not make the remark.

"I have heard," continued Matilda—"I do not remember where I heard it—but I know I heard it from somebody—that she is not particularly strict in the observance of the Sabbath—it is impossible a person can be a child of God, and break his positive commandments."

I thought it was one of the positive commandments that we should not bear false-witness against our neighbours. But I made no remark, at this time not quite agreeing with my friend; for, if Matilda did not know what she said to be false, she did not know it to be true; and if it was true, she had only assumed what she began with asserting, that Miss N. professed what she did not mean. How did Matilda know what Miss N. professed? In our recent conversation, confessedly the first she had ever had with her, I am certain she had not professed not to wear feathers, or not to go into company; and, supposing Matilda did not profess to speak no evil, and bear no false-witness, I considered that, however wrong I might regard them, both or either, I could not well apply to them my favourite word—a great disappointment to me.

Seated at tea in the balcony of our house, we were conversing one evening on a melancholy occurrence in a family of the neighbourhood, in which a young person had been reduced to a state of deep and morbid melancholy, by the effects of long-protracted anxiety, ending in severe and remediless affliction. It came to be considered, in the course of conversation, how far such a result was consistent with religious submission to the will of Heaven. It was very sapiently proved, that, by a mind entirely detached from the things of earth, the loss of earthly things could not consistently be felt—that a mind entirely trusting in the wisdom and power

of God, could not consistently suffer from anxiety—
that a mind totally acquiescent in the will of God,
could not consistently feel regret at the dispensa-
tions of Providence—and, above all, that where no
loss, or anxiety, or regret could be felt, the mind
could not consistently be deranged by them. These
were truths beyond all controversy, and we were
thence successfully going on to deduce the inconsistency of this helpless sufferer in particular, and
of every body else in general, ourselves excepted,
when the rolling of distant thunder in the horizon
announced a coming storm, called off our attention, and turned the conversation. The storm arose.
The young ladies became desperately frightened—
they did not know for what, but lest some harm
should happen to themselves, or somebody, or something that belonged to them. When I endeavoured
to soothe them by assurance that no ill would happen, they grew angry. How could I be sure of
that? 'Lightning often kills people—wind often
blows houses down—people sometimes lose their
eyes or their hearing in a thunder-strom—in short,
they thought it quite wicked not to be frightened
when there was danger, and distressed when there
might be suffering, to others, if not to ourselves.
The storm subsided—but not so the fears. They
had now, indeed, a definite object; very considerable damage was supposed to have been done on a
distant part of the coast, where they had property,
and they might possibly be very material losers by

the accident. Gloom, fretfulness, and anxiety pervaded the house through all that night and the succeeding day. With the hopefulness generally experienced by the uninterested spectator of others' anxieties, I represented to them every probability or possibility, reasonable or unreasonable, that their property might not have been injured—but they persisted in expecting the worst, in rejecting all palliations of the possible mischief. They would not eat—they would not sleep—they would not divert their minds by employment, or relieve themselves by conversation : and when they thought they perceived in me an opinion that they showed more uneasiness than was warranted by a yet uncertain ill, and more impatience under an imagined loss, than might have been reasonable even under a known one, they observed, that to be less anxious than they were, would be unnatural, insensible, impossible—in short, inconsistent with common sense. It did not happen to us at that time to renew the conversation of the balcony—of minds detached from earth—of trust that could not be shaken—of acquiescence that could not be moved—of that self-possession, in short, that could not be disturbed in a devoted and well-regulated mind.

Among our intimate acquaintance, there was one young person whose liveliness of manner and buoyancy of spirits made her the life of her family and the zest of every company she happened to mix with. She went gaily and cheerfully about every task that circumstance or choice imposed; she spoke of every thing with playful vivacity, and did every thing with an air of confident expectation; meet her when you would, or where you would, there was always brightness in her eye, and a smile on her brow, and activity and enjoyment in her whole demeanour. We allowed that this was agreeable, we confessed great pleasure in her society—but we could not approve her character—it was not consistent for a Christian to be always so light-hearted. The pilgrim, the penitent, the culprit, the suppliant dependent on Almighty pity, the combatant struggling through unequal warfare, the prodigal as yet almost a stranger in his home, the meek, the mournful, and the broken-hearted—emblems by which the Deity has described his people—are characters, we said, that consist not with so much gaiety and lightness of spirits, such sanguine, cheerful, fearless animation.

There was another, on whose brow the shade of pensiveness for ever sat supreme—she seemed to be always feeling, one might have said, always suffering—if there ever came a smile on her features, it was gone, ere you could be sure you saw it there—if there ever escaped from her a word of jest, the sigh came so quickly after, you felt forbidden to remark it: the liquid eye, and changeful colour, spoke intensity of feeling—but even in her feeling there was a stillness imperturbable—in her very pleasures, if she knew any, there was a tone of melancholy. Her affectionate softness we felt was

lovely, her gentle sadness interesting; we could
even have loved her, had we not seen her so very
inconsistent. A Christian who professes, as we supposed she did, to have found a real and substantial
bliss in grateful anticipation of eternal joy, ought
never to be melancholy—habitual sadness, an air
of habitual suffering, was not consistent with the
security, and peace, and joy, offered in the Gospel
to the believer, and professedly accepted by him.

There was a third person, whose busy, bustling,
babbling nature, happily set in motion by a disposition to good, was for ever talking, and for ever
doing; from sunrise to sunset, she was to be seen
in motion—assisting every body, exhorting every
body, teaching every body—sometimes laden with
books to give away, sometimes with work to be
done or clothes to be bestowed; her tables were
strewed with tracts and baby-linen—her basket was
filled with conserves and cough-mixtures—nobody
could live without her assistance, nobody could die
without her administration—it almost seemed that
nobody could go to heaven without her guidance.
The days were too short for what she had to do—
the hours were not long enough for what she had to
say; her busy head was always devising something
—her bustling step was always pursuing something
—her rapid finger was always making something—
her tongue outstripped them all; and of all, good
was the object, and benevolence the motive. Her
name was written in every record of humanity, and

sounded on every tongue, and engraven, doubtless, in many a grateful heart—but we did not like her, because she was not, as we said, altogether consistent—while engaged so much abroad, domestic piety was overlooked—while hurried up and down in perpetual activity of benevolence, private devotion must be neglected; there could be no time for reading or reflection; the religion of the closet was of more avail than all this bustle, and more consistent with the genuine spirit of the Gospel.

A fourth friend we had of an opposite character. She was never to be found taking part in the institutions of benevolence, or joining in public exertions for the propagation of truth. She was not known as the instructor of the ignorant, or the comforter of the afflicted; she was not known to belong to institutions or societies; she was very seldom heard to speak upon religion, and was very seldom seen in religious society. In private only might her piety be detected—in the peace and holiness that reigned in her family—the devotion that seemed to have its favourite dwelling in her closet—the silent study of the truth—the firm abiding by its precepts—the regulation of her temper by its laws—the tone, in short, of her whole feelings, habits, and desires, perceived though untold, betrayed rather than exhibited. It was necessary to know her intimately to perceive all this—we knew it, but it did not please us. If she was pious in heart. and devoted in private, why did she not come forward? Why did she not join with others of like feelings, and do as they do? It was not consistent that one who really loved the truth, should be supinely indifferent about its propagation—one who really feels must talk and act, must be anxious to impart what she knows and disclose what she enjoys: a barren and unproductive faith, so difficult to discover, and so fruitless, could not be consistent Christianity.

There was a fifth, whom birth and circumstances had accustomed to all the elegances and luxuries of life. A refined mind, a cultivated taste, and delicate habits, all conspired to make these things valuable and needful to her; and it was evident they were valued and enjoyed. She was nice in her dress, expensive in her establishment, stylish in the arrangements of her household. Her we condemned at once: so much indulgence and display, and care for things exterior, were not consistent with humility, self-denial and renunciation of the world.

A sixth, who, in a station of equal elevation and with equal means, was neglectful of appearances, homely in her habits, indifferent to the distinctions of society, whether from inclination, or from conscientious self-abasement, received from us no kinder judgment. It was not consistent in people of rank to look like housemaids, to live like peasants, to contravene the arrangements of Providence, by levelling the distinctions of rank and circumstance.

These, and such as these, are but instances of our ample success, in finding all our neighbours guilty of Inconsistency. In the full enjoyment of these discoveries, there came athwart me, Mr Listener, the recollection of your paper almost forgotten, and of my wish to help you. After all our talk about Consistency, and the want of Consistency, and the beauty of Consistency, where was the idea the word had stood for? Within me, and around me, I began to search for it. In my own mind, I could find nothing like an idea upon the subject—I had applied the word so indiscriminately to such a heterogeneous multitude of things, from the careless dropping of an unweighed word to the crime of grossest malignity, it was impossible for any one definition, or any one idea, to comprehend the whole. Around me—alas! in reiterating the charge of inconsistency on others, had we not amply proved it in ourselves?

No. XXI.

CONSISTENCY.

Dès qu'on se met à négocier avec les circonstances, tout est perdu, car il n'est personne qui n'ait des circonstances. La leçon qu'il importe le plus de donner aux hommes dans ce monde, c'est de ne transiger avec aucune consideration quand il s'agit du devoir.

DE STAËL.

MY readers may, I fear, become weary of a subject that has loitered unsuccessfully through three or four papers, with no better result than that of proving, what might scarcely need a proof, that a great many people talk of what they do not understand, or reproach others with the wrongs themselves unwittingly commit. Lest this should be, I propose, like other narrators, to tack a moral to my tale, by way of conclusion, and so abandon it. My object was not, as may have seemed, to prove every body in the wrong, but rather to exhibit the various modes of inconsistency; that, perceiving it and applying it, each one may correct their own. Some have said, Why expose the faults and inconsistencies of those whose principles are good, and bring on religion the reproach of all the inconsistencies of those who profess it? Let the shame be to the creature, and the glory to the Creator—what is good in us is His, what is evil is our own. But if it be true that these things exist, and that they are inconsistencies, shall we say—shall we leave it to others to say for us—that what, in the careless and the earthly-minded, we should condemn as faults, in those who profess more seriousness and devotion, we can gloss over and disown? It was said of one of old, that it was easier to believe that drunkenness was not a vice, than that he should be guilty of one. Far be from Christianity the adoption of so heathenish a principle! Rather say the spot is the blacker for the brightness of the surface on which it is seen—the stain the darker for the purity of the garment it pollutes: it seems so, and it is so. If we are ashamed of it, as well indeed we may, let us efface it, clean it, wipe it out—but not deny that it is there, or that it is what it seems. Christians think not themselves, they think not each other, sinless creatures. Should they desire to pass their alloy upon the world as pure and proven gold? But they say it is for the honour of religion, not their own, that they are so tenacious of the exposure of their faults. We are glad if it is so—but we would rather have this pious tenaciousness exercised in correcting the evils than in glossing them over, in lamenting than in denying them. So much, by the way, in reply to some remarks that have been made to us.

We hear of the beauty of Consistency; we repeat

perpetually, because we hear it, that nothing is so beautiful as a consistent character; but what does it mean? The sinner's consistency, alas! is sin—the false heart's consistency is falsehood—the villain's consistency is villany; but is this beautiful? It is a very common argument in the world, or rather a phrase that supplies the place of one, that it does not signify what religion a man professes, or what faith he holds, provided his conduct be consistent. Consistent with what? His errors? His perversions? That, alas! it is but too sure to be. The man who believes there is no God, is consistent when he breaks his laws, and sets his asserted power at defiance. The man who believes that there is no eternity, is consistent when he devotes himself to the things of time and sense; and is but the more consistent as he becomes more sensual. He whose perverted judgment and corrupted taste prefer the pleasures of sin to the peace of holiness, the interests of time to the bliss of eternity, is consistent when he takes the one and leaves the other—is consistent when he commits sin, is consistent when he defends it. The basest character on earth may be a consistent one. There cannot, therefore, be a more dangerous maxim; and I name it the rather as my young friends will hear it frequently repeated by the wise and prudent of the world.

A consistent character must certainly be that, which, having chosen the object of existence, employs the powers of existence to the attainment of that object: and in each particular, having formed a purpose, to do and to be what will promote that purpose. The inconsistency of the greater number of persons arises from their having conscience enough, and moral sense enough, to perceive what their object ought to be, and to determine their choice for good; while they have neither sense enough, nor virtue enough, to pursue it: and so the means and the end are for ever at variance, and the strangest inconsistencies are the result.

The world in general—I mean the decent and moral part of it, for the outlawed rioter in mischief we must leave to the full credit of his consistency—confess an end and object of existence which they do not pursue. We thus act exactly like a traveller, who, wishing to go to Greenwich, should, on reading the way-posts that direct him thither, turn off to the other hand, and proceed to London: of such a traveller we should say that either he could not read, or that he wanted understanding, or that he did not really desire to go to the place he professed to set out for. And so we may say in effect of all the inconsistencies of life and conduct—they arise in ignorance, misjudgment, or dishonesty.

I will illustrate my meaning by a few examples—not of the most important, perhaps, for it is not in great matters that we make the most mistakes—it is the familiar occurrences of daily life that make up the character and conduct of persons in ordinary life. When symptoms of physical disorder are to be

cured, the cause of those symptoms must be discovered and removed : so, when discrepancies of conduct
and inconsistency of character are to be corrected,
the better way is to proceed at once to the source
whence they spring : we all know by experience
how difficult it is to correct bad habits ; perhaps
the difficulty would be lessened, if, instead of attempting to cure the manifestation of the evil, we
were to descend into our hearts, see whence it arises,
and subdue the disposition there. The best method
of correcting our inconsistencies is to become better
acquainted with our own hearts, whence all our
conduct is derived. If it is with the conduct of
others we have to do, whether to judge or to correct,
the success of our endeavours, and the justness of
our judgment, mainly depend on looking beyond the
apparent inconsistency to its cause, and ascribing it
to its right source. Want of information, or a bad
judgment, claim very unequal censure, as well as a
very different remedy, from that which is due to
dishonesty of purpose.

I know a young person to whom circumstances
have given considerable control in her parents' house
—she devotes time and talents to the management
and education of her sisters, and says she has nothing so much at heart as their happiness and improvement. To effect this, she keeps the house in
perpetual contention—she makes their wishes and
tastes yield in every thing to hers—she finds fault
with every thing they do, complains of every thing

that happens to interrupt her purposes, condemns every thing that does not exactly meet her ideas— reasonable or unreasonable, nothing must take place in the family that does not exactly suit her convenience, and what does suit her convenience must be done at any rate. One of two things is the case— either she is dishonest in her purpose, and, while she seems to devote her time and attention to her family, she really desires nothing but the indulgence of her own self-will; or she wants judgment to perceive that always giving herself the preference is not the way to make others good and happy; and that the devotion of all her time, talents, and powers, to the annoying, contradicting, and molesting every one about her, is not a very consistent sort of sisterly devotion. If I were not indisposed to say any thing to any body above twenty years of age, I might just drop a hint that there are some devoted wives, and devoted mothers, and devoted mistresses, who do exactly the same thing. Did this traveller never mean to go to Greenwich? Or, on arriving at the way-post, and reading, " To London," did she conclude that that would bring her there?

I know another who seems very anxious to be sought and beloved by her companions in society, complains perpetually that nobody cares for her and every body neglects her, and she receives no attention and no kindness from any one. Mean-time, if she sees those people whose inattention displeases her, she goes across the street to avoid meeting them:

when she comes into company, she sits in dogged and sullen silence; or only speaks to declare that she hates all company, and is never happy but when she is alone, or to say something rude or impertinent to the society in general, or to some one in particular: if any offer of kindness is made her, she refuses it; if any particular attention is paid her, she attributes it to some sinister motive. Now, as I am satisfied from this lady's uneasiness that she is honest in her wish to be beloved, she must either, like the last traveller, think the way to reach her destination is to turn out of the road, or she must be unable to read, and really believe that L-o-n-d-o-n spells Greenwich — that is, she must think the way to be desired and sought in society, is to be very disagreeable, or that d-i-s-l-i-k-e-d really spells beloved, and so, with honest ignorance, takes the way to it.

A third I could point out, who desires, as I understand from herself, to improve her talents and inform her mind, that, when the transient beauty of her person shall have passed, and the zest of exterior amusements shall have passed, she may not be to others as a thing that has lost its value, to herself as one that has expended her possessions. But with ample powers and all means at command, she stands for an hour together at the fire-place, watching the reflection of the lustres—she begins to yawn at nine o'clock, and goes to bed at ten—is up, but not dressed, about the same hour in the morning—takes half an hour to put on her bonnet when she goes out, and another half hour, when she comes home, to take it off again; regretting, the while, that she has not time to improve herself. When any one about her is conversing upon serious and rational topics, she throws herself on the sofa and shuts her eyes, because she does not understand such things; forgetful that listening she might learn. When asked her opinion, or in any way addressed upon any subject, she says she is not used to converse of such things, she is not used to express herself, she wishes she were more clever; forgetting again it is difficult to be used to a thing one is determined not to attempt. She chooses her companions among those who are young, frivolous, and ignorant, because with those who are informed and sensible she feels herself inferior and embarrassed. In her studies and pursuits, especially reading, she does the same—she takes the lightest, the most frivolous, and the worst, because she cannot understand more solid works: she wishes she could understand them—then she should be very fond of reading. Now, really, I am at a loss how to class the inconsistency of this young lady—I am inclined to think she is not honest in her purpose—I believe, that in her heart, she likes London better than Greenwich—would rather be idle and frivolous, than a sensible, rational, and cultivated woman.

To ascend to higher matters, which yet affect our conduct in the smallest, there is one great source of inconsistency in the world, of which the features are too broad to be mistaken, of which the compass is wide enough to include every age, and character, and capability of human kind—the inconsistency of those who call themselves Christians and are not—who are travelling thither where they do not desire to arrive—who are going, as they say, to immortality, but neither know the road, nor ask it, nor will listen if you tell them: nay, there is not an obstacle that may oppose their progress, but they put it on their path—there is not a temptation that may divert them from it, but they hasten to turn after it; whatever reminds them of their pretended destination is mournful to them, whatever brings them nearer to it, is frightful. They allow the truth of every thing, and feel the importance of nothing—they admit the authority of Scripture, and deny every thing it contains—they call God their Father, and would be ashamed to bear the characters of his children—they acknowledge a Deity and an eternity, and live as if there were none. I need not designate them further. What consistency can be expected from such as these?

If, then, we would be consistent, we must first see that our object and our means of pursuing it, our path and our destination, are agreed. If they are not, let us examine where the evil is. Do we want information, do we want judgment, or do we want honesty? One or the other we want assuredly.

There is a character consistent in beauty, in holiness, in perfection. The features of it have been sketched, distinct though separate, in the records of eternal truth—the whole have been conjoined, embodied, realised, in the person of the incarnate Deity. Conformity to this standard is perfection — every departure from it is an imperfection — here perfect consistency would be perfect holiness. It is a standard no man has attained—yet it is the only one, consistency with which is desirable. When we seek consistency for ourselves, this ought to be what we mean—when we desire consistency in others, this ought to be the rule by which we judge them. But, I fear, for the most part, that is not our meaning. The only lawful code of conformity is abrogated; the only real standard of excellence, consistency with which is beautiful, and every inconsistency with which is a defect, is put out of sight; while we make to ourselves each one a standard of our own, moulded in our own prejudices, our own habits, our own peculiar taste and character; and by this we measure every thing, judge every thing, and too frequently condemn every body, for no better reason than because they are not like ourselves. In great things and in small things, from the important features of moral rectitude to the trifling ornaments of exterior propriety, Self is our standard, and all is right or wrong, admired or condemned, as it agrees with, or departs from, this standard, this household deity, that each one has made for himself, and fashioned to his own taste, that he may worship it.

Consistency, therefore, a word that in the language of Christianity should mean conformity to our Maker's will, has come, in common language, to mean little else than conformity to the narrow ideas of the individual who uses it.

No. XXII.

A FABLE.

O wad some power the giftie gie us,
To see oursells as others see us,
It wad frae mony a blunder free us
      And foolish notion!

                                    BURNS.

THE searcher after hidden wealth has sometimes found a treasure scarcely less valuable, though not the same as that he looked for. The blighted autumn leaf encloses a bud of future promise; and the hour of disappointment is the birth-time, not seldom, of a hope more fair than that which it extinguishes. Even so do the defeats of our baffled wisdom bequeath to us a jewel of no common price—a lesson of humility, self-knowledge, and forbearance.

Such was my reflection, as, in the closing sentence of my last paper, I alluded to that self-esteem which makes to itself an idol of the things that are its own, and desires to conform to them the things of others. And I determined to make it the subject of future admonition to those who even now are setting out on the passage of life, with these Penates in their bosoms; prepared to immolate to them every thing that is most lovely, most excellent, and most generous in human intercourse—justness, forbearance, concord, good-humour, kindness, liberality, affection, harmony, and peace.

An opposition of interests, each one's selfishness taking arms in defence of its own, is undoubtedly the source of much of the misery of life, and much of the contention with which it is distracted. But if we observe the various sources of disunion and disagreement that break the peace of families and the harmony of society, we shall find that opposing interests are not the only, nor perhaps the most frequent cause. We see the members of a family teasing, contradicting, and annoying one another perpetually, when all their real interests are in common: we see the members of society traducing, despising, and maligning one another, when it is the interest of all to live in sociability and peace. One very fruitful source of these disorders—but I would believe, not one that is irremediable, since a better knowledge and better government of our own hearts might surely correct it—is that self-esteem of which I spoke; that making of our own ideas the standard of all excellence. Hear a fable:—

The beasts of the earth, and the birds of the air, and the fishes of the sea, were living once — I do not think it was in Noah's ark—in peaceful community together; that is, they might have been peaceful if they would; being all fully provided, and secure in possession of their own.

But peace, it appears, was not to their mind. The Rein-deer, taking a walk one day to refresh himself, and being accustomed then, as now, to walk upon four legs, met with a Heron, who, as every one knows, walks upon two. "Yonder is a fine bird," said the Rein-deer to himself, "but the fellow is a blockhead; why does he not go on as many legs as I do?—I'll e'en knock him over, to convince him of his mistake;" and forthwith he ran his sturdy sides against the slender limbs of the bird; and if he did not break them, it was no fault of his.

A frolicsome Colt, playing his morning gambols, happened to come up to a young Bullock, entangled by his horns in a thicket, who, with groans and cries, solicited assistance to release him. "By no means," said the Colt; "it is your own fault. What need you be wearing those things upon your head —don't you see that we have none?" and kicking up his hoofs in the poor captive's face, he galloped off.

A Magpie, wishing to improve the society of the neighbourhood, sent an invitation to some Black-birds, to dine with him in a certain wheat-field, where, at much expense no doubt, a dinner of newly sown corn had been provided. The Blackbirds came in a full suit of black—the Magpie was dressed, as usual, in black and white; which, when the Blackbirds saw, great whisperings began amongst them. What a vulgar fellow!—how monstrously unfashionable!—could he not see that every body wears black ?—they wished they had not come; they gulped down the corn, half-choking with ill-humour; two of them died that night of indigestion ; the rest would ever after endure the pangs of hunger rather than alight in a field where a Magpie was feeding.

A certain Crab, cast upon the shore by the tide, and eager to regain his native element, was walking, as was his custom, sideways to the water's edge. By the way he met with an Eel in the same predicament; but he, like most other people, travelled with his head foremost. "I do not see, sir," said the Eel, " why you should refuse to conform to the customs of the world and the habits of society—therefore I will thank you to turn about, and walk like other people." The Crab maintained his right to walk as he pleased, more especially, as it was the only way he could walk. The Eel persisted. A quarrel ensued — mean-time, the tide went out, and neither party, backward or forward, being able to reach the water, they were left to die of thirst upon the sand.

" Hear those creatures," said a pretty little Thrush, who, just finishing his morning song, had alighted on a bough that overhung a bee-hive—" would you believe they take that noise for music ? The tasteless creatures! and pretend to have a concert! How I hate pretension! I will shame them into silence;"—and forthwith the Thrush resumed his loudest song. The Bees, however, happening to have more taste for honey than music, a concert not in their thoughts, went buzzing on, totally unconscious of the rivalship they had excited. The Thrush grew wroth—they were actually trying to out-sing him—that was not to be borne—and down he pounced upon the Bees, as one by one they soared above their hive, and struck them to the ground with his beak: they trying in vain to pierce his close feathers with their sting — though some historians are of opinion he did not escape altogether unhurt.

"Pray, sir," said a Goat to a Sheep, as they chanced to meet one day upon a narrow path of a declivity, but just wide enough to allow them to pass—"may I take the liberty of asking why you wear your hair curled, while I wear mine straight?" The Sheep, not remarkable for his reasoning powers, had no particular reason to give —it answered his purpose, and, if each was content with his own, there was no need of argument. The Goat thought otherwise — people ought to have reasons for what they do, and be able to explain the grounds of their conduct—and if they have not brains enough to discriminate, they ought to follow the example of those that have—therefore, to convince him that there was a reason why long loose hair was more advantageous than close curled wool,

he should take the liberty of putting his horns into
his fleece, and rolling him down the steep; which,
if he had worn hair, he could not so easily have
done.

It happened that a beautiful little Spaniel formed
a strong attachment to a certain Rabbit he was in
the habit of meeting in the beds of his master's
garden.   The Rabbit felt extremely much flattered
by the protection of so superior a person; but there
was one subject of difference between them that was
not easily to be adjusted.   The Spaniel assured the
Rabbit it was excessively vulgar to live upon vegetable diet—no rational creature did so—it was food
only for brutes —he hoped, now he had chosen the
Rabbit for his friend, he would try to acquire more
polite habits.   The Rabbit modestly suggested that,
besides that he had no teeth to masticate animal
food, and possibly no organ to digest it, he did not
exactly know how he was to get it.   The Spaniel
generously promised to remove the latter difficulty,
by sharing with him his own food—as to his teeth,
if he could not masticate the meat, he might swallow
it whole; it would save appearances, and nobody
would know whether he digested it or not.   The
ambitious Rabbit, eager to place himself on an
equality with his friend, and willing to imitate him
in every thing, most assiduously swallowed the meat
the Spaniel brought him; and, if he did not enjoy
his meals to the full as much as when he fed on
cabbages and parsley, the idea of growing more

genteel quite reconciled him to the privation. But, alas! nature prevailed, and poor Bunny died.

A Fly, who had been born and bred among his kindred, behind a drawing-room curtain, determined to go forth and see the world, and make himself better acquainted with the beings that inhabit it. On his return, he was observed to be morose and melancholy—he shut himself up in the creek of the ceiling, and could scarcely be persuaded to go out in search of necessary food. His friends, greatly concerned, questioned him upon the cause of this sadness; to which he only answered, that what he had seen of the world had so disgusted him, he was determined to have no more intercourse with it— he would rather stay in his creek and starve. His companions, who had seen nothing in society so much amiss, except a few Spiders, continued to express their surprise; till the poor fly explained, that during his recent intercourse with the world, he observed that the animals had the folly to wear their eyes in the front of their heads—of all the living creatures he had become acquainted with, there was not one, besides themselves, that could see behind him—he would sooner starve in solitude than associate with creatures so senseless; and he is supposed to have died of cold soon after; because he would not go to the hearth to warm himself, lest he should meet a creature without the eyes at the back of his head.

My readers, I am sure, must feel much affected

at the mournful state of society in the animal creation at that period; at sorrows that overwhelmed
alike the innocent and the guilty. I can imagine
that nothing, while they read it, stays their tears
from falling, but the hope that such a state of society never has existed. I cannot certainly pledge
myself to the historical truth of what I have related
—though it appears to me quite as probable as many
things that are believed—but I can assure you, I
have seen something very like it, in the state of
society among certain young ladies and gentlemen
of my acquaintance in various parts of the habitable
earth: I say *young* ones, more especially—because
it is an evil the experience and self-knowledge of
increasing years tend, in some degree, to correct.
But habit not unfrequently perpetuates what began
in folly; which makes it the more necessary that
early habits—habits to which ignorance and inexperience mostly tend—should be watched, and, as
far as may be, restrained; lest, confirmed by repetition, and become insensible to ourselves, the fault
remain when the excuse is gone.

Young persons, ignorant of the world and mostly
ignorant of themselves, receive from their parents
or their governess, or from the combined circumstances of their education, a certain set of opinions,
ideas, and habits—very good ones, perhaps; but
confined, as the sphere in which they are collected.
This set of notions is made into a standard of excellence, differing materially according to the differ-

ence of education—but every girl thinks her own standard the best, or rather the only one, for she knows no other; and she comes into society fully prepared to measure all and everything by her own set of notions. If to discover her mistake and correct it were the only results, it would be very well —the best and easiest remedy for a temporary evil —but this is not all. Censoriousness, contempt, impertinence, ill-humour, contention, and injustice, are the abundant progeny; and self-esteem is the parent of them all. Too high an opinion of ourselves, and too low an opinion of others, is the certain position assumed by a mind so conditioned— the very worst that can possibly be maintained, for all that is most lovely and valuable in the human character.

I observe a young woman who has been brought up in a London school—she has been taught to do every thing by the rules of politeness—she walks by rule, and talks by rule, and eats by rule, and thinks by rule—and she is withal a very polite young person. She goes into the country and meets persons who have had an education quite as good as her own; but they do everything as nature suggests, with the careless freedom of home and a country life. She decides at once that they are coarse and rude. She treats them with contempt, speaks of them with ridicule, and decides that it would be an outrage upon her good breeding to become their companion and friend. She is mistaken—they are neither coarse nor rude—there is more elegance very frequently in their ease than in her mannerism —more grace in their carelessness than her high polish. They have feelings as refined, and minds as well cultivated, as her own. And these too return her the compliment of aversion—they call her fine, affected, artificial—they think she can have no simplicity of feeling, or honesty of heart, under an exterior that betrays so much design. They are unjust too—she is not affecting any thing or designing any thing—her heart is as open and as true as theirs—but artificial refinement has, by education and habit, become natural to her.

Again, a girl has been brought up abroad—under skies where lighter spirits, and less thoughtful minds, and less cautious temperaments, give to the manners more ease and cheerfulness : and the feelings, from their very want of depth, acquire an appearance of more warmth and vivacity. She goes into society in England, where more thought, more feeling, more moral sensibility, encumber the mind whose intrinsic value they enhance, and give to the manners a degree of restraint, reserve, and heaviness. Now, if this young lady says these manners are disagreeable to her, she is not used to them, and cannot enjoy such society, that is very well, and she may be free to avoid it. But if she affects contempt for her countrywomen, exults in her own superiority, fancies they are admiring in her what she desires in them; or believes that they are not ten times more agreeable to each other than she is to them, she is mistaken. They have turned the glass; and at the very moment she is rising in her own esteem, on the comparison, they are seeing her bold, flippant, heartless, imprudent, indelicate: not at all more just than herself, they attribute to character what is mere manner, or do not make allowance for circumstances in their estimate of character. Both parties seeing themselves in the other's glass, had gone away humbled, perhaps; but having looked only in their own, exalted in their own esteem, they have separated highly pleased with nothing but themselves.

Here are persons brought together by providential circumstances—they might be the happier for each other's friendship; the better for the counterbalance of each other's peculiarities; mutually improved by the very opposition of character; but they despise each other when they meet—cold civility and haughty distance ill conceal their aversion; when apart, they ridicule and traduce each other without mercy.

The woman, who, with considerable natural powers, has been placed in a situation to cultivate them highly; whose taste for literary pursuits, never checked by the claims of domestic duty, or encumbered with attention to the homely necessities of existence, revels in the full delight of intellectual employment, and, while she indulges her own inclination, fulfils the wishes of those she loves, and gratifies by her improvements and talents all around her—comes in contact with some quiet, domestic girl, whom smaller powers, or smaller means, or different example, has consigned to other occupations, and other pleasures : her business is the direction of household affairs, and the plying of the indefatigable needle ; her amusements, the weeding of her garden, the feeding of her canaries, or a five miles' walk in the mud : the comfort no less of those about her, the cheerful and useful assistant of her parents, the prudent adviser of her inferiors, and the affectionate friend of her equals. What should these be to each other but objects of mutual kindness and admiration, each fulfilling her own destiny, improving the peculiar talents committed to her charge, and contributing to the happiness of those around her?   And what are they to each other?   The clever and accomplished woman turns her back on the useful, domestic friend ; repels her friendly intimacy ; wonders she wastes her time in work when she might be improving her mind ; laughs at her amusements ; despises her plain good sense ; and, when not restrained by the civilities of society, treats her with disregard and impertinence.   The other does not remain her debtor in this reckoning of mutual depreciation.   She thinks women should keep their sphere—better be a good housewife than set up for a great genius—it is waste of time to be always reading—why does not her friend do something that is useful?   She does not approve of learned ladies—she cannot bear *blue-stockings*—it is only for display women learn so much—

it is not consistent with feminine modesty to be so much distinguished for talents and attainments.

To speak more generally of what I have thus evidenced by a few examples: Young people think every one who does not know what they happen to have been taught, is ignorant — every thing they happen not to have learned, is useless—every thing that is not the custom of the society in which they happen to have moved, is vulgar—every one who does not like what they happen to like, has bad taste —every one who does not feel what happens to affect them, has no heart—every one who is not employed as they are, wastes his time—every one who does not conform to their estimate of right, has no conscience—every one whose opinions are not like their own, or their mamma's, or their governess's, is mistaken. If it ended here, we might live very happily in our self-esteem; and society, if not in unanimity, might remain in peace. But it does not. We are never contented in our fancied superiority—offence is taken where it is not given, or given where it is not provoked—kindness is coldly withheld, or rudely repulsed, or ungratefully repaid with ridicule—pain is inflicted unnecessarily, where all have of necessity enough—innocent feelings are mortified, and innocent enjoyments marred. Instead of being, as we ought to be, the variously wrought parts of one providential whole, to support, to counterbalance, to assist each other; to communicate to others what we hold in pre-eminence; to avail ourselves in others of what in us is deficient: it seems to be the very essence of our existence to depreciate and despise others; while our minds become at once narrowed and inflated by admiration of our own supposed advantage ground.

No. XXIII.

EGOTISM.

Communément le plus simple et le plus sûr est de ne jamais parler de soi ni en bien ni en mal sans besoin : l'amour propre aime mieux les injures que l'oublie et le silence.

FÉNÉLON.

I NEVER pass by without attention any suggestion given verbally by a friend, or conveyed anonymously by letter. To such hints I am indebted for many of the subjects of my papers—sometimes by direct request, sometimes by the accidental expression of a wish that things were not so: and sometimes in company with my younger friends, I venture to confess my subjects are stolen from observation of habits that to themselves I am not at liberty to remark: and when this happens, when some young lady finds in my pages her own words, or her own follies. I am persuaded she reads them smiling, and without offence—even as if we told her her ribbon was untied, or her feathers about to blow away; it had escaped her observation—she cannot see herself as others see her—the mirror once presented, she can judge of the justness of my remarks.

And as, in the hubbub of this noisy world, there
is much passing that I may not hear, I am happy to
let others listen, and insert with pleasure the following paper, which has my entire approbation.   If I
add to it some observations of my own, it is not by
way of amendment, nor because I am determined
to let no one else have all the *say*.   But, alas! my
young critics are so difficult to please—if the Listener happens to be shorter than usual, they say it is
a fraud—if it happens to be more grave than usual,
they say it is stupid—if any one but myself has listened, they say I am asleep—if it relates to men and
women, forgetting they shall sometimes be men and
women themselves, they say it is of no use to them.
Wherefore, in the attempt, never in the records of
humanity successful, at pleasing every body, I am
often induced to spoil the composition of my friends,
by tacking it to something of my own.

The following paper, on a subject it has long been
my intention to touch upon, needs no apology for
its introduction : it refers to habits that may as well
be the habits of youth as of age—indeed, if they
exist in after life, it is almost certain to be because
they have been indulged at its commencement.

Has it ever happened to any but myself, to listen
to I, I, I, in conversation, till, wearied with the mo-
notony of the sound, I was fain to quarrel with the

useful little word, and almost wish I could portray
its hydra head, and present it in a mirror to my
oracles, that they might turn away disgusted for
ever with its hideous form? If so—such will have
sympathy with my tale.

I was the companion, one morning, of an invalid
young lady, of rather respectable mind, and who
was sufficiently recovered to take an interesting part
in conversation, when her medical attendant was announced. A young gentleman entered, whom I judged to be about twenty-five: his pleasing appearance
and studious countenance attracted my attention;
and after the few necessary medical inquiries were
dismissed, I was alert on his introduction of topics
more general. I listened for some time even more
than willingly, and from the wisdom of his remarks,
I should certainly have given him credence for a
man of reading and of thought, and as such, should
have judged he gave the preference to literary society, without the unceasing assurances of these facts
from his own lips. But to convey to my readers
a clearer idea of my disquiet, I will give the outline
of the *closing* part of the conversation, assuring them,
however, that the *preceding* discussion did more
credit to the doctor's pretensions.

Dr R.—Have you seen that ponderous work of
Mr S.? I sat up till past midnight reading it. It is
a most delightful thing ; and I can never lay aside a
book in the midst, when I am interested.

Miss H.—I have not seen it, but from your recommendation shall be glad to do so, particularly as in this country place I can find but little society.

Dr R.—True—literary society is the charm of life : I mingle with no other (excepting indeed professionally); and then [introducing a splendid list of literati] with such men as these, one can find mental reciprocity : and I have the honour of their intimate acquaintance.

Miss H.—I have read the works of C—— and of S—— you have just named. What kind of man is C—— in the parlour?

Dr R.—O, quite charming! I was very intimate with him—he exceedingly regretted my leaving town—I must stay and dine with him whenever he got hold of me ; and then B—— and F——, they were my inseparable associates : after such companions I can scarcely have patience to listen to common talkers.

Miss H.—It is well for those who cannot find society to their taste, that there are books.

Dr R.—I read constantly : I am quite a devourer of books, all books that I can obtain; I can pick something good out of all ; but my time is very precious this morning, and my visit has already been extended ; but when I get into an *interesting conversation*, I, I——And, thought I, as he made his retiring bow, with the *interesting subject* SELF, doctor, you are not soon weary.

I will detail one other demand on my patience from this ill-favoured propensity ; and I would that

these were isolated passages in my *listening* history :
but perhaps I may have been peculiarly consociated
with egotists. At all events, I know I am a great
favourite with them, and that, whatever they may
say about literary conversation, they always prefer
my attentive ear.

I took up my abode for some time with a lady,
whose habits of benevolence were extensive, and of
whose true philanthropy of heart I had heard much.
I expected to follow her to the alms-house, the hos-
pital, and the garret ; and I was not disappointed ;
thither she went, and for purposes the kindest and
most noble ; she relieved their pressing wants, minis-
tered consolation in the kindest tone, and gave religious instruction wherever needed. But then she
kept a strict calendar of all these pious visitings,
and that, too, for the entertainment of her company :
all were called upon to hear the history of the appalling scenes she had witnessed, the tears of gratitude that had fallen on her hands, the prayers, half
articulate, that had been offered for her by the dying ;
and to hear her attestations of disregard to the opposition she had to encounter in these her labours of
love. Who, with such an appeal, could withhold
their commendation ? I therefore, of course, as I
listened again and again to the same tale to different
auditors, heard many pretty complimentary speeches
about magnanimity, &c. ; and getting somewhat
weary, I drew nearer to the lady's guests, till I
actually thought I heard from one (he was a clergy-

an, I believe) an inward whisper, that he would like to refer his friend to the first four verses of the sixth chapter of Matthew, but that it would be unpolite. If my listening powers were too acute when I heard this, let me now lay aside my title, and, turning monitor at once, assure my young friends, if they would have their conversation listened to with pleasure, they must be economists with *self*, as their subject.

ANTHEMIS.

THERE is one point on which God and man are agreed—their hatred of Selfishness: with this only difference, that God hates it every where, and man hates it every where but in himself. There he feels it not, knows it not, and never would discover it, did not the prominence of the same quality in others come in perpetual and painful collision with it in him : and many a hard rub, and many a rude knock, must his self-love suffer, before he discovers what part of him it is that has been wounded. Amid the thousand forms that Self assumes, in its influence upon our thoughts, and words, and deeds, the least harmful it may be, but certainly not the least offensive, is that in which it affects our conversation. We have indeed, like Anthemis, listened to the I, I, I, till we have thought it the worst-sounding letter of all the English alphabet; only halting, in our opinion, between it and its compound companion, the *my, my, my,* with which it rings in everlasting changes.

On behalf of the very young, we certainly have it to plead, that they know very little of any thing but what is in some sense their own. If they talk of persons, it must be their parents, their brothers and sisters, because they are the only people they know —if they talk of any body's affairs, it must be their own, because they are acquainted with no other—if of events, it must be what happens to themselves, for they hear nothing of what happens to any body else. As soon, therefore, as children begin to converse, it is most likely to be about themselves, or something that belongs to them ; and to the rapid growing of this unwatched habit, may probably be attributed the ridiculous and offensive egotism of many persons in conversation, who, in conduct, prove that their feelings and affections are by no means self-engrossed. But the more indigenous this unsightly weed, the more need is there to prevent its growth. It has many varieties—the leaf is not always of the same shape, nor the flower of the same colour—but they are all of one genus; and our readers, who are by this time, we trust, most excellent botanists, will have no difficulty in detecting them, however much affected by the soil they grow in. The *I's* and *my's* a lady exhibits in conversation, will bear such analogy to her character as the wares on the stall of the Bazar bear to the trade of the vender. Or, if she have a great deal of what is called tact, she will perhaps vary the article according to the demands of the market. In fashionable life it will be *my* cousin Sir Ralph, *my* father the Earl, and *my* great-uncle the Duke—the living relatives and the departed fathers, the halls of her family, their rent-rolls, or their graves, will afford abundant *étalage* for any conversation she may have to furnish out. Among those who, having gotten into the world they know not how, are determined it shall at least be known they are there, it is *my* houses, *my* servants, *my* park, *my* gardens—or if the lady be too young to claim on her own behalf, *my* father's houses, &c. &c. will answer all the purpose. But happily for the supply of this sort of talk, rank and wealth, though very useful, are not necessary to it. Without any ostentation whatever, but merely from the habit of occupying themselves with their own individuality, some will let the company choose the subject; but be it what it may, all they have to say upon it is the *I* or the *my*—books, travel, sorrow, sickness, nature, art—no matter—it is, *I* have seen, *I* have done, *I* have been, *I* have learned, *I* have suffered, *I* have known. Whatever it be to others, the *I* is the subject to them; for they tell you nothing of the matter but their own concern with it. For example, let the city of Naples be spoken of—one will tell you what is seen there, what is done there, what happens there, and make her reflections upon all, without naming herself; you will only perceive by her knowledge and her re-

marks. that she has been in Naples: another will
tell you how she came there. and why she went, and
how long she staid, and what she did, and what she
saw: and the things themselves will appear but as
accidents to the idea of Self. Some ladies I have
known, who, not content with the present display of
their powers, are determined to re-sell their wares
at second hand: they tell you all the witty things
they said to somebody yesterday, and the wise remarks they made to a certain company last night—
I said, I remarked—the commodity should be valuable indeed to be thus brought to market a second
time. Others there are, who, under pretext of confidence, little complimentary when shown alike to
all, pester people with their own affairs—before you
have been two hours in their company, you are
introduced to all their family, and all their family's
concerns—pecuniary affairs, domestic secrets, personal feelings—a sort of bird's-eye view of every
thing that belongs to them, past, present, and to
come : and wo to the secrets of those who may chance
to have been in connexion with these egotists !—in
such a view, you must needs see ten miles round.

There is an egotism of which we must speak more
seriously. Faults, that in the world we laugh at,
when they attain the dignity and purity of sacred
things, become matter of serious regret. I speak
nothing of the ostentatious display of pious and benevolent exertion, too well depicted in the sketch of
Anthemis, to need our further remark. We live at

a time when religion, its deepest and dearest interests, have become a subject of general conversation.
We would have it so—but we mark, with regret,
that Self has introduced itself here. The heartless
loquacity—we must say heartless, for in matters of
such deep interest, facility of speech bespeaks the
feelings light—the unshrinking jabber with which
people tell you their soul's history, their past impressions and present difficulties, their doctrines and their
doubts, their manifestations and their experiences—
not in the ear of confidence, to have those doubts
removed, and those doctrines verified—not in the ear
of anxious inquiry, to communicate knowledge and
give encouragement—but any where, in any company, to any body who will listen—The, *I* felt, *I*
thought, *I* experienced — *my* sorrows, *my* consola-
tions. Sorrows that, if real, should blanch the cheek
to think upon, mercies that enwrap all heaven in
amazement, they will tell out as unconcernedly as
the adventures of the morning—the voice falters not,
the colour changes not, the eye falls not. And to
what purpose all this personality? To get good, or
do good? By no means: but that whatever subject
they look upon, they always see themselves in the
foreground of the picture, with every minute particular swelled into importance, while all besides is
merged in indistinctness.

We may be assured there is nothing so ill-bred,
so *ennuyant*, so little entertaining, so absolutely
impertinent, as this habit of talking always with

reference to ourselves. For every body has a Self of
their own, to which they attach as much importance
as we to ours, and see all other matters small in the
comparison. The lady of rank has her castles and
her ancestors—they are the foreground of her picture—there they stood when she came into being,
and there they are still, in all the magnitude of near
perspective; and if her estimate of their real size
be not corrected by experience and good sense, she
expects that others will see them as large as she
does. But that will not be so. The lady of wealth
has gotten her houses and lands in the foreground—
these are the larger features of her landscape—titles
and the castles are seen at a smaller angle. Neither
lady will admire the proportions of her neighbour's
drawing, should they chance to discover themselves
in each other's conversation. She again, whether
rich or poor, whose world is her own domesticity,
sees nothing so prominent as the affairs of her nursery or her household; and perceives not that in the
eyes of others her children are a set of diminutives,
undistinguishable in the mass of humanity; in which
that they ever existed, or that they cease to exist, is
matter of equal indifference. And she who holds her
mental powers in predominance, to whom the nearest
objects are knowledge, and reason, and science, and
learning—she takes disgust at the egotism of the
former three, and does not perceive that the magnitude she gives to her own pursuits, seems as ill proportioned to them as theirs to her. And if there be

one who is disabused alike of all, of wealth, and rank and learning; and, having taken just measure both of what she has and of what she has not, has placed all in the obscurity of the distance; and in nearness to her heart and pre-eminence in her contemplation, has placed the great things of eternity—right though she is, and just though her drawing be, even she should be aware that others see it not so. The shades that overcast her landscape, never hung on theirs—the sunbeam that lights it, never shone on them. In time and season she must speak to them for good—but when good is not the object, she, too, must be aware of offensive egotism, in speaking of joys and sorrows that they never knew, and exhibiting contempt for things that she despises, but they cannot.

It is thus that each one attributes to the objects around him, not their true and actual proportion, but a magnitude proportioned to their nearness to himself. We say not that he draws ill who does so—for to each one, things are important more or less, in proportion to his own interest in them. But hence is the mischief—we forget that every one has a Self of their own, and that the constant setting forth of ours, is to others preposterous, obtrusive, and ridiculous. The painter who draws a folio in the front of his picture and a castle in the distance, properly draws the book the larger of the two : but he must be a fool if he therefore thinks the folio is the larger, and expects every body else to think so too. Yet nothing wiser are we, when we suffer ourselves to be perpetually pointing to ourselves, our affairs, and our possessions, as if they were as interesting to others as they are important to us.

END OF VOLUME FIRST.